¶

DEATH UNDER THE STEEPLE by Ruben D. Gonzales transports readers back to the picturesque town of Black Mountain in western North Carolina to solve another murder. In this book, as in the others in the series, Gonzales has created well-developed characters with intriguing backgrounds, as well as numerous suspects with believable motives. Its protagonist, Emma Shaw, is someone readers will root for— she's intelligent and independent and makes good use of the keen observational skills she's developed as a photographer. Her family connections to the town allow her to access relevant clues while also providing a strong motive for her amateur sleuthing. Another great entry in the series, this book can easily be read as a stand-alone. Lovers of traditional mysteries who enjoy realistic depictions of small-town life, intriguing plots, and well-crafted characters should definitely check out DEATH UNDER THE STEEPLE.

—Victoria Gilbert, author of the Blue Ridge Library Mystery, the Booklovers B&B, and the Hunter and Clewe mystery series

***

In his third mystery set in his Black Mountain Series, DEATH UNDER THE STEEPLE, Ruben Gonzales does not disappoint.

Emma Shaw, photojournalist and now photography shop owner, feels compelled to once again stick her unwanted nose into a police investigation. A well-loved, charismatic preacher is found dead in the church baptismal with a bullet wound in his head, and since Emma's father and the reverend had had a disagreement, the inept sheriff is determined to pin the murder on him and refuses to look for other suspects.

Determined to prove her father innocent, Emma enlists the help of her sort-of boyfriend, Jeff and sets out to find the real killer or at least another suspect.

¶

Though she's threatened and physically attacked on more than one occasion, she doesn't give up even when her father hides, not only from the police, but from her, too.

Will Emma be successful in finding the right killer, so an innocent man doesn't have to pay for a crime he didn't commit?

—Agnes Alexander, prolific writer of over 50 books in the mystery, romance, and western genres including the recent, THE FRIENDLY CREEK - 5- Book Series.
All of her books in print can be found on Amazon.

***

A feisty heroine, a mountain community with colorful characters, and a twisty mystery make *Death Under the Steeple* a compelling read. Emma Shaw has solved murders using her ability to see auras, but this time the main suspect is her father. Was the young preacher murdered, or did he commit suicide? The future of the church, as well as the land, depends on the answer, an answer Emma has to find to clear her father's name.

In this third installment of the Black Mountain Mysteries, Ruben Gonzales once again fills his story with a wealth of detail, bringing to life the people and the world of Black Mountain.

—Jane Tesh, author of the Mountain Lodge Mysteries.

Death Under the Steeple

By

Ruben D. Gonzales

Deep Indigo Books
Published by Indigo Sea Press
Winston-Salem

¶

Deep Indigo Books
Indigo Sea Press
302 Ricks Drive
Winston-Salem, NC 27103

For information regarding bulk purchases of this book, digital purchase and special discounts, please contact the publisher at indigoseapress@gmail.com

Manufactured in the United States of America
ISBN 978-1-63066-567-8

"To everyone who loves small-town North Carolina."

—Ruben D. Gonzales

¶

Chapter One

Monday

It's a cumbersome process, working with my computer, especially for me, the two-finger typist who avoided girls' business class in high school like the plague. Technology was on the cusp of exploding and the ambitious flocked to high school computer classes where they taught all about binary code and stuff. Of course, it was a boy thing back then. The mountain communities lagged behind the rest of the world and only boys were expected to go into computers. After we graduated, we girls were expected to put our hair up in a bun and be a secretary to some male business manager somewhere. Most of those same men laughed when I quit my job at the newspaper and told them I wanted to return to my hometown to go into the photography business. More than a few men snickered and rolled their eyes, implying what did a woman know about running a business? Luckily, I've never been one to listen much to what others have to say, especially men.

Pa found me working in my Black Mountain Main Street studio. After saying howdy, he paused. I caught the first look of distress on his face, normally bright and happy, with a steady dark blue aura about him, indicating a calm and thoughtful person, but in the fading mountain afternoon light, his aura faltered and clouded over into darkness, indicating a troubled soul.

I've been able to see the auras of most people since I was a kid. When concentrating on a person their aura appears to me, radiating out in a rainbow form, in a spectrum of color depending on their mood. I use my gift, a hand-me-down from my Cherokee ancestors, in my portrait photography. When I snap the camera shutter at the moment of a person's brightest

1

aura the resulting images appear so lifelike, you'd think the person was breathing, or so a critic once said.

"What's going on?" I asked him, stopping my task and trying to give him my full attention. I hadn't seen Pa a lot these last couple of months. I'd been busy with my new business and here lately even our normal Saturday suppers had been canceled more often than not. The business had improved over the last year, although not to the point I could lose a sale to a 'proud of the grandkid', grandparent.

"It's about Pastor Bennett," he said.

"Reverend Bennett," I asked, wondering where the story would lead, "your pastor?"

"No, gal, young Bennett, over to *Living Waters Church*, down by the lake."

"Oh, well, what's up with him?"

"He's dead."

Okay, this was important, "What…?"

"Emma, they found his body in the church," he explained, taking a seat at the table, "shot in the head."

"What?"

"Yeah, he's dead. The cleaning committee found him around noontime today. They're a bunch of elderly ladies who volunteer and get together on Mondays to clean up from the day before services. They'd only just arrived when they found his body down in the baptismal fountain. I heard it from Wendall Hawkins, he does the maintenance over there, and was with them."

"Wait…in the baptismal fountain?"

"Yeah, they got one of those big ones, looks like a swimming pool, about three feet deep, sits down in a hole under the church steeple. I'm surprised no one else has fallen in over the years and drown."

"How in the world? Was it suicide?"

"They don't know for sure."

"Did they find a gun?"

"No, and that's the other thing."

"What?"

"If it was suicide, someone could have taken the gun to make it look like murder."

"Who said anything about murder?"

I'd seen plenty of death over the years. Growing up in the mountains you just expected to see it. Hogs and cattle are slaughtered to refill the freezer or to provide meals for a summer week-long tent revival. If you hunt, you'll see it, if you're lucky. Accidents kill people too. There're feuds in the mountains, among family, and friends. I'd also seen my share of death during a tour with my National Guard unit in Afghanistan. The bodies may all be different colors, but the blood all runs the same red, people and wild things alike. Years had passed since I did my duty, but those images are burned in my mind, like a forest fire can scar the side of a mountain if it runs on long enough, blood-red in the heat of the fire, then black as night after. It takes years before the green of life grows back, years. I imagined it would take a bunch more years before time could bury those images deep enough in my memory, so I didn't regularly relive the nightmare.

I knew about the Bennetts. The family came into the valley with the early settlers and founded one of the largest farms in the valley. Their descendants branched out into other walks of life, including the ministry. The older of the two Bennetts preached at Pa's church, Swannanoa Baptist, but the younger Bennett, the son, preached at a church down by the lake that had gathered quite a following of people into its fold, young and old alike, my two elderly aunts included. The large congregation made it the most attended church in my hometown of Black Mountain. I'd heard they were planning to build a big new sanctuary, you know one of those glass-walled mega-churches with a stage for a rock band.

I had seen Pa upset about death before, like after Mama died. Then again when my brother Early was murdered two

3

years before. Both occasions were tough on him. It's tough to lose a spouse, but from what I saw, losing a son might have the edge. It bothered me to lose my big brother, but it near killed my pa. Losing a child had to top the cake. That was probably something I didn't have to worry about since I didn't think I'd ever get married much less have kids.

I didn't know how I felt about the Pastor's death. I mean with a religious man, you expect he'd have already paid for his passage to heaven. "Did you see the body?"

Pa paused when my dog, Blue, the friendly black Labrador I got as a gift a year back, came over and rested her head on his lap. Blue's young but she has a way with people. Somehow, she knows when people are under stress, and I got the feeling Pa was under some stress. "Ah, no, by the time I got over there the Sheriff had gotten Gilmore's Funeral Home to pick up the body."

"Not before the State came in to investigate?"

"He said he's not calling in the state, said it was an obvious murder. He said with the body soaking all night there wouldn't be much evidence on it anyway."

"Well, the Sheriff may be right, it's got to be murder."

"That's kind of what I'm afraid of."

"What do you mean?"

"Well, when the sheriff starts to ask around I'm afraid my name might come up."

Pa was distant kin of the Bennett ancestry, through the line of the Shaw family tree. The Bennetts married into the Shaw family back when the Shaws started running the town of Black Mountain in the early 1800s, when they first came into the Valley of the Three Forks. The Shaws own the local lumber mill where most of the men in town work. They also own most of the businesses in town including the real estate company, the hardware store, the insurance agency, the bank, and the biggest vineyard on this side of the Blue Ridge. What they don't own they control through intimidation.

4

"Why would the name of Logan Shaw come up in connection to Young Pastor Bennett?"

"You see, we had words yesterday evening."

"What kind of words?"

"The kind that gets you put in jail for murder."

***

My pa, Logan Shaw, grew up in Black Mountain but didn't trace his lineage straight down from the Shaws that run the town. Oh, he's a Shaw in many respects, being tall and broad with piercing gray eyes, but he has thick black hair that had only turned white around his ears, instead of the balding crowns most Shaw men bear. Also, aside from his moonshine days and alcoholism, he's a fairly straight arrow. For a while, people knew him and mama as the town's leading Holy Rollers, and he never got far away from that even after Mama died, so I found him having crosswords with Reverend Bennett, or anyone for that matter, a little hard to believe. Pa did serve in Vietnam, and I'm sure developed the military mantra of kill or be killed, but that had been long ago. Don't old soldiers leave that behind them, eventually?

I had just finished shooting action photos of a high school Junior Varsity boys' soccer game when Pa came in and caught me struggling with the computer program. After shots of a game, I transfer the photos from my digital camera to the desktop computer, and then to the auxiliary hard drive where I store all my pics before transferring them to my studio's website. I usually have Sue Ellen Shaw come in and help, but she had to finish a paper or something for her high school history class, so I gave her the afternoon off. She can download the pics, sort them, put them on the website, and post them on my social media platforms faster than it takes me to just open the darn program. I would have waited for her to do that the next day, but several parents told me after the game

5

that they wanted to see the shots of their boys so they could order some prints and I didn't want to lose the sales, so I decided to load them myself. Call me greedy.

"Why don't you tell me about it," I suggested.

Pa sat back in his chair, ran his hands through his hair, and settled in a minute before answering me. Ever since he went sober, he made a point of getting settled before launching into an oration of a Bible verse or in this case, a confession. Blue looked up at him, encouraging him to go on.

"You know Clare Bennett?" Pa asked me, scratching under Blue's chin.

"Some," I said, only recalling a spry woman about the same age as Pa, but closer to the Shaw tree. "Why?"

"She'd been attending First Presbyterian Church but several months back she started going down to *Living Waters* because of all that new-age Christian dogma."

"Where the young Reverend Bennett preached?"

"That's right, and well, she's been trying to get me to go over and sit with her in a service."

"What?"

"You know, go with her to meeting."

"You and Clare Bennett?"

"It's not like you think, Emma. It was just an afternoon in the church."

"But you went?"

"Not right off, but they have a Sunday evening family service and she invited me over to that."

"What time did you leave?"

"About nine o'clock."

"That's kind of late, no?

"Yes, and that's what I was getting at."

"What?"

"Well, after the service they have a social hour, down in the basement activity room. That's when young Bennett and I had words."

"What did you say to him?"

Pa leaned on the worktable and gathered his weathered hands together. He'd spent forty years at the Shaw mill and every one of them showed. When he finally retired on the meager pension the Shaws doled out, his back was spent and he walked with a limp that only slightly improved, even after years away.

"Well, the social hour had broken up and most people had left but a couple was talking to the Pastor, and I overheard something he was saying about the scripture he quoted in his sermon."

"What scripture?"

"Jeremiah 29:11"

"Oh," I said, nodding my head like I knew the verse, "what did you tell him?

"I told him he had it wrong, the verse interpretation. It's often quoted but most people don't know it all. It just so happened I was reading on it a couple of weeks back and was familiar with it. Most people can only vaguely recall it in terms of a promise that we will all prosper and be cared for if we only believe, but when you don't know the complete text, you miss the Good Lord's point. The way young Bennett quoted it left the main point out and distorted the Word of God."

"What did you tell him?

"I told him he was distorting the Word of God."

"I bet that didn't go over well. What did he say?"

"He accused me of being an unbeliever."

"What's that got to do with Clare?"

"Well, she spoke up in my defense. Said that if Logan Shaw said something about the scripture, then it was right."

"Then what happened?"

"Young Bennett told Clare to mind her own business. He went on and on about her not having faith and whatnot. To tell the truth young Bennett just went darn crazy about it and made a scene. It hurt Clare to the bone, the pastor saying things like that, and she a church-going lady for sixty years. She told him they were hurtful words and she'd be reconsidering her support of the church. He tried to apologize then but, well, you know, I couldn't just let him talk to her like that, pastor or no pastor, so I let him have a piece of my mind."

"I bet."

"Yep, and unfortunately there were other people down in the room at the time and they witnessed the ruckus."

"What all did you say?"

"I can't remember half of it, but I got into him pretty good."

"Then what happened?"

"We left right out of there and the Pastor was still alive when we did."

"So, you figure Sheriff Banner will set his sights on you as a suspect?"

"Since they didn't find a gun at the scene, I would…wouldn't you?"

***

Pa looked like he could use a walk and a cup of coffee so I attached Blue's leash to her collar and we headed down the sidewalk to the *Coffee Bean,* a recent addition to downtown Black Mountain commerce. Though Main Street had seen better days it was making a rebound spurred by the industrious spirit of the area's mountain craftsmen, farmers, and homegrown small businesses. A Shaw family renovated waterwheel complex with a bakery and gift shop on the Swannanoa River, sat on one end of town, with a new town-built farmers market across from it. A batch of new tourist shops interspersed with commercial businesses flanked the downtown district for two blocks east and west, with Town Hall and the town's one stoplight, in the middle, and a small park with gardens opposite. Storefronts, including my photography studio, filled every available space between there and the hospital. The new businesses lent the whole downtown a contagious vitality.

Though most of the town men still worked at the Shaw lumber mill, many others found jobs at the new businesses in town, at busy construction companies, at the tech company that opened a new call center down on Lake Nebo, or at a smattering of vineyards that had sprung up along the mountainsides and valleys of the Blue Ridge Mountains, the Shaw Winery included. I was happy to see the transition of the town from Shaw family-owned and run to a more egalitarian economy that rewarded the entrepreneurial spirit.

May Shaw, a daughter-in-law in the Shaw family tree, opened the *Coffee Bean* a couple of years ago across the street from the hospital. Previously, the location housed numerous businesses over the years, too many to remember. Now the bright coffee shop settled in successfully, offering a local gathering option so no one had to frequent the chain operations out on the busy highway.

Logs burning in a big fireplace warmed the place in the fall and winter. They always put out stainless steel water bowls for the dogs that followed their owners out of the weather, a necessity in a mountain town where every family has a dog, frequently more, and where most men spent more time with their dogs than with their wives.

The aroma of fresh-brewed coffee and burning hardwood greeted us as we entered the shop. We ordered coffee and a calorie-loaded homemade cinnamon bun for us and took a fresh-made doggie biscuit for Blue. May kept a big jar of them on the counter for the wayward hungry dog that came into the shop. Suitably armed, we settled into a table looking out onto Main Street.

"You know," Pa said, "I've said this before, I just don't see how a man can charge more than a dollar for a cup of coffee."

"And I've explained this before, Pa, it's a better cup! Now

drink up and eat your bun!"

An eclectic group of customers crowded in the large room laid out to seat fifty patrons. The rustic room featured exposed ceiling beams, young people on laptops or heads bent down looking at cell phones, and a number of older folks looking for a place to gather out of the cold and read the latest edition of the Black Mountain Post.

It might have been a little late for coffee, but even a strong cup usually didn't keep me awake at night. Other things like my new business, my on-again-off-again romance with Jeff Carson, my new dog in my life, or my still uncompleted apartment above the studio, things like that kept me awake, but not coffee.

"Now Pa, about this Pastor Bennett thing," I said when we had settled in our seats and had a chance to reflect, "don't you think you are overreacting a bit? You haven't even heard from the Sheriff."

"No, I think you need to get ahead of this before the trail gets cold."

"What do you mean, me?"

"I want you to look into this thing before the Sheriff hauls me off in irons. I don't have time to sit in the county jail while they sort this out."

Two years before I moved back to Black Mountain permanently, I looked into the mysterious death of my big brother, Early Shaw. He was the town's Chief of Police at the time and the accident that killed him looked suspicious, so when the town fathers failed to show any interest, I investigated. During my feeble attempt at playing detective, I discovered the town's finance director was cheating on the books and I used my aura reading gift to catch him in a lie. We discovered that he killed my brother when Early found out about the man's money skimming.

"Now, Pa, you know the ATF boys played a big part in that."

"Yep, but you solved that Barbara Walker thing on your own."

Pa was referring to the case the previous fall when I found the wife of a prominent area businessman floating dead in Lake Nebo. In that case, I used my gift of aura reading again to separate the liars from the truthful, but science played a role in that case as much as anything.

"Now, Pa, there was a lot of high school biology involved with that," I explained, keeping the aura reading out of it and referring to a blood test that implicated the guilty family member.

Pa and Ma knew about my aura reading, but I didn't let many in town in on that ability of mine. To a naturally skeptical culture, mountain folk just find it hard to believe in something they can't see. So, getting the science right in that case was important. Back in high school, a group of girls in a pretty but dumb clique accused me of seeing ghosts when I tried to explain my aura reading to them, calling me the *ghost whisperer*. The misinterpretation drove me from town and I pledged to never come back. Never say never.

"I know, you bring a lot to the table, that's why you are so good at this kind of thing."

"What kind of thing?"

"Detective work!"

"Pa," I said, "keep it down." A few people were already looking our way, attracted by Pa's loud voice.

"Well, okay, but look," he said leaning across to me, "with the Sheriff out to get me I can't be going around asking questions and all. I've got to stay out of sight."

"Okay, okay, so…" I paused knowing the next few words out of my mouth would set the stage for me for the next week or so and I'd be fairly consumed by it, "so, if not you, and not suicide, who do you think killed the good Pastor?"

"Well, from what Clare tells me, there's a rift in the *Living Waters* faithful."

"What do you mean?"

"Oh, Clare told me Young Pastor Bennett came up with a plan to expand the church."

"I heard that."

"Well, the congregation is divided between those who want to expand the church and its ministry and those who want it to stay small. People are passionate on both sides of the matter so, there's bad blood and jealousy down there."

"Enough to kill the pastor?"

"He was set on the expansion."

"That's not enough!"

"Maybe not, but I need you to take a look at this before the Sheriff shows up at my door."

"Okay, okay, but won't it wait a while?"

"No, you know I'm in the middle of the corn harvest. Remember, a lot of people are counting on that."

Pa reminded me of the cornmeal giveaway he started. He and a few of the valley farmers planted corn in unused fields this past spring and hoped to harvest, mill, and give away the cornmeal to area food banks and church pantries ahead of the winter months. An extremely thoughtful and needed endeavor, especially for the Black Mountain community where usual actions are routed deep in "what's in it for me" attitudes.

"This is the first year of the program and I can't afford it not to be a success. You know we talked about it."

"I got it, Pa, really, but I'm swamped myself. I got the business to see to and then my still unfinished apartment. I don't know how much time I can devote to this. Can you let me think about it?"

"Okay," Pa said, getting up from his seat and picking up his cardboard coffee cup with a fancy *Coffee Bean* logo printed on it, "but don't take too long."

"Why?"

"Because the Sheriff is coming down the walk and I'm heading out the back way."

Chapter Two

After I solved the mystery of my brother's suspicious death and got him buried, Mayor Franklyn Shaw followed through on a long-sought-after reorganization of the town's police department, he closed it! Yep, after years of putting up with Early's tough-nosed–no-give administration, the Mayor entered into a contract with the county sheriff to provide public-safety service for the city. He let them have the former police office in Town Hall as a satellite office, but no one ever used it. The county sheriff's deputies assigned to the town made a drive-through a couple of times a day but that is about all. The Mayor likes it that way and it helps that Sheriff Banner is an in-law to the Shaws, having married into the family via a Shaw first cousin. Some things in Black Mountain never change.

Sheriff Banner stood well over six feet and the extra fifty pounds he carried around added to his stature. He played football on the Morgan City High School team. In his senior year, he led his team over the Black Mountain Broncos in a major upset that knocked us out of the state high school championships. People still remembered that game, but not fondly.

After high school Banner went on to play a couple of years at State, but an injury ended his playing days. After getting his degree in Public Safety, he came back and joined the County Sheriff's Department. The Sheriff didn't care much for me, a fact I found out while looking into Early's death and confirmed when I was poking into Barbara Walker's case. I guess the Sheriff didn't appreciate that someone, especially a woman someone, was undermining his authority.

From the doorway, I could clearly see the Sheriff's earthy brown aura ballooning out from him as he yanked the coffee shop door open. Followed by an equally large deputy, they came in and made straight to my table, their eyes hidden behind dark sunglasses.

"Where's Logan?" The Sheriff asked as a way of greeting.

"Good afternoon, Sheriff," I welcomed the man, slowly reaching across the table and pulling Pa's paper plate to me before the Sheriff recognized that two people had been sitting at my table.

"Don't, *good afternoon* me, Emma," the man said, "Where's your pa?"

"Why? What's this about?"

"Don't play dumb, Emma, you're too bright for that."

"Now, Sheriff," I said, "I don't know what you are getting at, but you'll have to give me more if you want me to take part in this conversation."

"This isn't a conversation…this is an investigation!"

"An investigation of what?"

"A murder!" the deputy said, speaking for the first time.

"My pa's murder?"

"Don't be silly," the Sheriff said, whipping off his Stetson and sitting down, taking the seat opposite me that Pa had just vacated, and leaving the big deputy standing, "someone killed young Pastor Bennett."

"How?"

"Looks like a handgun shot, small gun, small round, in the head, didn't go through. We'll send the slug off to the State to get confirmation."

"Maybe it was suicide?"

"No, what's he got to be depressed about? The growing congregation, the new church being planned, happy family, why would he shoot himself?"

"Did you find a gun?"

"No, no gun, so no suicide."

"Someone could have taken the gun to make it look like murder."

"Where'd you dream that up?"

"I saw a few of cases like that when I was with the Piedmont Paper."

"Not this one and as I said, the Pastor didn't have any reason to kill himself."

"We never know the burdens people carry around, Sheriff. I wouldn't be eliminating the possibility the Pastor was under some strain and maybe, just maybe, he took his own life."

"Dream on, Emma, until I see evidence to the contrary, I'm looking at this as a murder."

"Maybe it was a robbery?"

"No, there was nothing taken. I had the church staff go through the place and nothing is missing besides the Pastor's Bible. Besides, that place doesn't have much. Nothing worth taking anyway. No, there's a murder here all right. The only question is who did it? Once we find the 'who' we'll know the 'why'."

"What time did it happen?"

"Gilmore said he couldn't be accurate with the body soaking all night but sometime yesterday evening."

"Soaking," I asked, playing along like I didn't know details.

"They found him down in the baptismal fountain."

"Baptismal fount?"

"Yeah, they got a big one under the steeple. It's got steps going down in it you have to walk down if you want redemption."

"Oh…"

"Yeah, and that's why I want to speak with your Pa."

"Sherriff, Pa doesn't go to *Living Waters*," I said, picking up Pa's uneaten bun and taking a big bite, feeling the effects of the sugar rushing to my head, "he belongs to Swannanoa Baptist, been going there all his life."

"I know where he goes to church, Emma."

15

"Then how would he know about anything happening down at *Living Waters*?"

When the Sheriff saw how the direct tactic wasn't getting anywhere he paused in his tirade and looking around at the crowded coffee shop, decided to try a softer approach, "Look, Emma," the man said, leaning across the narrow table close enough I could smell his Old Spice aftershave and continuing in a quieter voice, he said, "your Pa was seen having words with Young Pastor Bennett last night after church service and I need to question him on it."

"What kind of words?"

"Insulting words."

"Threatening words?"

"Yes, threatening words."

"Threatening like how?"

"I don't have the exact wording, but a half-dozen people said it was threatening enough that the Pastor was afraid."

He probably *was* afraid, afraid that Clare Bennett would take her money elsewhere. "Just what brought all that on?'

"Well," the Sheriff paused, probably mulling over how he wanted to answer, his aura pulsing a muddier shade of pink. Although a bright pink aura can indicate great passion, even love, the darker hue can be a sign of emotional imbalance, deceit, someone struggling with the truth.

I needed to have the Sheriff lay out facts of the case, so it would look like it all came from him, and I didn't get anything from Pa. "Looks like your Pa got into it because of Clare Bennett."

"Clare Shaw Bennett," I said, playing dumb this time, "has the big farm over off State 220?"

"You know any another Clare Bennett in town?"

"I just wanted to make sure we were speaking about the same person, Sheriff, so far you've been pretty sketchy with the details on all this."

"Look, young Pastor Bennett said a few things to Clare,

and it caused your Pa to butt in and that's what started it all. Next thing we know, young Pastor Bennett is dead, and we have a murder on our hands and your Pa's the main suspect."

"Well, sounds like you need to speak with Clare."

"We tried but can't get a hold of her."

"Oh..."

"But we questioned everyone who was there last night and they all confirmed the argument between your Pa and Young Pastor Bennett."

"Did they say argument, or was it more a discussion?"

"What's the difference?"

"A lot, one might lead to further thoughtful discussion and the other might lead elsewhere."

"Well, this one led elsewhere and that's why I want to talk to your Pa."

"And when did all this happen?"

"That meeting broke up at 9:00."

I was thinking over the time frame the Sheriff gave me and how it fit with Pa's.

"So, where is he?"

"I don't know Sheriff, I'm not a little girl anymore and I live on my own. Pa's a free man and doesn't tell me of his coming and going."

"You don't know where he is?" The Deputy said, his voice rising above conversation level, high enough that Blue got up and growled at the man.

"I told you, I don't know where he is right now," *which was true.* I didn't know where he was at that moment. Now, if the Sheriff had asked if I'd seen Pa recently, I may have had to answer differently.

"Look, Sheriff, I can see you are just doing your job on this, but there must be other suspects out there with more motive to kill the Pastor. Pa can't be the only one in town that had a beef with Young Pastor Bennett. It still could have been a suicide."

"It wasn't suicide, Emma, and I can't think of anyone else in town who would have a beef with the pastor big enough to kill him. From what I understand everyone loved the man."

"Just the same…"

"Look, we'll follow up if any other suspects pop up," he said, looking down at Blue, who growled at him too, "but in the meantime, your Pa is the first one up."

"Come on Sheriff, my Pa, a killer?"

"I don't know much about your Pa, Emma, some say he used to run liquor through the hills."

"That was a long time ago, Sheriff."

"Just the same," the deputy said, "we need to talk to him."

"And who are you," I said to the man who had been standing silent behind the sheriff, tall and broad, but seeing him up close I could see he carried more fat than muscle.

"This is deputy, Ross Banner."

"Ross? Your boy? Why, isn't that convenient?"

"Don't trouble yourself, Emma, the Sheriff can hire anyone qualified, including family, and Ross took all the Public Safety courses at Catawba Tech. Besides, you're one to say anything, the way the Shaw's have packed the town and county government."

I bristled at the Sheriff's notion that just because I carried the Shaw name I took after the Shaws in manner. I didn't agree with the way the Shaws ran their empire, but I figured it wouldn't mean anything to him so I said, "Well, look, Sheriff, as you can see, Pa's not here right now, but when and if I see him again I'll let him know you are looking for him and I'm sure he'll be in touch."

The sheriff took off his sunglasses and looked at me with dark blue eyes, but when Blue growled at the man he scrunched up his mouth and nose and put his hat back on. Without another word he got up and walked to the door, his son following, both trailing a brown aura I often saw in people who are uptight and carry chips on their shoulders. If he had stopped and asked anyone in the room about Pa, he may have gotten a lot of different answers, but no one volunteered. People in Black Mountain have long memories when it comes to losing football games.

***

To tell the truth, I didn't know where my Pa was at that moment, but if he wanted to stay out of the Sheriff's way he could. Pa didn't talk much about his time in Vietnam, but I knew it had a lot to do with search and destroy. With that background and his knowledge of the area, he could disappear up in the mountain easy enough. No, sir, if Pa had taken to the hills the Sheriff would never find him.

After talking with the Batman and Robin sheriff duo, I got hold of Blue and we went back up the walk toward my studio. Halfway there I came to the Fish and Game shop that Jeff Carson's family has run in town for several generations. I could see Jeff inside, sitting behind a counter, at a workbench, hard at work, a trait I admired in the man.

"Hello, stranger!" I called out when I entered the shop, Blue charging ahead, squeezing between display counters, and jumping onto Jeff's lap. I don't know how I felt about my dog getting more excited about seeing Jeff than I do.

"Emma Louise," Jeff said back, adding my middle name that people who know me use when they want to make a point. "I just saw you for dinner last night!"

"I know," I agreed with the man. Jeff and I had taken up again with a left-over high school friendship. I'd hardly been back in town but I was back in the game, chasing love in my mid-thirties, enjoying what I had missed while trying to escape my mountain upbringing past. The only surprise in it all was Jeff still being available.

"You told me you'd be busy all day today so not to expect to get together."

"And you believed me? Don't you know that's exactly when a woman expects you to reach out to her, more than ever?"

After a pause as Jeff roughhoused a bit with Blue he gathered himself and said, "No, I expect I missed that Women Studies class when that was explained. Looks like I have some remedial reading to attend to."

Jeff is tall and broad, the opposite of my short and lean. Lately, he'd been clean shaved. He used to hide his face behind a thick beard but when I told him it was rough on my skin when we kissed, he shaved it off. Now his bright blue eyes shone out of rosy cheeks and his aura pulses a light green demonstrating a person balanced between nature and personal being. I liked that color.

"Don't worry, I'll keep you up to date."

"Good," he said getting up from the bench where he was loading shells for sale in the shop. "I don't have time for reading. So, what's up, are you taking Blue for a walk?"

Walking a dog was a new experience for me. Growing up on a farm we let our dogs run free but living above my studio I didn't have that luxury. I didn't think the downtown merchants would appreciate a seventy-five-pound dog romping up and down the sidewalk scaring away paying customers. Getting up with the roosters to walk Blue in the morning was getting old, but I needed to do something. If I'd known what a domesticated pet required in terms of care I might have hesitated a bit before accepting the dog gift from Dan Walker. He said it was a reward for solving the case of his wife's murder the year before, but more and more recently I suspected it was more of a punishment.

Jeff had helped me out on the two cases I looked into. He even roughed up a couple of characters when I got in over my head. I have always been capable of taking care of myself. I lived alone for many years and my National Guard training and service made me confident in handling most situations, but Jeff came to my rescue when fancy moves, and feminine wiles weren't enough.

"Actually…"

"Oh, no," he said, worry wrinkling his forehead.

"Now, don't look like that, I haven't even explained it yet."

"Emma Louise, what are you up to?"

"Now, Jeff, you know I don't go looking for trouble it just seems to find me."

"This have anything to do with Young Pastor Bennett's death?"

"Why would you ask that?"

"He's the only person turn up dead lately."

"You heard about that?"

"Some, just a few words here and there. Word is he committed suicide, shot himself in the head."

"Is that what people say?" I asked.

"What else could it be?"

"Sheriff says it might be murder."

"Why?"

"They didn't find a gun at the scene," I explained. "No gun, no suicide."

"Someone could have taken the gun to make it look like murder."

"You think?"

"Now hold on, Emma. So that's what this is about? Investigating this thing? Now, why get involved in this? Young Bennett was no kin to you like Early was, and I don't believe the church held a mortgage on your Pa's farm, so they can't be threatening to have him evicted. So, what reason would you have to get involved with this? Just let the Sheriff get on with it and you can sit this one out."

"Well, you see, that's the problem."

"What's the problem?"

"Turns out…if it's not suicide, then Pa's a prime suspect."

"Oh, no, how in the world…?"

"Seems like he and Young Pastor Bennett had words and the Sheriff heard about it."

"What kind of words?"

"The kind that can get you arrested."

"Oh, that kind."

"Yep and the Sheriff is out looking for Pa."

"A little presumptuous of the Sheriff. There must be something else pushing this."

"Like what?"

"I don't know, but come to think of it, you'd better go on and start your case."

"Oh yeah, why?"

"If you recall from previous experience, our fine Sheriff generally takes the easiest route to the end of a case, facts aside and it appears your Pa is the low-hanging fruit for picking in this one."

***

I appreciated Jeff saying he'd help me out if I needed him. The man looked genuinely concerned and worried when Blue and I left. That streak of empathy was another reason I liked the man.

We headed back to the photography shop. I had purchased the business the year before from the town's old photographer and moved back home permanently after years away. When I went off to college I swore I'd never move back to my small-town mountain home, but when I quit my job at the city newspaper because of a merger, I was looking for an opportunity and the chance to be my own boss seemed too good to pass on, so I returned home to be an entrepreneur.

The business came along with the old building sitting on a corner of Main Street with the studio on the first floor and enough space on the second floor for an apartment. I laid out a floor plan on the second floor with two bedrooms in the rear of the space and a great room that overlooked Main Street. I designed an open floor plan with the kitchen at one end, a dining area in the middle, and a seating area at the opposite side, with a proposed fireplace. I say proposed because it had been months since the apartment had been completed, but not the fireplace, and outside of a leather sofa I bought at a discount store, I still hadn't furnished the place. In the meantime, to cover the hole in the wall, I had put up a sheet of plywood and painted a red brick fireplace on it. I painted a mantel and everything. From a distance, it looked like the real thing, from a distance. Last Christmas I even nailed two stockings up, one for me and one for Blue.

Saunders Photography had been a town fixture for fifty years. From the days when he developed his own film and printed out his own photos up to the dawn of the digital camera and now the phone camera, and the subsequent decline in the photography industry. More than a few laughed at my business venture, some even remarking if there was even a need for a professional photographer these days. But there is still a need for fine photography, and I filled my menu of services with sports photography, special occasions, recording family events, and occasional weddings. I wasn't as busy as I wanted, but maintaining a tight business and personal budget, I passed the breakeven point and was looking forward to a profitable year. All I needed was to keep my nose on the business and not get sidetracked, like getting involved in another murder investigation.

Blue and I had just reached the business stoop when I noticed Mayor Franklyn Shaw's big SUV still sitting in its parking place outside Town Hall. The fall evening was approaching fast and businesses up and down the street were turning on their evening lights. The fall leaf season had been in full color for a good four weeks and weekend tourists had flocked into town to stay at the bevy of bed and breakfast places that had sprung up since the Shaws had renovated the big waterwheel house on the river. Somehow the town got the thing on the National Register of Historic Places and that helped spur tourism. A bunch of young people even opened a microbrewery, Black Brew Brewery, in an old building near the river. Of course, with the surrounding hills filled with local moonshine history, it was only a matter of time before brewing came down out of the mountain and became legal on Main Street.

I let Blue in the studio and closed the door on her and walked across the street to Town Hall. She set to barking but I knew that no dogs were allowed in Town Hall. The grand structure with columned portico had stood strong and tall for over a hundred years. Built from granite hauled down the mountain by imported Italian laborers, it looked as good as the day it was built, inside and out. From a town budget the Mayor said couldn't support a police department, there always seems to be enough to maintain the building in "A" shape, down to polished floors and dust-free chandeliers.

I saw a light at the end of the hall in the Mayor's office. I didn't know what had kept the man late on a Monday. The reception desk where the Mayor's pretty new wife usually sat was vacant so I went down the hall.

"What are you doing here?" Mayor Franklyn Shaw growled seeing me standing in his doorway, as he struggled to his feet to greet me. The Mayor's aura beat the steady shade of dark brown I always see with hard-driven businessmen. The color is commonly associated with greed and with the mayor and the Shaws in general, it was accurate.

When the mayor sat down his chair moaned under his weight and I worried for the chair and the mayor's health. The man who once quarterbacked the high school football team looked like he put on thirty pounds since he got married, on top of the fifty he carried before that.

"I saw your light burning. What are you working on so late?"

"The bank's board meeting is coming up and I had some

figures to go over. What's your excuse?"

"I ran into Sheriff Banner a while ago and he was telling me about the Pastor Bennett case."

"Oh, like what?"

"Yeah, he said he's looking into the case as a murder and not a suicide."

"Who said anything about a suicide?"

"That's what everyone is saying."

"Since when do you pay attention to what anyone says?"

"I like to listen to all perspectives," I told the Mayor, knowing his comment referred more to me working from intuition rather than hard evidence. This was more of a defense mechanism because even though I can see a person's aura, I don't let on about it. My grandmother, Louise Look Bird, a Cherokee midwife that brought me into the world, warned me a long time ago that people wouldn't understand the gift so I needed to be careful how I used it. Only a few people knew about my gift, Pa and Jeff of course, and I liked it that way. I just preferred people thought I could see ghosts.

"Well," the Mayor said, "the Sheriff is looking at this as a homicide, not suicide."

"Why is that?"

"Even though it's none of your business, it's because there was no gun at the scene. I don't know how a person can shoot themselves in the head and then manage to hide the gun they shot themselves with."

"Well, Franklyn, I'm afraid it is my business."

"What are you talking about?"

"Sheriff Banner is trying to pin this on my Pa."

"Where did you get that idea?"

"He caught up with me at the *Bean* and was looking for Pa. It seems that Pa and the good Pastor had some words and the Sheriff thinks it's enough to get out a posse."

"Now, don't exaggerate, Emma, I'm sure Banner is only following up on a lead."

"He's following a lead all right, to my Pa. Now, Franklyn, you know Pa wouldn't have anything to do with something like this so you need to get the Sheriff to back off."

"Look, Emma, Banner has clearance to look into anything here in town, especially a murder, so let's let him work through the process. He'll find out Logan didn't have anything to do with this. Your Pa has an alibi for his where-a-bouts when Young Bennett was killed, doesn't he?"

Alibi? I actually didn't know about an alibi. Pa didn't offer to provide one. I just assumed he had one.

"Sure, he does," I lied, glad the Mayor couldn't read my aura right then. I'm sure it was throbbing in the dark pink range of untruthfulness.

"Then you got nothing to worry about."

"All the same, Franklyn, I think…"

"No, Emma, don't be thinking about this at all."

"What do you mean?"

"You need to stay out of this with your amateur sleuthing skills and let the Sheriff do his job. That's what we are paying the man for."

"Look, Franklyn, I got to make sure this thing doesn't get out of hand. Maybe I can help?"

"If you really want to help, then stay out of Banner's way. You know he didn't appreciate it when you stuck your nose into the middle of the Walker case."

"He was way off base on that one. I was two steps ahead of him the whole way."

"Don't get sassy, Emma, you got lucky on that one."

"I believe in creating my own luck, Franklyn."

"Look Emma, you let those people down there bury their pastor and get back to their lives. Why do you want to go stirring up things? Those people got enough on their plates and now with their pastor dead…"

"Just what are you talking about?"

The mayor paused at that point. He maybe thought he

already said too much, I didn't know, but the Shaws knew about anything and everything that went on in town. Granddaddy Shaw once told me that if a man took a piss in the river he'd know about it. I knew that was an exaggeration, but only just.

"Come on, Franklyn, what's going on? You know I'll find out about it soon enough. What do you know?"

"Look, Emma, I can't be getting into the *Church of Living Waters* stuff, but I know one thing."

"What?"

"You be careful where you go sticking that pretty nose of yours, you're likely to get bit."

I didn't much like the mayor's attitude about my looking into the case. When he asked me to investigate the Walker murder the year before he was all appreciative of my effort. Of course, he had a business deal pending on that case, and with money on the line, it made a difference. On this matter, it wasn't costing him anything so having Banner stumble through the motions didn't bother him. Or, *was* there money involved? No telling with the Shaws, they always had money riding on any deal in town.

It bothered me though since Pa was involved. I might be overreacting, I mean, I was sure Pa had a solid alibi. It just bothered me that Pa hadn't mentioned what it was.

Chapter Three

With not much more to do in the studio, I decided to lock up and go up to the farm to talk with Pa. I told myself it was just to see how he was doing, but it was also to check on his alibi. We really didn't have the time to discuss all the circumstances of Young Bennett's killing before Sheriff Banner came looking for the man. I could see the timing of everything would be important.

Leading Blue to my Jeep we climbed in and drove out of town and into the foothills beneath Black Mountain. The mountain, so named for a dark green rhododendron face covering, that loomed over town, rose out of a gentle valley fed by three rivers that emptied into Lake Nebo before meandering toward the coast. Old lore from the Catawba recorded a time when you could canoe all the way to the ocean by way of Columbia, South Carolina. People take the interstate now of course and the thought of meandering for a month or so to the beach by way of river and stream never crosses a mind.

Pa's little farm sat adjacent to the national forest. When young, my brother Early and I spent any free time we had running and playing in the deep woods. The Cherokee call the forest, *Nantahala*, or *"Land of the noonday sun,"* because the trees are so thick there that you had to wait for noontime before the sun's rays could get to the forest floor.

By the time I was ten or so, I already knew how to shoot and track. Many a night Early and I would follow my old dog, Big Bay, as he chased a critter in the dark. I'd done a lot of things since then; fought in the desert, hiked through the Rockies, canoed the Colorado River, surfed the Pacific, but chasing a big raccoon with your brother through the black of night ranked near the top in excitement.

By the time I reached the farm, the darkness took hold of the night permanently, the house a shadow against the black forest curtain. Pa liked to go to bed early but not that early. Fact is, with the trouble, I expected to see him up late worrying about the Pastor Bennett thing.

The thought of turning around entered my mind but I decided I'd go all the way up to the house. Pa might have dozed off when reading his Bible and didn't realize how late it was, maybe he was sleeping there in the dark.

I parked out in front of the house next to Pa's old truck and got out. I went to the Jeep's middle door to let Blue out. Uncharacteristically, when I got the door open a crack, she squeezed out and took off barking into the forest. I worried about her going off like that, especially in the thick woods, but she seldom acted that way so I wasn't prepared with her leash. I called after her to no avail hearing her scramble into the underbrush, after what I couldn't imagine.

I figured I was in for a romp in the dark but of course, I didn't have the proper footwear. In a hurry to leave town I was still wearing a cheap pair of flats, ill-suited for rough tracking over roots and fallen limbs. I needed better shoes so went onto the porch and called out for Pa.

When the man didn't answer I went to open the door and of course, I found it ajar like snooping characters find in scary movies or bad mystery books. I went into the dark house and flicked the light switch by the door to the on position, but no light came on, surprise, surprise. I took out my phone and using its flashlight tool, worked my way around the house, flipping up light switches as I went, but with the same no light results.

Confused a bit, I went back to my old bedroom where I still stored a few leftover clothes. My old moccasin boots were in my closet, so I used the phone light to find them and dragged them out. I sat on the edge of my old bed to pull them on. A red State bedspread covered the worn mattress. When I first moved back to town I stayed at home for a while until I could get into my renovated apartment. I still hadn't moved everything out of Pa's house. I guess I was stalling. Something permanent about moving your seventh-grade underwear out of your parent's house.

I went back out and down the short hall to the front door using the phone light to guide me. On my way out, I noticed Pa's 12 gauge was missing from the place where it usually hung over the door. I paused just a moment but when Blue sounded off somewhere outside I rushed through the doorway.

On the near pitch-black front porch, I ran into someone big. Bouncing off, I scrambled away as the person reached out and tried to get hold of me. I knocked their hand away and while at it pivoted around and cranked out a *Taekwondo* sidewinder back kick into the general direction of the person's midsection, hoping to make enough contact to forestall a serious attack.

"Hold on, Emma," Jeff shouted out in the dark after my kick found his tummy. "Take it easy there!"

"Is that you Jeff?"

"Of, course it's me, who do you think it is?"

"What are you doing out here in the dark?"

"Getting kicked in the gut."

"Jeff!"

"I followed you out here. I saw you leave town when I was closing up."

"Why?"

"I thought you'd be coming out here to talk to your Pa, and well, I was kind of interested in hearing what your Pa had to say about Pastor Bennett."

"I wanted to talk to him but he's not here. The power's out in the house. I only went in to get my boots because Blue ran off and I have to go look for her."

"Why's the power off?"

"I don't know."

"Where's the main electrical box?"

"Around back, on the porch."

I led Jeff around back and we found the box open. Using the flashlight on his phone he pointed out the main breaker was open. "Someone flipped off the power," he said, turning the main breaker back on, and every light connected to a switch I turned to the on position, lit up the house. "Why would he cut the power?"

"He wouldn't, not with deer meat and whatnot in his freezer. He'd never cut the power. And, where is he? It's not like him to run off."

We went around to the front of the house and found Blue sitting in the doorway, her tail thumping on the wooden planks, her tongue hanging.

"There you are," I scolded, and before she could run off I hitched her to her leash and led her into the house.

"Do you remember which light switches you tested when you came in?'"

"Why?'"

"Just something I'm thinking about."

"Well, I hit this one here by the door, then the one by the hall door, and then the one in my room."

"Jeff walk through the house flicking light switches off as I mentioned and I followed. The last one he flicked over, turned off the light in my bedroom but it wasn't the last light on in the house. When we went back into the kitchen area the light over the kitchen table was glowing brightly.

Pa had made that table for Mama right after they moved into the house. He used long planks cut from an old oak tree that came right off the land. Early and I spent a lot of hours at that table eating and doing homework. Mama always oversaw our studies. She knew the secret to getting out of Black Mountain was going to be education and she was determined we do our best in school. Of course, Early earned his way out with a football scholarship, and I got an academic scholarship,

31

but Mama was proud of our efforts. I wondered how she'd feel about both her offspring ending up right back where we began.

Pa made a lot of the furniture in the house. Growing up we weren't exactly poor, but there was little extra money. Pa worked up at the mill all right, but he also ran a still for liquor before he got sober and learned to farm.

The light showed down on the tablecloth Mama stitched herself, and there was only one thing on the table, Pa's Bible.

"There's his Bible," I said, pointing, "he always kept it on the table here for studying. The only time it wasn't sitting there was when he took it to bed."

"The chair's pulled out too."

Moving around the kitchen/parlor area Jeff said, "Well, I think I can see what happened."

"What?"

"I think your Pa was sitting there at the table reading his Bible quiet like, probably right after dinner," he added pointing to a coffee cup and plate in the sink drain basket. "Then the power goes off."

"Then what happened?"

"I figure he went out to check."

"I don't know…" I said.

"Then what got him up?"

"He got up all right and went out, but he knew something was up."

"How do you know?"

"Well, he was in a hurry because he left his Bible behind."

"Well, whoever it was, they and your Pa are long gone."

"And another thing…"

"What?"

"He expected trouble when he went out.

"How do you know?"

"He took down his shotgun when he went out."

***

On the drive back to town I had some time to think over what happened. Pa must have been scared off that's why he disappeared and why he left his truck behind. I didn't know about what. As far back as I remembered there wasn't much that could scare Pa. Still, someone or something spooked him, so suddenly he didn't take his Bible, but still left him enough of his wits to grab his shotgun on the way out the door. It was a puzzle to me. My primary question was, did it have something to do with Young Pastor Bennett's death?

Jeff had followed me down the mountain and when we got back to Main Street I expected him to veer off for his family home, but instead, he followed me right to the front of the studio.

"Aren't you ready to call it a day?" I asked the man when we both got out and stood out in the cold. I was hoping Jeff wasn't hanging around for any romantic reasons. I was too worried about my pa and wondering what happened to the pastor to have romance on my mind at that moment.

These days I wasn't sure what I felt about Jeff. There was a time when just being around him made my knees weak and I usually developed a stutter. But here lately, after being back in town for over a year, we had settled into familiar roles of beau and gal. But although the infatuation luster had dimmed, I could still get goose bumps when Jeff held me in his arms.

"I'm bushed for sure, but there's one thing I wanted to tell you."

"What?"

"About your Pa."

"I know, that's just not like him. I wouldn't worry though, if Pa is up in the mountain he'll be okay. He knows those hills like the back of his hand."

"No, it was something else. I should have told you before but…"

"But what?"

"Well, it may look bad for your Pa. That's what I wanted to talk to him about. You know, just clear up a loose end, a big loose end."

"What loose end?"

"Emma, I sold your Pa a little .32 handgun a week back."

Chapter Four

Folk in the mountain just gravitate to guns as if they're a birthright. I grew up with guns and they didn't scare me. I learned to shoot with a little over and under .22/310 rifle my Pa had. It wasn't good for much. Later, when I could shoulder and handle the recoil, I used a .20 gauge for bird hunting, and eventually, Pa showed me how to shoot the 30/30 for deer and wild boar. Of course, the killing part always bothered me. Sometimes it seemed a waste, but as long as you put up the meat for eating then it almost made sense, almost.

I got my marksmanship medal in basic training and joined a rifle platoon for deployment. There weren't many that could score higher than me. Pa was proud of that.

I know a lot of people are uncomfortable around guns, but even a really poor family will have a rifle or shotgun around the house. But I never saw the need for a handgun, and from what I remembered, Pa would have had to be rolling in dough to spend a dime for a pistol of any sort.

"Pa never used a handgun," I said to Jeff when he told me about Pa buying a pistol. If true, it might look bad for Pa, but it had to be a coincidence that Young Pastor Bennett was shot with a small-caliber handgun. Of course, we'd have to have the ballistics back from the State Bureau to confirm that.

"I know, it surprised me that he even wanted to look at one. But you know we keep that cabinet full of used pistols we've traded for or bought at gun shows over the years. The markup is really high and we get a lot of collectors looking at them. We put them up on the website and we have people from all over the country inquire about them. A collector came over from Texas last summer and bought an old Colt M1848 Dragoon that Confederate officers carried during the Civil War. It was in good condition."

"Where did you get that?"

"The Patterson family had it up in their attic. Belonged to their great grandfather who got it from his grandfather who served in the South. The thing was a hundred and fifty-some years old but I cleaned it up, added some oil, and got it working like a clock."

"So, what did Pa buy?"

"I sold him an S&W Snub Nose .32 revolver, you know a small handgun, like all the old detectives used to use. They don't make them stateside anymore. Most people use a 9MM for self-defense."

"Self-defense? Pa told you he wanted one for self-defense?"

"That's what he said. Oh, it was an older model but still usable."

"I don't understand, Pa wouldn't need a pistol for self-defense, he would as soon beat someone to death with his boot as to shoot them with a handgun."

"I know, Emma, but he dropped in a couple of times before settling on the little revolver, and he didn't haggle over the price, paid cash. I ended up giving him a preferred customer discount and threw in a box of shells we hand-loaded. It's hard to find shells for a gun like that."

"Well, that doesn't make sense. When did you say all this happen?"

"Couple of weeks ago, more or less, but I can check the license application if you want. It would have the exact date."

"Go on and check, we may need to know, although I just can't figure any of this."

Chapter Five

Tuesday

With the revelation fresh in my head that Pa possessed a handgun just like the gun that maybe killed Pastor Bennett, I went to bed and tossed and turned all night. I had heaped a pile of blankets atop the bed against the fall nighttime cold. Once I got the real fireplace installed in the upstairs apartment I'd have heat, but until then the uninsulated plywood over the fireplace opening in the wall wasn't much of a deterrent. The cold air happily seeped in, keeping the room only a few degrees above the outside air.

Blue never let me sleep in beyond 6:00 AM. About a quarter to the hour, she started moaning and fidgeting for me to get up and let her out. Once the hour turned, she commenced to barking. I couldn't complain though. She only had a couple of indoor accidents the first week I got her and since then she had a regular routine. Of course, it started at 6:00 AM with a walk along the river and usually ended with a long walk around town in the evening. Once in a while, when I felt full of energy, we'd go all the way down to the lake about a mile away and we'd jog a little.

I got up and put the same jeans on I wore the day before and slipped into my wool socks and moccasin boots. I put on an old State sweatshirt and pulled the hoody over my head and Blue and I stumbled down the staircase in the dark. I put her lead on her and we went out the back door.

Main Street Black Mountain paralleled the Swannanoa River but stood on high ground with Mill Row between. The Shaws built the row of mill houses back when most of the men in town worked at the mill and needed cheap housing. The row of small cottages sat neat and well kept on both sides of the street. There used to be only retired mill worker families living

37

there but with the general revitalization of the town's economy the small homes grew in value and young people began buying them up and renovating them. Now you could hardly find one for sale. Mostly you had to wait on an old retiree to die off before a cottage would come available.

The mill workers never owned their homes, and neither did the retired folks. They all lived there under an agreement with the Shaws, and once they moved out or died, the properties reverted back to the Shaws. Before the recent property value increases, the homes weren't much more than slum quality, but now the Shaws were making minimum repairs and selling them for huge profits. The Shaws weren't anything if not shrewd business people.

A few of the homes on the row fell into serious disrepair before the gentrification of the street began, so the town demolished them and left the lots vacant. The double empty lot at the end of the street turned out to be Blue's favorite. I didn't know why, maybe because the river flowed closest there, but whatever it was, Blue held her business in until we reached the lot. Lord help me if it was raining that morning because it was her favorite spot, rain, snow, or sunshine.

Back in the studio, we went up the steps to the apartment and I fed Blue a cup of dried food and turned the coffee maker on. I hustled into the bathroom and slammed the door behind me and turned on the hot water nozzle in the shower. I didn't have to wait long since the water heater was in the closet on the other side of the bathroom wall. I designed it that way on purpose. After years of waiting on hot water to get to me, I decided early on to make sure that was one detail I got right in the renovation.

By the time I got my clothes off, the shower water was running hot, and I stepped into the shower closing the glass door. The room quickly steamed up. I let the water run off my head and back feeling wonderful. I pulled off the rubber band I had used to bundle my long braid and after unwinding my thick black hair, I shampooed. I let the water run another minute or two just because I could. Even though the apartment lacked heat, the hot water ran hot. After nearly a year, I had yet to run the hot water down and I was beginning to think it might be an endless supply.

I finally gave in, turned off the water and grabbed a towel and rubbed myself down. I wrung out the excess water from my hair and then using another towel, wrapped it tight and looped it over my head. I dried off with a separate towel and wrapped that around me as well. I peered into the mirror to see what I looked like but couldn't see my reflection in the steamed up mirror, so I put on my heavy robe I kept hanging behind the door and with a "burr", stepped out into the cold room, my skin still tingling and flush from the shower.

Blue had disappeared. I knew she'd gone on back to bed but I couldn't. I had a good business day ahead of me. I had two appointments in the studio to get ready for and then a girls' middle school soccer game to shoot that afternoon. I had landed a contract with the school system to provide photography services for all their sports teams. The after-school jobs kept me busy during the school season with high school varsity and junior varsity sports and an equal amount of middle school sports as well. On the weekends, the area youth sports league contributed to my business cash flow line that until then was headed in the wrong direction.

A bonus from the school contract gave me the opportunity to sell photos of the players on my website. I sold regular action prints, framed shots, posters, novelty items, and resin blocks that grandparents seemed to love to purchase. I knew going into it that the portrait aspect of the business would take time to develop but everything I read said the side stuff like weddings and special events, would make up an equal revenue stream, and what I read turned out right. I'd even been toying with the idea of using the latest technology of drone photography for a number of uses that paid particularly well, including just about everything associated with real estate.

So, with the day ahead of me I poured a cup of coffee and went back to my bedroom to get dressed. I needed to look professional on the job but thank goodness the physical nature of the job allowed for some flexibility in my attire. Never a fashion diva to begin with, being more comfortable in jeans and boots, I settled on several fleece jogger suits. The comfortable-fitting outfits gave me the freedom to squat, lie, and crouch in awkward positions as I searched for different subject angles in the studio work but also allowed me the freedom to run up and down the sidelines of a school sporting event.

I blew my hair dry and pulled it back into a ponytail that hung down near my waist. I looked into the mirror on my dressing table and settled on rubbing a dab of lotion for my face and hands but nothing else since my Cherokee ancestors provided enough color that I didn't need extra.

I shook off my robe and towel, slipped into underwear, and put on a clean navy-blue outfit with a fitted top and tapered legs. I stepped into a pair of running shoes, grabbed my coffee, and went downstairs where I had heat in the studio, to get ready for the morning. Blue had taken to continuing his nightly sleep by curling up on a mat she dragged over to a heating vent in the corner of the reception area. For the most part Blue ignored me while in the studio, but she always got up to inspect clients when they came in. After she decided they weren't there to kill me or anything, she'd retreat back to her bed.

Until my first appointment, I busied myself with the new orders that came in on the computer since yesterday, arranged my two studio spaces for the morning sittings, and tried not to think about my Pa and the dead young Pastor Bennett.

Chapter Six

The photography studio management software system I installed connected my website and all the utilities I needed to operate including an integrated calendar. Potential customers could make appointments and after, order prints right online. You could set the interval between appointments, and I took advantage of that to give me time between shoots for working with customers on orders. The system displayed the digital photos on a big screen and allowed for an extended review for mothers and grandmothers to pick out just the right poses. I could tell by the number of booked appointments that the approaching holiday season would be busy.

Most of my family shoots were on the weekend and the appointments for every Saturday booked quickly, but I had an occasional weekday shoot.

That morning the Spencers were coming in. Mack and Mabel Spencer, 70 years old and counting, came in dragging four toddler great-grandchildren, three boys, and a pretty red-headed girl. Mack and Mable had six children of their own and I don't know how many grandchildren but between the schools and the youth leagues I worked there must have been twenty athletes out there with the Spencer name. The only other more prominent name I saw playing was Shaw.

Mack spencer was retired from the mill, but Mabel had been an assistant teacher with the school system for forty years. When you added all the second-grade students she mentored through the years, Mabel probably had a family of over a thousand children that loved her. We should all be so lucky, and not that I was rushing her, but whenever she got around to dying, the crowd at her funeral would probably fill three churches.

"Mabel," I said to the grand lady when she came in

through the door, Mack and the four great grands trailing behind, "You look wonderful today." The lady wore a medium-length gray wool skirt and a bright red wool sweater with a turtleneck top. At only about 100 pounds, but at close to six feet tall, she resembled a well-dressed stork, and I spent the next hour chasing the toddlers and trying to find the best look for their holiday photo card. I juggled arranging lights and shades against a blue background. Thank goodness for digital photos as I would have wasted several rolls of the old 35 mm film on the shoot and still wouldn't have been sure of the results. But with the digital system, I could check my camera as I shot to make sure I was getting the right poses. Afterwards, Mabel could use the computer to look at the sixty or so shots and insert a make-believe background chosen from an index too numerous to count, so I got off cheaply, and she chose just the right one.

The second appointment that morning was with Darlene and Charles Paulson, both eighty years old. They wanted a photo to attach to an announcement of their sixtieth wedding anniversary. When they sat in front of the blank green screen their auras seeped out and blended together in a warm lavender that I had only seen once or twice before. I'd never been an expert at aura reading but I knew that color was associated with deeply spiritual people.

Early in my photography career, I discovered that I could use my aura reading skill to pinpoint the exact moment in time when a subject's countenance is most vivid. It doesn't work with everyone. Many people are capable of hiding their auras, either by choice, like they hide feelings, or just by nature, like naturally shy people, but most of the time, as a subject's aura yoyos between their inherent color ranges, that magic moment comes.

The grand couple looked almost regal in brand new clothes. I could see a sales tag dangling from Charles's coat sleeve so figured they would be returning the outfits to

Miller's fine clothes, the main clothing store in town, once they got the photo they wanted. My hunch was further confirmed when Darlene shouted, "Don't sit down!", at Charles every time he tried to sit down and run the risk of wrinkling the new pair of pants.

Knowing they were a church-going couple I asked them if they heard about Young Pastor Bennett.

"Of course," Darlene said, "we've been going to *Living Waters* for a couple of years now. Ester Cook called me and told me all about it."

"It's a shame what happened to the Pastor," Charles said.

"Well, it's always a shame when someone dies," Darlene said, "but he brought it on himself."

"What do you mean?" I asked.

"The Pastor carried the weight of the church on his shoulders. No one could stand under that weight for long before it'd wear you down."

"Are you saying you think the Pastor committed suicide?"

"Of course, dear."

"The Sheriff says it was murder."

"Who'd want to kill the poor pastor?" Charles asked.

"I don't know. I'm just telling you what the Sheriff has been saying."

"Well, I don't know anything about that," Darlene said. "I just know the pastor was under a lot of stress lately and him up and killing himself wouldn't be much of a surprise to those that know what all he's been going through."

"What kind of stress?"

"All kinds. He had the new sanctuary project to worry him, the fundraising campaign, the church budget, then that deal with his brother…"

"What about his brother?"

"It wasn't too long after Pastor Bennett was hired, he brought him over from Hickory and put him on as assistant Pastor over operations, and not many agreed with that."

43

"What's there to say?"

"People had a lot to say. It really caused the first real rift in the Elders."

"Oh, Darlene," her husband said, "you are just speculating on that."

"Now, Maxine Waters said as much just last week. It's the reason Clare Bennett called for an audit of the church's books."

"Well, he cared too much for the flock," Charles said, "and that brother of his was no help."

***

Once the morning rush was over, I started to work on the sports orders from previous athletic events. The system held a backlog of orders, and I worried that I wouldn't be able to catch up, even with Sue Ellen's help. God forbid, the notion of hiring someone else to help with printing and production, even crossed my mind. I calculated some preliminary numbers, costs of the wages versus the predicted profit and it made sense to hire another part-time person. Someone to print out the posters that appeared to be gaining in popularity.

The system was in the middle of a print run when a loud beep filled the room indicating the printer was out of ink. When I checked the supply cabinet I almost swore. The ink cartridge box was empty and a yellow post-it note on the box showed my "order more" reminder that I had forgotten about.

The nearest store that carried the printer cartridge I needed was thirty minutes away at the shopping center on the highway near Lenoir. I quickly calculated I could make the round trip there and back in plenty of time to get to the school soccer game at three o'clock. Besides, I needed the ink if Sue Ellen was going to run any prints in the afternoon, otherwise, she'd be downloading more orders on top of what we already had.

I grabbed Blue's leash and took her out back for a quick

"do it" run, put her back in the studio with instructions to *guard the place*, then went out front and got in the Jeep for the ride over to Lenoir.

I hated going out of town for supplies. I was determined to support the local businesses as much as possible, but the office supply section of the Shaw General Store on Main Street only carried a few standard ink cartridges, so I had to shop out of town for anything professional. I had bought a few things online but deemed it better for the area economy to at least keep the revenue in the state. The only trouble with shopping at the busy shopping center was Joanie Shaw worked at a dress shop right next to the office supply store and likely as not would see me pull up and make it a point to talk to me, or as she had in high school, torture me.

Joanie Shaw had run the high school, *we are the pretty girls, and we know it,* clique. Even after the years between, she still thought of herself as the leader of the posse. It was her group that started the false narrative that I could see ghosts, the *Ghost Whisperer*. It was my own fault since I divulged my aura reading ability to someone I thought was a friend who went and told the group. Dense as they were to not understand my ability, I let the rumor spread, at the time thinking it was just better to laugh it off as a joke instead of trying to explain just what exactly this gift was that I possessed.

It was also no secret she always had eyes for Jeff. My return to town created an obstacle she thought she did away with back in high school. Oh well, best-laid plans, right? If I was lucky she wouldn't see me. I wasn't.

"Well, if it isn't little Emma Shaw!" Joanie exclaimed, coming out of the fancy dress shop and smiling wide after she saw me pull in, almost like she was waiting on me. She had somehow managed to stuff herself into a much too small low-cut red blouse and tight black fashion jeans. Her red heels made her tower over me even more than her normal height. Her long shoulder-length hair tended to run in the blond range, but at that moment it looked positively red.

"Hello, Joanie," I said, stepping on the sidewalk and moving quickly down toward the office supply store entrance, "how have you been?"

"We're just hammered lately," she told me, following along as I walked. "Everyone getting out and shopping early for the holidays. So, what brings you to town?"

"I need a printer cartridge for the studio."

"Oh, that's right…little Emma, the entrepreneur. So, how is business?"

"It's growing," I said, surprised she even knew the word entrepreneur. I bet she couldn't spell it.

"Well, I'm glad something is."

"Umm … yes," I said and moving quickly added, "and I've got to get going because I have an appointment this afternoon."

"So, how's Jeff?"

She knew that would get me to pause.

"He's fine," I told her, stopping to face her, and just to dig it in a little I added, "we went out Saturday night."

"Where did you go?" she asked smiling down at me.

"That new place in town, the micro-brewery, Black Brew Brewery."

"Oh, I just love that place. They have a great beer list, even carry some brands out of Asheville, and they have live music once in a while."

"Well, I'm mostly a chardonnay gal, but I like an occasional beer if it's locally brewed."

"I know, it seems to be really catching on, who would have thought, a micro-brewery in Black Mountain?"

Then, I couldn't help myself, but interested in her dating life asked, "Do you go there often?"

"Oh, yes, once or twice a week. You meet a lot of men there, which reminds me, did you hear about Young Pastor Bennett?"

"Yes, I did," I told her but didn't offer any details. "How does going out to a bar remind you of Pastor Bennett?"

"Oh, the good Pastor liked a cold beer now and again."

"What?"

"Oh yes, a left-over habit from his years down at State."

"I didn't know," I said and wondered about what other habits the good pastor might have developed in his youth.

"Yes, indeed, I've seen him there several times."

"But wasn't he married with kids?"

"Yes, he was," she said, and smiled down at me, but didn't offer anything more.

After my run-in with Joanie, I finished up my shopping, including purchasing a ream of poster paper, and started back to Black Mountain. I looked at my phone and could see I was ahead of schedule so wondered if I could make a quick stop at the *Church of Living Waters*. You know, just to get a look at the murder scene.

***

The Church of Living Waters had stood proudly for some 100 years. The old wooden structure occupied a corner of a country road intersection, across from Lake Nebo. The church's whitewashed steeple poked proudly out of the forest trees and its cast iron bell could be heard miles away, both beacons of truth and redemption to its faithful. A small cemetery took up the north side of the property, parking took up the south side, and the lake stood across the road, about a hundred yards to the east. To the rear, a thick forest loomed, and a rusted chain-link fence cordoned off the privately owned forest property from the church land. A bright green lawn that someone took pride in maintaining, surrounded the church. Several newer looking, *no trespassing signs*, were posted prominently at short intervals along the fence, warning people to stay out of the forest.

I'd never been much of an architect or engineer but looking at the church's location I wondered just how the congregation expected to expand the property to build a larger sanctuary.

I parked on the side of the church where a recently added wood-sided church annex with church offices, was connected to the church proper. A sign, planted in the green lawn said, *Living Waters Church* – William L. Bennett, III – Pastor. The little lot stood half full and I had to park several rows back. People were coming and going between the little office complex and the church, and I began to question my timing in stopping, what with preparations for the services for young Pastor Bennett. But since I was already there I decided to go on and see if I could talk to someone about the incident.

I decided to skip the main office and followed an older group of parishioners as they made their way to the church's rear entrance.

Darkness crowded the sanctuary. It took my eyes a minute to adjust, but the group I followed appeared to be the cleaning team, busy with a loud vacuum and mops, the scent of Lysol in the air.

"Hello," I called out, trying to get someone's attention. An older man and woman heard me and came over to talk, but when they realized they wouldn't be able to hear me above the noise, they directed me outside.

"Hello," I said again, once outside, "I'm Emma Shaw."

"Hello, I'm Wendell Hawkins," the man nodded. "Nice to finally meet you in person."

"Oh, do we know each other?"

"Not really, but I see you driving around town in that Jeep of yours, you and your dog."

"Oh, yeah, that's Blue."

"A black lab, right? Good dogs, I've got a whole brood of them."

"I love her, although we're having a little difficulty adjusting to city life, you know, living above my studio."

"Well, glad you could come by, and on such short notice."
Not knowing what he meant I nodded my head. "Yes, sir,
I was sure sorry to hear about young Pastor Bennett."

"Yes, we are all so sad," the woman said, a bright violet
aura ticking from her, the color related to spirituality, "as you
can imagine. The pastor had many followers, so we want to
make sure we honor him properly at the funeral service."

"Yes, I understand he was well-loved."

"Of course," Hawkins said, his aura a dark tone of the
same violet, "as are all the children of God."

I wanted to ask if I could take a look at the crime scene,
but as the team was actively cleaning the whole area, I doubted
there would be any evidence left to discover.

"I supposed you want to look at the renderings?" the man
asked.

"Renderings?" I asked in return, hoping I didn't look like
a complete fool.

"Yes," he said, turning and looking back to the church.
"The pastor loved this old church, but he told us many times
that the future of the congregation depended on building a
larger sanctuary and the Board of Elders agreed, so we want
to remind the parish by including some slides of the project.
You know, just enough to remind the congregation of how
much the Pastor wanted the expansion and how much he
would want us to move forward with it."

"Not all of us," the woman said. "We are all not in unison
when it comes to moving forward."

"No?"

"No, we are not."

"Now, Sister Ester, I'm sure the young lady isn't
interested in the goings-on at *Living Waters.*"

The man was growing on me, especially as he referred to
me as a young lady. It had been a while since I was addressed
that way. Of course, compared to the elder set, I guess I was
young.

"So," I asked, "why isn't the congregation set on moving forward?"

"Money of course," Ester said. "We may be a growing flock, but the big money in town still attends First Presbyterian. I don't know how the Pastor expected to pay for a new church. We can barely keep the lights on as it is."

When neither offered any more I asked, "So, about this presentation, I'm not sure I understand?"

"Oh, we know it's a bit unusual," the man said, "for a funeral, but I think the Pastor would approve. Most of these slide shows always deal with a recently departed person's past. Here we want to show what the Pastor's vision for the future looked like. Don't you agree?"

I am not usually so dense, but I finally figured out what the man was talking about. He was referring to me preparing a slide show about the church's plans to build a new sanctuary. Somehow, he figured I'd come early for a proposed appointment to get the details. They must have gotten word that I ran the photography studio in town, and I'd make a good choice for preparing the presentation.

"Clare Bennett highly recommended you," the woman said.

"She did?"

"Yes," the man said, "she was quite adamant. Anyway, let's go over to the office, you'll want to speak with Pastor John."

"Pastor John?" I asked.

"Associate Pastor John," the woman said with emphasis on the associate title.

"Yes," the man said, "Pastor William's older brother. He's taken over duties until the Elders can decide on who will lead the church permanently."

"He's taken over a little too much if you ask me," the woman spoke out.

"Now, Ester, let's not be judgmental, someone has to take

charge and he *was* second in command, so to speak."

I followed the man, weighing the options. I could tell him I was completely unaware of what he was talking about, or I could hold off a bit and see how Clare Bennett fit in with all this. Maybe she knew something about Pa? Maybe she knew where he was? Maybe she knew who killed the good Pastor Bennett? I should be so lucky.

"Here we are," the man said when we entered the crowded room. There was little noise in the room, as befitting the occasion, but plenty of activity.

"Where's Pastor John?" the man asked a pretty young lady. "We need to see him."

"He's in the office," the young lady said, tears clouding her eyes, "follow me." Her aura radiated out of her in a broad orange swath, a color I usually associate with sexuality.

"Here we are," the young lady said, as we entered a small but plush office. Pastor William Bennett's name still adorned the office door and a desktop plate, with the deceased pastor's name, still occupied a place on the wide dark desk, but the man with his head in a file cabinet was someone else.

"Now, Candace," the man said hearing her announcement but not turning around, "are you sure the pastor kept his Bible in here? I can't find it anywhere."

"Pastor John, this is Emma Shaw," Mr. Hawkins introduced me. "Come to look at the renderings."

"Sorry," he said, turning around and seeing us standing there, "I didn't know I had visitors."

"Oh," the young lady said, "I only just now sent the email."

Thinking quickly, I said, "I just got it over my phone and since I was in the area, I thought I'd stop by on a chance I could see about this today."

I could see the young woman working the timeline over in her head, but she rushed off, putting the question behind her before another wave of crying could overtake her.

"You'll have to excuse Candace," the man said, "we are all still a bit overwhelmed by Williams's death."

"I can understand."

"Well, this is very prompt of you," the man said more brightly still, taking a seat behind the desk, "coming around so quickly, we do appreciate it."

With the introductions over, Hawkins left me and the Pastor alone.

"So, Clare Bennett recommended me?" I asked the man while I sat down in a chair across from him.

"Yes, Sister Clare sits on the Services Committee," he said, closing a large ledger book and getting to his feet again, moving across the room to a filing cabinet. "This morning when we were looking at the budget for the services, she recommended you. It's too much of course, to organize everything, but we are pushing on. So," he asked after putting the ledger in the cabinet and closing it and with a push, pressing the locking button, "can you prepare a nice slide show?"

"Oh yes indeed, as long as I have something good to work with."

"Well good, here are the renderings," he said, picking up a thick brown folder stuffed with files and handing it to me, "Clare left these for you, elevations and such of the future church campus. William had an architecture firm over in Asheville design the new church. There are several renderings and elevations in there and we'd like to have those made into slides for the funeral service. Now, we haven't selected the music yet, and if you have a recommendation we would look at that, but I think a two-minute show for this part is all we need. Don't want to bore anyone, right?"

"Right, two minutes."

"Now," he said sitting down again across from me and smiling, "we are looking through a pile of other photos, from his youth and ministry, some family stuff, and when we get all those together, I'll get Candace to run them over to you. Altogether a five-minute loop should be sufficient. Now, we are planning on a Friday night viewing and Saturday afternoon service. Will that give you time?"

"No problem," I told the man, finally on top of the task.

"So," the man said, sitting back and smiling even wider still, "what will be your fee?"

"Well, Pastor John, I couldn't charge you for this, I mean it would be the least I can do."

"Are you sure? We are not without means here at *Living Waters.*"

"I couldn't think of it," I said, remembering what good Sister Ester had said about the church's finances.

"Well, then bless you, and we look forward to seeing what you can do. Now remember, not too gloomy, okay? We want people to feel like we are still pressing forward with William's vision."

"Right."

I took the materials out to the Jeep and started toward town. It surprised me a little that I agreed to the service, especially for free, but now I needed to find out about Clare Bennett and why she thought I'd be a good choice for this job. As far as I remembered, I'd never met the woman. I think it had to do with something other than my skill as a photographer. I also wanted to find out a little more about the smiling Pastor John and his brown aura. I usually only see that color around people not associated with doing good, like the Shaws.

Chapter Seven

Rushing back to my studio and got there with just enough time to take Blue out for a quick walk and to get my gear together for the soccer game. Blue gave me a look that told me she was not happy about me going out again without her.

"I'm sorry, girl," I apologized, as I loaded a bag with stuff, "we'll go for a long walk this evening, okay?" Blue was not satisfied with the promise, but I had to leave her. I'd taken her to a game or two early on, but it proved problematic as she barked loudly through the whole match, thoroughly annoying the spectators. The months since I came into possession of the dog reminded me why I had never gotten a dog before, it was too much responsibility. I could barely take care of myself. How was I supposed to take care of a dog too? If it weren't for her big sad brown eyes, I would have given her back a long time ago. Now it was too late for that. Now I was stuck, for better or worse, just like being married, well, maybe not as bad.

"I promise," I told her again as I remembered to leave the ink cartridge on the computer desk for Sue Ellen to see and headed for the door. "I'll be back in a couple of hours."

The Black Mountain Middle School soccer match was against a team bused over from Boone County. It went down to the wire and ended in a one-all draw. The league rules didn't allow for a penalty kick decision on the winner of the match. I guess someone high up decided if two teams fought hard enough to end in a tie then it should stay that way. I know the two teams of girls liked it that way. When the match ended, the two teams formed lines and walked by each other fist-bumping and smiling at each other with both sides happy, as opposed to the opposite attitudes if one of the teams had lost.

After the game, I hustled out to the parking lot and passed

out flyers. I found out the previous season that the visiting team parents and grandparents turned out to be good customers, so I made it a point to let everyone know that action photos of the players were available to order through my website. I knew that I'd get a handful of orders overnight. The revenue stream was so important that I found myself shooting as many action shots of the opposing teams as the home team, even though my contract to provide photography was with the home school system.

By the time the last car left the area and I climbed into my Jeep, the sun had set, and darkness began to swallow the mountain. As I made my way back to town in the gloom, I started thinking again about Pa and how he could fit in with the death of young Pastor Bennett. It didn't make sense that anyone could think a small argument could result in violence. But why did Pa buy that handgun?

Back at the studio I pushed through the door and heard the printer going in the back room, and as always, I heard Blue's feet come rushing down the hall. When she got within striking distance, she launched herself at me, knocking me down on my rear end, licking away at my face.

"Blue, get off me," I yelled at the big and growing dog. Pushing her off, I struggled to my feet.

"That you Ms. Shaw?" Sue Ellen called from the workroom.

"Sue Ellen, how are you?" I asked my part-time helper. Sue Ellen had taken the place of Laney Shaw who went off to college back in the spring. She wasn't as good with the customers as Laney had been, especially with the babies, but I liked her. I appreciated her bright green aura, signifying an emotionally balanced being, and one with the world around. She was also a whiz with the shop's photography software program and invoicing. Both tasks I didn't gravitate to naturally.

"I'm fine Ms. Shaw, I'm trying to catch up with the

orders. Would you like me to load the game's shots on the website?"

"Yes, please," I gladly agreed, walking into the room, and handing her my camera bag, then thinking of my earlier cash flow calculations I added, "Say, Sue Ellen, do you know anyone who that might want some part-time work? I'm thinking about getting someone in here to help us out. What do you think?"

"I don't know, you wouldn't be cutting my hours none?"

"Oh, no, just someone to run the print jobs and help us out on the weekends. You know I used to have an extra person last year. Also, I've been wanting to add delivery to our services, so someone to make deliveries would help out a lot. What do you think?"

"Well, sure then. In fact, my boyfriend is looking for work, you know he's got a truck."

"Ask him to come by and we'll talk. Tell him I'll reimburse for his gas."

I took Blue out back for her evening walk in the dark. The river seemed to make almost no sound, its heavy flow moving as one, almost a thing, the lights of the homes on Mill Row reflecting off its black mass, giving it brooding life.

When done we went back to the studio and Sue Ellen, and I worked steadily until I gave in and let her go around 7:00.

Sue Ellen was a distant relative of some sort. When the first Granddaddy Shaw came into the valley, he fathered eight boys and two girls and since then the Shaw progeny spawned countless lines of heirs. You'd need a genealogy chart six-foot-long to trace the varied branches of the Shaw tree, and then there was the Bennett line who got in through the marriage route. When you added them to the mix the brew was too well stirred to make much sense of.

Blue and I walked Sue Ellen to the door where she bent down and gave the dog a big hug and told her she'd see her tomorrow. At that moment her boyfriend pulled to the curb. I could see in the streetlamp over the stoop that he drove an old but well-kept truck, a good sign that he was a responsible young man. Sue Ellen climbed in the passenger side and I saw her scoot over to the middle space and give the boy a kiss. She stayed there as they drove off. Ah…young love I thought, trying to remember how that felt, but it had been so long ago I couldn't quite recall the feeling. The feeling in my stomach was probably hunger telling me I hadn't eaten since breakfast.

I followed the truck taillights as it went down the street, passing the Fish and Game store where lights still shone brightly out of the windows. I knew Jeff would be in the shop, hard at work. His family had run the store for the past hundred years or so. Before the valley was permanently settled, the Carsons were well known for gunsmithing. Through hard work, their business grew along with the town. It was a source of pride for them that they were one of the few businesses in town that the Shaws didn't own.

I glanced back into my shop, dreading going back up to an empty apartment just then, so putting a leash on Blue, we went up the walk to the Fish and Game.

"Hey," I called out when I opened the shop door and a bell announced my arrival, "can I buy you a drink?"

Blue rushed in, crawled beneath the counter, and jumped into Jeff's lap as he sat at a worktable loading gunshot into hulls. A long glass counter, filled with guns and knives of every shape and size, separated the space between the customer side and the work side. On the customer side several rows of clothes, hunting, and casual wear, crowded a single aisle. Fishing gear took up the far end and racks of rifles took up available space on the back wall.

"I don't know about a drink, but I could use supper."

"Okay, I'll buy."

"I can pay."

"Oh, sure, I know, but let me treat you."

The only place in town open at that hour was the *Coffee*

Bean. All the other places, closed up early, except for Shaw Diner, on the outskirts of town. But at that hour, it would only be serving its 24-hour breakfast special for the truckers coming off the interstate looking for diesel fuel and something heavy to eat.

Jeff went around and put a ledger into a file cabinet, but before we got out, the door swung in, and a big man dressed from head to toe in camouflage came in with four other similarly dressed younger men behind him.

"Not closed, are you?" the older man asked.

"Just about," Jeff said back, "you caught me just heading out. Emma, do you know Sam Lawson and his boys, from up Beulah way?"

"Yes Sir, Mr. Lawson," I greeted the older man and waved at his boys who had taken up a position at the front of the store, two on either side of the doorway. I could see the boys' ages ranged from mid-twenties up to their thirties, and all big and broad. I thought I recognized the oldest one. I also saw they were all armed with some firearm, including the elder Lawson who had an old revolver in a holster belted through his pants.

"You Early Shaw's little sister?" the man asked, referring to me in a way I'd never outgrow, no matter how old I'd gotten.

"Yes, sir!" I answered the man and noted his dark green aura that indicated someone at home with nature. "Did you know my brother?"

"No, not really," he said, "but I heard you did a good job solving his murder case."

"I got my two cents in," I said, as I saw his aura tint to the pink hue of deceit, surprising me. What I found out over the years about aura reading was that it was hard to pin down what exactly a person was trying to lie about. With Mr. Hawkins it could have been a lie about knowing my brother or a lie about having heard about my *good detective work.*

"Humm…" he said, pausing to take a good look at me, like sizing up a piece of meat.

"Well," the man said, turning to Jeff, "I need a box of 30.30s if you're still open to taking my money?"

"Sure, one box enough?"

"Better make it two, my eyesight isn't what it used to be, especially when I get up in my stand. For some reason, those deer won't stand still."

"Where do you have your stand?" Jeff asked the man.

"We built one up in an old oak tree, down by the lake, near the church.

"*Living Waters Church?*" I asked him.

"Yep."

"Do you go there?" I asked, surprised.

"The missus goes and makes me and the boys tag along, she works up in the office there."

"Then you heard Pastor William died?"

"Yep, really broke up the missus. Suicide, was it?"

"They don't know for sure."

"Who doesn't?"

"The Sheriff. He says it could be murder."

"Is that right? Well, as long as I can still hunt down there."

"Now, Mr. Lawson," Jeff asked the man, "you're not hunting on church land, are you?"

"No, sir, I've got our stand a way back in the woods north of there."

"You own that land?" I asked him.

"Me? Heck no. It belongs to the Porter family. Do you remember them? I went to school with Julie and Jolene Porter, and they let us hunt down there."

"I thought the Porters moved away?" Jeff asked.

"They did, down Florida way, couldn't take the cold up here anymore. Can you put the shells on my account?"

"You know Mr. Lawson," I said, "the church is planning to expand down there."

"Oh, I didn't know," the man said, his aura still pulsing a shade of muddy pink. "What's it to you?

"Sheriff's been looking into the Pastor's death."

"Yeah, so you said, and…?"

"My Pa's involved so I'm looking into it."

"Well," Lawson ended the conversation, picking up a bag with his shells, and heading to the door, "that's got nothing to do with us."

After Lawson and his boys left, I asked Jeff, "How common is that, hunting on other people's land?"

"Most people would complain big time if they caught you hunting on their land. That kind of thing got many a man shot for trespassing."

"Well, then how come no one has never said anything to Mr. Lawson?"

"Maybe they are an absent owner, you know, just an investment company owns the land. A group like that wouldn't know what was going on down there."

"I'm not sure about that," I said.

"Why"

"First time I went down there I noticed there were brand new "No Trespassing" signs on the fence that separates the forest land from the church grounds, like they had just been put up. Someone local is looking after that land, for sure. The only question is who doesn't want the word getting out on who owns the property?"

"I wonder who?"

The one person I knew in town who would know about that property was Thomas Shaw, the manager of the Shaw family real estate company.

We left the shop and walked down the walk. Blazing logs from the fireplace greeted us when we went into the *Bean* and the nearly full place bustled with activity. We read the *Bean's* limited nighttime menu, printed on a black chalkboard easel standing at the front of the entrance. Not known for their cuisine they did offer a selection of delicious homemade soups and hot Panini sandwiches.

After ordering we sat at a table and a waitress brought our order, Jeff started in with a vigor I'd grown accustomed to.

"You're not eating?" he asked me when he saw me picking at my food.

Since I'd been busy that afternoon, I really hadn't had a lot of time to think about Pa and the Pastor Bennett mess.

"It's this deal with Pastor Bennett and Pa."

"What are you thinking?"

So, I told Jeff about Joannie Shaw, my meeting with smiling Pastor John at *Living Waters*, about the seemingly split congregation on continuing with the church expansion, and how Clare Bennett recommended me for the task of preparing a slide show for the weekend services.

"Maybe your Pa told her about you and your photography studio and she's just trying to throw some business your way?"

"Maybe."

"What was that about Pastor Bennett and going bar hopping?"

"Seems like the good pastor had a leftover college vice or two."

"I don't see it, he seemed like a good family man."

"Don't they all? But I'm not sure of any of it."

"What are you going to do?"

"I'm going to talk to Clare Bennett and see what gives between her and Pa."

"What makes you think there's anything there?"

"Call it woman's intuition."

"Oh no, not that again."

With dinner done we went back up the sidewalk and Jeff walked me to the studio's doorway. He bent down and gave me a kiss when he left, but my heart wasn't in it.

Once inside I went up the steps to the apartment, put a scoop of dry dog food into Blue's metal bowl, and stretched out on my bed. I heard Blue's bowl clanking on the linoleum floor in the kitchen area and when it stopped, I braced myself. A minute later Blue leaped onto the bed, bouncing me around, shaking covers everywhere. When settled and arranged again I tried to relax after my long day. The last thing I remembered was the smiling face of the dead pastor's brother, John Bennett.

Chapter Eight

In the morning I realized I slept in the same clothes I had worn the day before...all day. If blue noticed she didn't seem to care since she stood at the foot of my bed waiting for me. Being dressed saved me the trouble of shrugging on something warm to take Blue out. At least I took off my shoes before falling into bed.

I ignored Blue and got up, putting on a bathrobe and the red fluffy bedroom slippers that used to belong to my mama. I snitched them from Pa's house the year before. It was nice having something of Mama. She used to love flopping around in the slippers in the morning while she drank coffee. Although Mama wasn't my birth mama, she was the mama I identified with as my mama. My birth mama died giving me life. I had a vague vision of my birth Mama from Pa and Louise Looking Bird, my grandmama, but it was more a perception of what she was, a bright dream of a woman that loved me enough to die for me. How was that for a burden to carry?

Somewhat awake, Blue and I went downstairs where it was warm. I was getting tired of that hole in the wall where my fireplace was supposed to be. I didn't like to think about it, but I might have to just bricked it in. I could still get one of those fancy wood stoves. It wouldn't be as romantic as an open fire, but it would be better than freezing. I had already gone through one unheated winter, and I didn't relish going through another. The older I got the less I seemed to tolerate the cold. I was beginning to understand why Mr. Saunders sold me the place and moved to Florida.

Blue's morning routine took longer than usual. I swayed half asleep as she inspected a particular tree for several minutes, before deciding the area was right, then squatting for her morning business. Once done we retreated back to the studio.

I smelled coffee when we climbed the back-porch steps and went slowly into the delivery area. Almost certain I hadn't turned the coffee maker on, I paused and slowly peeked around the corner, and the sight of Jeff sitting at my desk with a cup of coffee about scared me to death.

"What are you doing here?"

"Drinking coffee."

"You scared the …you know what, out of me."

"Shouldn't have, where's that dog of yours."

Blue followed me in, let out a weak bark, then rushed over to Jeff for his scratch behind the ears.

"What kind of watchdog you got? She should have smelled me a mile away and warned you."

"She isn't a watchdog."

"What kind of a dog is she?"

"She's more a lap dog."

"Kind of big for that."

"I'm growing into her."

"Humm…"

"Say, how'd you get in here?"

"The front door was unlocked. I saw the back door ajar and figured you had Blue out so I went up and got the coffee going. Did you know your door was unlocked?"

"Of course, I did," I lied. "I've been up for hours."

"You must be busy, not having time to change out of the same clothes you wore yesterday."

Looking down at myself and Mama's red slippers, I swore.

"What was that?"

"Nothing," I smiled at Jeff, then holding a hand up to him said, "hold on a minute, I've got to run upstairs."

I left Jeff sitting there and took the steps two at a time up to the apartment. I rushed into the bathroom and looked into the mirror, "OMG…" I looked like a harried housewife with four school age children on a Monday morning. Weighing it would take too much time to take a quick shower, I splashed water on my face, roughly dried off, and then brushed my teeth.

I stripped off my clothes and donned fresh undergarments, a pair of clean jeans, and slipped into sneakers. I brushed out my hair that looked like a den of squirrels had taken up living there, pulled it back into a ponytail, and tied it with a red scrunch. I skipped any makeup. Jeff wouldn't know the difference anyway.

"I'm back," I said, back down in the studio space.

"I'm glad," he said smiling, "I just love to see you in the morning."

I wasn't exactly sure what Jeff meant. He could have been kidding, or he could have been serious. Either way it kind of scared me.

"Here's a cup of coffee," he said.

"Thanks, so, what are you doing up so early?"

"I was walking up the sidewalk to the shop and saw a light on in here so was going to see if you wanted to get breakfast. How about it?"

Quickly going over in my head what was on my schedule that morning, which was nothing, I said, "Sure, but I'm buying."

A morning crowd crammed into the *Coffee Bean*, but we snagged the last available table and Blue took up a position at my feet. With good coffee and a couple of fresh country ham biscuits, we settled in for a nice morning, at least until Sheriff Banner came in and walked right to our table.

"Where's your Pa?" the Sheriff asked as a way of saying good morning.

"Good morning to you too," I said, and Blue growled at the man.

"Don't good morning me, Emma, you said you'd tell your Pa to get in touch with me."

"I said if I saw him, I'd tell him you were looking for him, but I haven't seen him."

"You haven't?"

"No," I told him again. I was about to say something about going out to Pa's and finding him missing, but that might make it look like he run off, so I didn't say anything.

"Isn't that a bit unusual, you not seeing your Pa?"

"He's a grown man, Sheriff, I don't expect him to tell me about his days and what he's up to. Do you tell your mama everything you do? Why don't you look for him?"

"I did," he said, "Went up to his house yesterday but there was no sign of him."

"Maybe he's gone out hunting," I said, looking for a reason he'd be gone.

"Could be, as a matter of fact I checked with our local Wild Life agent and he said Logan was licensed. He has one of those Lifetime permits."

"Okay then, he's probably off somewhere on the mountain."

"What's this about?" Jeff asked although he knew very well what it was all about.

"Well, if it's any of your business, I'm investigating Pastor Bennett's killing."

"So, you think Logan Shaw might know something about it?"

"I don't know what he knows. That's why I want to talk to the man. The sooner I talk to him the quicker I clear this up."

"What's the hurry? A case like this could take months."

"I don't have months, so if you don't mind, I need to follow up on a few more leads."

With that, the Sheriff turned and walked out.

"What leads?" Jeff asked.

"I don't know, but thanks for not letting on about Pa."

"That's okay Emma, but you are in a bind here."

"What do you mean?"

"I mean the Sheriff sent that bullet that killed Pastor Bennett off to the State. Once the results come back he's going to know what kind of gun was used. When he has that information, he'll look at all the licenses issued for that kind of handgun here in the county and it's going to show that your Pa bought that gun from me."

"Are you sure?"

"I filled out the paperwork myself. It's in the system and the Sheriff is only a click away from seeing it."

"I wonder how long we have?"

"What's this *we* business?"

"We, as in, *you and me.*"

"Not again, why is it I'm always getting myself involved with your little investigations?"

"Just lucky."

"I guess."

"Besides, you never can tell when I might need someone roughed up."

"Okay, Emma, I'll do what I can, but I can't stop that license from showing up."

"Looks like I'd better get busy."

"And one more thing."

"What?"

"Remember how we pieced together your Pa running off last night?

"Right."

"Maybe it was our friend the Sheriff trying to sneak up on your Pa? He didn't look so happy right now about your Pa disappearing."

"So, I guess I'd better see Clare Bennett."

"Why?"

"Because I think there might be more going on between them than Pa is letting on."

***

The Bennetts didn't till the land like they used to, so they left their rambling farmhouse and moved into town. They lived across the river with all the upper class in Black Mountain. By upper class, I mean all the Shaws and those related to the Shaws. The Bennetts are connected to the Shaws by way of great-granddaughter Evelynn Shaw marrying Horace Bennett, some hundred years ago. Since then the Bennetts laid claim to the Shaw empire with about the same rights as regular Shaws, although control of the town still rested with those descended in a direct line from Walter Shaw, the first Granddaddy Shaw.

The big Bennett Federal style house stood on a pretty four-acre parcel of land overlooking the Swannanoa River. A forest of hardwoods, their leaves a brilliant mixture of red, yellow, and brown colors to match the season, surrounded the house. From that vantage point, one could look down on the town in one direction and out through the Valley of the Three Forks in the other.

I drove around the wide circle drive of the house and parked. The brick structure loomed over me, making me feel small. I supposed that was always the intention of big, large, homes. It certainly wasn't meant to house a large family. I recalled, the Bennetts only had two daughters and they only had one son between them. I couldn't recall which of the daughters was the spinster. If it was Clare Bennett, I wondered if she was planning to break out of her spinsterhood with the help of my Pa?

I gave Blue a pat on the head and went up to the door. Up close I could tell the house was well cared for. A tall man, wide in the shoulders, in work boots, jeans, and a flannel shirt with sleeves rolled up to the elbows answered my door ring. I'd seen the man around town some, always with an armful of something. He was easy to remember, seeing as how he was big and with a gnarly beard which stood out, even in a town known for gnarliness, if that's a word.

"Hello, I'm Emma Shaw," I said, putting on my best smile, "is Mrs. Bennett at home?"

"Who?"

"Mrs. Bennett."

"No, who are you?"

"I told you, I'm…"

"I heard your name but what do you want?"

"I want to speak with Clare Bennett."

"Why?"

"It's personal."

"Personal?" The man repeated, like a parrot.

"Yes, like between me and her. Personal."

After pausing for what seemed like a full minute, during which time I could almost see the clock works in his brain turning over, he let me into the two-story foyer of the home. A thick carpet ran the length of the hall dividing the house in two.

Before he disappeared, the man showed me into the first room on the right, a sitting room with old but comfortable-looking furniture. A fire in an ornate fireplace roared out of the far end of the room, letting off almost no smoke, indicating it was drawing efficiently.

Two walls contained floor-to-ceiling books, all looking dusted and well cared for. A glass topped display case sat in each corner of the room. I worked my way around examining their contents. A Confederate officer's hat and uniform were on display in one case. A long saber and several medals, still shining after all these years were in a second case. A third case contained an assortment of old pistols, looking like new in every style from a small derringer looking thing up to a long barrel revolver. The fourth case contained a collection of letters, preserved but yellowing. Lines of neat script covered the pages. I wondered what stories were written there.

"It all belonged to our great-great-grandfather," a tall stately seventy-something woman said. The man who greeted me led the lady by the arm.

"Clare Bennett," I asked the lady, well dressed in gray wool and low heels.

"No, my dear, I'm Ruth Bennett," she said as the man helped her into a chair. "Thank you, Zachary," the lady said to the man. "You can go now but, wait…my dear, would you like a cup of tea? Zachary is surprisingly good in the kitchen, maybe coffee?"

"No, thanks, I'm fine."

"Alright then. Zachary, make sure you poke the fire upstairs in my room. I think I'll take a nap after this."

When the man left she said, "That big old lug is Zachary, my son, I couldn't get along without him. He does everything here. The grounds outside, the housework inside, and looks after matters in general."

"I can see he's detail-oriented if he takes care of your wonderful collection of Civil War memorabilia," I told her, sweeping my hand about the room.

"Thank you, he's conscientious, but I'm afraid the Southern cause has lost much of its luster. I do like to remember the era as a time of gallantry, no matter how misplaced it was.

"Clare is my younger sister," the lady said.

"Oh, I'm sorry, I don't know Clare myself, so I took a guess. So, could I speak with Clare?"

"No, no, I'm afraid Clare is not here."

"Oh, no, I should have called ahead. I was hoping to catch her."

"That wouldn't have helped, my dear, you see Clare is away at the moment."

"Away where?"

"Well, actually, I'm not sure."

"You're not?"

"No, you see, we have a house down in Charleston and also one in Naples. The cold up here is more than we care for, so we spend time away after the holidays."

"The holidays are some time off."

"Yes, I know. Clare must have gotten restless and headed out early. It has been cold here you know."

"I'm surprised she didn't tell you where she went."

"Oh, well, I'm afraid Clare and I had a bit of a feud, and she went off in a huff."

"Oh, about what?"

"Well, my dear, that is much too much of a family matter to go into now. So, just who do you know that is familiar with Clare?"

"My father, Logan Shaw."

"My dear, I'm sorry, I didn't recognize your name, you must be Emma Louise?"

"Yes, I am. Do you know my father?"

"No, not well, but we knew your mother, Dorothy."

"You knew my mother?"

"Yes, of course, you know, when young, your mother was the prettiest girl in town. A shame she had that episode with Cousin Lawrence."

"Yes," I nodded, but didn't want to go into the circumstances of my mother's unwanted high school pregnancy, and how my brother Early was subsequently raised by Pa, and not by his birth father.

"Of course, it could have been quite a scandal back then but the family managed to keep it quiet. We all ached for poor Dorothy. Thank God your father came to the rescue."

To change the path of the conversation I said, "You have a beautiful home."

"Grandmother and Grandfather loved it," she said, looking around the room, a smile on her face, maybe thinking of the past. "Clare and I spent summers here and when

71

Grandfather died I moved back to be with Grandmother. Then when Grandmother died, Clare came back as well. Mother, of course, hated it. Once she went off to Bennett College she never returned."

"I might know a little of what she felt, I never wanted to come back."

"Oh?"

"Yes, the ghosts of the past are a bit much for me."

"But, my dear," she said, getting to her feet to show me out, "here you are?"

"Yes, never say never."

The lady walked with me to the door and out onto the wide stoop. Garden beds bordered both sides of the brick pathway. A mixture of fall perennials, Aster, Goldenrod, Chrysanthemum, and tall bright-red Franklinia, filled the space.

"Your gardens are beautiful."

"Yes, the gardens were grandmother's pride, I think she planted the mums herself."

"That's right, the rose garden in the town square was donated by the Bennett's and the Town Hall garden as well?"

"Yes, Grandmother and Grandfather insisted on keeping up with the gardens. Grandma had it written in her will that we continue with the many garden projects they founded and the other environmental causes they always supported. Great grandfather sowed the family's interest in horticulture. You know, his farm was the first in the valley to practice crop rotation."

Kneeling down she reached for a stray weed and yanked it out. "I'd do anything to protect the plants. Grandmother expected that we would continue the tradition of gardening both for beauty and education."

"Including the church gardens," I said. "I remember now, the First Presbyterian memorial rose gardens were donated by the Bennett family."

"Yes, Grandmother had those put in some sixty years

ago. She was a staunch supporter of the church and I continue to support the parish as well."

"Your sister Clare doesn't have the same allegiance to First Presbyterian?"

The lady paused, looking like she had just sucked on a lemon. She may have been holding back out of just good manners that cover not airing out family troubles to strangers, but finally said, "Why do you say that?"

"I know she attends *Living Waters*, by the lake."

After another pause she said, "Yes, she does, although I don't know why. Dreadful people there, with some kind of rock band on a stage and all the congregation in casual dress."

"What does Clare find so appealing about the church?"

"Heaven knows, my dear, she was brainwashed by that Pastor down there."

"Young Pastor Bennett?"

"Of course, who else? He was a distant relative, several lines removed."

"So, you heard he's dead?"

"Yes, I heard. You know, he even talked Clare into donating some land down there."

"Land?" I asked, surprised. Did Pa know that Clare had pledged to give the church land? Was that how the church was going to expand?

"Yes, they are planning on building some God-awful monstrosity, right on the lake. You know, *Living Waters*, I can just see it now, all-glass, stainless steel, and rock music."

"Is that what you argued about, donating the land?"

"Yes, and thank God I don't have to worry about that anymore."

I didn't have the heart to tell her that it looked like Pastor John was planning to move forward with the building project, no matter how monstrous it looked.

Chapter Nine

Wednesday Afternoon

On the Jeep ride down the mountain, I saw the folder with the church renderings sitting on the passenger seat and remembered I hadn't received the photos for Young Pastor Bennett's slide show. Someone was supposed to drop them off but hadn't. With only a couple of days before the memorial service, I needed to complete that project, so I hoped the photos turned up sooner than later.

When I turned up the street I saw a big red truck parking in front of the studio. The truck was lifted high and colossal mud tires completed the aftermarket upfit.

"Hello," I said, recognizing the driver from the church. The young lady used a step to climb down from the tall cab. "You're Candace, right?" She wore cowboy boots, jeans, and a tight fleece top, markedly different from the prim church attire she wore the day I met her in the church office. Red still rimmed her eyes from crying.

"That's right," she answered, handing me an envelope, "but people call me Candi. I'm sorry it's taken me until now to get these pictures to you."

"I was wondering about those."

"Yeah, well, I should have dropped them off before, but I couldn't get away."

"I guess you've all been busy, with...you know, preparations."

"It's been so depressing, Pastor Bennett getting killed."

"Is that what you think?"

"The Sheriff said it was murder."

"The jury is still out on that."

"If not murder then what?

74

"The Pastor could have killed himself."

"Suicide?"

"It's been known to happen. A man gets stressed out and out of the blue something drives him over the edge."

"Not the Pastor, …he had too much to live for."

"Look, Candace…"

"Candi," she corrected me, "only the church folk call me Candace."

"Okay, Candi, now…I don't know, who knows what lurks in the hearts of men? Did you see anything lately from the Pastor that would indicate he was under some stress? Maybe the stress of building the new sanctuary?"

"What's it to you about the way the Pastor died?"

"I'm looking into the matter."

"Why?"

"My Pa might be involved so I'm checking into it."

"Well, no, the Pastor was on top of things. He had a way of balancing everything, always in control and he loved the idea of building the new church. He used to tell me the new church would be a beacon for all those in the valley. A beacon calling the people to a new birth, a new life of faith in Christ. He never would have taken his own life. He had too much going for him."

Tears filled the young lady's eyes again, so I paused to let her get control before asking, "Did you know Pastor Bennett long?"

"Not too long," she said, wiping up tears, and moving to the Jeep and reaching into where Blue was to give her a pat, "just since I've been going there."

"How did you come by working at the church?"

"It's no secret, the Church sponsors a drug intervention program and we met there. He figured a job would help keep me out of trouble, keep me busy."

I didn't need to ask the young lady about the drugs, illicit or doctor-prescribed. It didn't seem to matter.

"Has it kept you out of trouble?"

"It's keeping me out of one kind of trouble, but there are all kinds of trouble."

I knew all about trouble.

"Speaking of trouble," I said, taking a wild stab at something that had been bothering me. "I think we have a mutual friend, Joanie Shaw?"

"You kin to Joanie? Of course, you are, both Shaws, right?"

"Just distant cousins. We went to high school together, although we didn't run in the same group."

"I wish I would have stayed in high school."

"You didn't finish high school?"

"No, I'm working on my GED though. Pastor Bennett wanted me to finish high school."

"That's good!"

"So, when did you talk to Joanie?"

"I saw her a couple of days ago and she mentioned the new brewery in town and how she loves going there."

"My favorite place, I see her there a lot, we play there some."

"Play?"

"The band and I. They let us play on off nights."

"A music group?"

"Kind of country rock but we play Country Gospel too. The Pastor let us play Wednesday nights at church youth group."

"I hear Pastor William liked the place?"

"Who told you that?"

"Joanie mentioned it."

"Well, he showed up once in a while. I think, looking for lost sheep, more than anything, you know?"

I wondered what else the good pastor was looking for in bars.

After an awkward pause, she gave Blue a hug and turning

said, "Well, I've got to run."

"Okay," I said, unable to think of anything more I could ask to keep the conversation going.

I watched the young lady climb into the truck cab and start the big rig up. I got the church folder out and slipped the envelope of photos in. I pulled Blue out of the Jeep, and she whimpered a bit as Candi backed up and drove away. I kind of agreed with her. Candi certainly looked like someone you would want as a friend.

***

Back in the studio I took the church folder over to my desk and dumped the contents out spreading paper and files everywhere. Amidst everything I found the renderings of a fancy, mostly glass, modern-looking church, sitting on the edge of the lake. The new Church of Living Waters – the *beacon of hope to be in the valley.*

Pastor William had big dreams for the church. I wondered if his dream was what got him killed.

I gathered the various files and stuffed them back in the folder. A last piece of paper eluded me and fell to the floor where Blue jumped on the little sticky note. We played take away for a minute until I finally cornered her and grabbed the note away.

I saw that the saliva-soaked and partially torn yellow note was written by Clare Bennett. *"Emma, everything you need is in this file...C. Bennett."* I was again thankful that Clare Bennett had recommended me for the job. Who knew? It could turn into a new revenue stream. Too bad more people didn't get murdered in Black Mountain.

I put the note back in the folder, shoved the whole thing to a corner of my desk, and went upstairs to get a yogurt cup from the refrigerator. Part of a weak plan I was formulating, was to lose five pounds by next spring. For flavor, I added some nuts and a spoonful of frozen blueberries to the cup. I poured water into Blue's bowl and went back down to look at my appointment schedule.

I had my under 10 boys football practice that afternoon. The fall before, the Mayor had talked me into coaching the young players flag division team. All the other team Dads were busy coaching their older sons, so the youngest league was short of coaches. Because of the CTE concerns the league started a flag division at the youngest age. To save the sport, many leagues were paying cursory attention to medical evidence and hoped to relieve some of the fears of the parents about their boys getting brain injured knocking heads around every fall Saturday.

I think the Mayor thought if a woman was coaching, the mothers in the league would feel better about submitting their sons to the chance of brain hemorrhaging. I was hoping they'd consider raising the flag requirement up to the older levels. CTE was a problem. I thought it even had something to do with the problems Early got into the last few years of his life.

I checked my phone and saw there were several text messages about orders to process. The photography studio program's messaging system sent out text messages to the management team, informing me, *the management team*, of waiting orders.

I had other texts. One about an opportunity to upgrade my phone plan, another offering to sell me life insurance, and one telling me they wanted to buy my house. I laughed at that last one since I didn't own a house. I guess my building was listed somewhere as residential. Maybe they hacked into the county Building Inspections database and saw the permit issued to build out my apartment.

Real Estate values were skyrocketing in the valley, ever since a big tech company built a distribution center across the lake. The Shaws owned just about all the vacant land in the town. They used to own all the land around Lake Nebo but ninety years ago, during the depression, Samuel Shaw sold the eastern half of their land to the state for a dam. He used the money to consolidate the Shaw holdings in town but now, years later, I'm sure the Shaws regretted the move. Who knew land around the old lake would be worth millions?

Eventually, other Shaw Lake land was sold off for various reasons. The last big sale was to generate cash so they could upgrade the lumber mill. The Shaws always went on about the mill losing money and they were always threatening to close it down and put everyone out of work. They never did, of course, they just used it as a scare tactic to keep everyone in line.

From what I understood from family gossip and eavesdropping on conversations, the Shaws still owned many parcels around the lake. If anyone knew the value of the property today it would be the Shaws and maybe they could tell me how much that Bennett land was worth. Was it worth enough to get someone killed?

Cousins to the Mayor ran the Shaw Real Estate company. Not directly descended from the Walter Shaw line, they still laid claim to the ancestry. To appease the distant kin, the Shaws gave them the opportunity to participate in the empire by managing the family landholdings. Never rich enough to own their own land, it gave the clan a sense of importance to play landlord, collect rent, and represent the true line of landed wealth that they would never actually possess.

Located at the opposite end of Main Street, I grabbed Blue's leash and after hooking her up, went out the front door, turned right, and walked up the street.

Like most property the Shaws owned, the Real Estate office stood prominently on a corner about a block up from Town Hall, diagonally across the street from the bank. Someone had posted photos of the different houses and lots for sale in town on the business office windows so anyone walking by would see the current listings. Like most of the businesses along Main Street, a sign on the door said "Pet Friendly," a concession to the mountain folk who owned dogs, or tourists who traveled with dogs. I surmised that people with dogs were the most likely customers the office had. In other words, people looking for land out in the middle of nowhere, where dogs had room to roam, not like an upstairs apartment where you kept your dog caged all day and felt guilty about it.

A bell over the doorway rang out with our entry, but no one sat at the reception desk to greet us. I could hear a printer running somewhere and called out, *hello,* announcing our presence.

"I'm sorry," Thomas Shaw said when he came out, I didn't hear you come in, I'm printing some flyers in the back." Then, after getting a good look at me he said, "Emma Shaw, is that you?"

"Hello, Thomas," I said to the man, tall and broad, sporting a shaved head, a camouflage for the trademark balding of most Shaw men, whose foreheads looked like ski slopes in summer, "how are you?"

"I'm doing great," he said, looking down at me, somehow making me feel small in the small room. "Well, I don't think I've seen you since your brother's...you know."

"I thought I saw you there, at the viewing, I was kind of in a daze, don't remember everyone that came, but thanks for going."

"Oh, sure, we're all one family, right?"

I didn't really know how to react to his sympathy. Last I remembered Early talking about Thomas Shaw was when he was describing the man as a scam artist who conned a bunch of old people into investing in a housing project that never got off the ground. Early told me he was going to arrest the man, but in a deal, brokered by Granddaddy Lawrence Shaw, he got the man to settle with the victims and the Shaws swept the whole thing under the rug, and life returned to normal in Black Mountain. At least normal for the Shaws.

"Good looking dog," he said, seeing Blue at my side.

"I hope you don't mind my bringing her in?"

"No, no, all dogs welcome here, especially one as good-looking as…"

"Blue, her name is Blue."

"Well," he said squatting down, trying to maybe pet her. When she growled at him, he slowly stood up and stepped back.

"Sorry about that," I said, "she can be a little protective."

After backing away, he went over and stepped behind the reception desk, giving himself some space between him and Blue. His aura vibrated out from him, in the earthy color of brown, a character color I see in people who are uptight and nervous.

"So," he said, "I've been meaning to drop into your shop and congratulate you on the renovation of the studio and your apartment above."

"Thanks."

"Yes, sir, that was a shrewd move, buying that place and fixing it up like that. Great investment."

"Drop by anytime," I said, and just to show I wasn't a businesswoman to let an opportunity pass I added, "maybe we can get you and the family in for a holiday sitting?"

"Sure, I'll ask Caroline if we have another plan in place."

"Great and tell her she can make an appointment online."

"Okay, I will," he said, and with the pleasantries dispensed with he asked, "So, what can do for you?"

"You hear about young Pastor Bennett?"

"Oh, yes, a terrible thing."

"I was talking to Franklyn about the whole matter."

"Franklyn?"

"Yes," and being as vague as I could I continued, "and he told me a little about the situation with *Living Waters Church.*"

"Situation?"

"Yes," I continued the vagueness, but dangling a little more bait in front of him said, "you know, about the land deal down there."

"The land deal, you say?"

"Yes," I said, and thinking I might have him hooked, added, "how much are we really talking about? Franklyn said you'd know the real value of the land."

The man hesitated and I saw his aura tick into the fringes of pink, a sure sign he was preparing to tell me a whopper – then, unexpectedly, the color blended back into a violet that indicated a serene state.

"Well, I don't know anything about Franklyn's involvement with a land deal, but with any deal down there we'd be talking about big money."

"Would we?"

"Yes," he said, warming up to a familiar topic, "as you know, land values have been on the upswing. Last month we sold a small lot that two years ago we couldn't give away but sold it for four times its tax value. Three people were bidding on it."

"Where?"

"Down by the lake. The lot is barely large enough for a hut, but for anyone looking for lake view it was apparently a bargain."

"Lake view?"

"Yes, not lakefront. Lakefront property is going for ten times tax value. When the new County property values are reset, there's going to be a lot of sad landowners out there."

"Including the Shaws?"

"Well, the family has always considered land a long-term investment. We've managed to keep property values below market for years because we sit in the majority of county commissioner chairs, but times are changing. A lot of landowners like the increased value which makes selling what you have easier and more profitable."

"If you can afford the taxes."

"That's the trick."

"So, what's land worth down there?"

"Maybe a million an acre."

"That much?"

"Sure, a condo project down there, twenty units or so, $200,000 per unit, you do the math."

I tried, but in my head, I couldn't get it. I'd have to take his word for it.

"Yep, big money," he said, just getting started, "and that is lake view. You can times that by four for lake frontage. I'd kill for some lakefront property down there."

"Do you know the Bennett land down there that fronts the church?"

There was that pause again and his aura flickered pink, "A little."

A little? He knew the details of the lake property, why wouldn't he know the details of a relative's land, even a distant relative's land?

"Isn't the church negotiating with the Bennetts about buying their land for a new sanctuary project?"

"Oh," his aura beating a steady pink, "I hadn't heard anything about that?" which could have been an outright lie.

Since the colors in a person's aura didn't change immediately with an emotion change, as the color blended from one emotion to the color of the next, Thomas could have been lying about not knowing about the sale or he could be lying about not knowing about a new sanctuary.

"Well," he said, looking at his watch, confirming he wasn't being honest with me about something and was looking for a reason to end our little talk. "I've got a showing, so I'll have to cut our visit short. You don't mind?"

"No, that's okay, I've got a practice to go to."

"That's right," he said, walking me to the door and changing the subject, "you've been coaching the league's under ten flag team. How did you get talked into to that?"

"In a weak moment I let Franklyn talk me into it." Which was exactly what happened.

"Do you get any complaints from the parents?"

"About what?"

"You know, about flag football as opposed to regular tackle."

"No, I think the parents appreciate the concept, and the league likes it that it keeps the boys playing another year before the parents decide to quit the league and move their kids to soccer. I hope they raise the flag age bracket up. Better for everyone."

Pulling a set of keys from a coat pocket Thomas Shaw opened the door for me and said, "I bet that will go over like a lead balloon."

Showing me out, he locked the door and moved the hands around a cardboard clock he hung on the door to indicate he'd be back in a couple of hours.

Just outside the door, I reminded him about sitting for a holiday family card.

"Sure," he said, smiling, "let me check with Caroline about that."

I didn't have a lot of time if I wanted to follow Thomas Shaw, so I hustled down the walkway toward the studio pulling Blue along. It was going to be fifty-fifty. Thanks to the town's enforced 10 miles an hour Main Street speed limit, if Thomas drove south through town toward the lake, I'd have enough time to get to my Jeep and follow him. If he went north the other way, he'd be out of town and could get to the highway before I could catch him. I had a hunch he'd be going through town though and he did, giving me the time necessary to tail him, you know, like in the movies.

As I followed Thomas Shaw at a respectable distance, he drove east toward the lake. I was mildly surprised when he got on Lake View Road and went straight out to *Living Waters*.

Pastor William's death was still a mystery to me, and I didn't know if the man committed suicide or was murdered, but Thomas just proved to me that the land had to be at the center of the whole thing and that told me enough.

***

Black Mountain fielded a team for every age division during the Little League Football season. I initially tried to refuse the coaching offer, using inexperience as an excuse, but the Mayor knew I had been a sports photographer at the Piedmont Paper and with my family background in football, he knew I could handle it.

I had wondered about the job and the innovation of flag football, and how it would go over, but all the mothers thanked me for taking on the job, and I was hoping maybe the league would think more critically about CTE. Also, as all the dads say, *when mama's happy, everyone's happy.*

Soccer was another story. More and more families were directing their sons toward the soccer fields. Youth, pre-teens, and teen teams were filled with the athletes that used to grace the football fields. Now, parents who were aware of concussion issues, opted for the relative safety of the soccer pitch as a legitimate alternative to the traditional head-butting game. When soccer first exploded on the scene, the mountain communities fought the trend, but statewide mandates forced the high schools to include the sport. It didn't take savvy school administrators long to also realize that it was not only less dangerous, but it also costs less to field a soccer team.

I dropped Blue off with the promise that after practice we'd go for a long walk. It was a consistent lie I hated telling her. For most practices, by the time I'm finished, I'm lucky to make it to the Jeep, much less go for a long walk after. Blue looked at me with those big brown eyes. I knew she was on to me because she only snorted and ambled over to her bed to settle in for the afternoon.

"Now, you be a good girl while I'm gone," I admonished her, repeating the words I'm sure all mothers speak to their daughters at one time or another, and I heard from my own mother many times growing up. Thinking back to my own youth, I was glad Blue didn't know how to unlock windows.

Before the season I studied up on flag football rules and best methods for youth teams, and I developed a practice routine for the boys that proved successful. Early on, a few unconvinced Dad's staked out spots in the parking lot to watch the practices. But after starting the season 3 and 0, no one doubted my ability and I think the mothers got a big kick, no pun intended, about a woman coaching in a man's game. Even if it was flag football.

After another good practice the team's team mom, came out with snacks and drinks for all the players and I rounded up all the equipment. It had been a long day and I still had a mystery to solve.

Chapter Ten

Thursday Morning

For most of the month, the weather had been seasonal, bordering on cool for the fall, but when morning came it brought a blast of cold air. Football weather, hardy fan weather, and by that I meant the freezing weather had arrived. The kind that takes your breath away when you come out of a warm house and are not expecting the mountain cold. The kind you meet with hot coffee and flannel nightwear, and I had just what I needed, a pair of flannel pajamas that used to belong to my mama.

I didn't have much that had belonged to her, the mama who raised me. I inherited the ability to see auras from my birth mama and her generations of Cherokee ancestors. But the mama who raised me wasn't one to hoard things and didn't abide by consumerism for the sake of collecting. The day we found her dead in bed she was wearing one of the few dresses she owned. The one she only wore on Easter Sunday. I couldn't blame her for wanting to look good when she met her Lord.

Blue, of course, loved it, the cold weather, not the pajamas. The cold didn't affect her at all. In fact, even with the temperatures hovering in the teens, the dog panted around with her tongue hanging out like she had just crossed the Sahara Desert.

Leashing her up, we went out into the morning air to make her rounds. The night before we didn't take that long walk I promised her. Another broken promise I made to my girl. What a terrible mother I was. Luckily it wouldn't matter if my poor example of motherhood rubbed off on her since she was fixed and wouldn't be raising any problem children.

The saving grace of doing bad by your dog is that they are all about the moment and if you can give them something in the moment to make them happy, they again pledge their undying love. Not like most people who tend to never forget the smallest transgression and will more than likely carry the memory of it to their grave.

I carried my clothes for the day down to the business level and changed in one of the studio rooms where the electric floorboard unit kept the heat above freezing and I could change out of my mama's flannels and into long johns and jeans without my teeth chattering. I just had to do something about that upstairs hole in the wall.

When dressed, I powered up my computer to check my appointments and the only thing on the schedule was the varsity boys' soccer game at 7:00 PM. *Great,* it should be really cold by then. I hesitated to look at the weather app on my phone, but opened it up and thanked God for small favors, no rain was predicted. The only thing worse than cold weather is cold wet weather.

With the whole day on my hand, I decided to follow through with the long-promised walk for Blue, remembering to save some time to get to that slide show for Pastor Bennett's service the next night. Gathering a few things into a day pack and a water bottle, I hitched Blue up and we went out the back door down to the river. We made a circuit along a trail that zigzagged about a quarter way around the lake then turned back. At the turn around point we stopped to eat a snack. I took a few photos of the sun coming over the mountain top, pouring light down through the valley that lit up the fall foliage, just past peak color.

Suitably tired by our trek we ended up back at the trailhead and stopped for a drink of water. I poured Blue a bowl of water and sucked on a plastic nozzle connected to a hydration bladder in my pack. We started back up to town but at the fork in the trail, where one fork led up to town and the other, to Mill Row, I turned down Mill Row. The old road followed the river for a quarter mile in either direction and my aunts Maybelle and Laura, lived down the eastern end of the street in a house built on stilts, a protection from the frequently flooding Swannanoa.

Aunt Maybelle and Laura, and their recently departed sister, Martha, lived and were raised with mama right on the row. At one time or another, all the sisters married and moved away and then for whatever reason found their way back home. Though a little touched, as they say, I liked my aunts and tried to visit when I could. Being the last of my Mama's relatives, I wanted to stay in touch, but that morning I was more interested in their thoughts on the goings-on at the *Living Waters Church*

I'd been looking into the case for a couple of days and so far, I hadn't reached any conclusions, except that my Pa looked guilty of murder. His disappearance didn't help the situation. It was a ridiculous notion of course, but being stubborn, I couldn't talk him into coming in and setting it right. The fact that Clare Bennett also seemed to have disappeared was becoming an unfortunate coincidence, or was it?

Aunt Maybelle and Laura were born in the same year, one in January and one in December. Although not technically twins, they looked close enough to fool most people, and in their old age, fooled even more. They kept their hair in a gray bun, wore the same wire-rim round spectacles, and dressed alike.

"Why Lordy," Aunt Maybelle said on the other side of her screen door after she opened her front door and saw me standing out on her porch, "Sister Laura," she called, "look who's come to visit."

"Well," she said, opening the door for me, "you come on and bring that dog of yours in before we let all the heat out of the old place. Have you ever seen such a cold spell?"

"I told you it wasn't all that cold," Aunt Laura said when she came into the room, beginning the familiar course of disagreement on all matters between the two. I used to wonder about the arguments but decided a long time ago it was just their way to communicate, "not like it can get."

I could tell from their auras, which usually glowed in the rainbow range, that it didn't matter what came out of their mouths, they always had the love of sisters between them.

"Still, Sister, it is cold out. Emma why are you and that dog out and about so early?"

"I promised Blue she could visit with Oscar," I told the ladies, referring to their old bloodhound. "You don't mind if I put her out back and let them play?"

"Heavens no," Aunt Laura said leading me to their back door. A wide porch sheltered the backside of the house and Oscar took up a southside corner where if there was going to be sun, he'd get his share. When Blue smelled the old dog, he let out a bark, and Oscar raised an ear from a bed of old blankets and remnants of carpet. I turned Blue loose knowing that nature, and a great deal of sniffing, would take care of the rest between the friends.

"Sit down and let's have a cup of coffee," Laura said.

The old kitchen remained as I knew it for the last thirty years. Generations of Brown family men and women had sat at the old table, having their morning coffee before heading out to work at the Shaw Lumber Mill.

After I took off my pack and heavy coat and we settled in I said, "Sorry to hear about young Pastor Bennett."

"Oh, my," Belle said, "we just can't believe it."

"I'm not surprised," Aunt Laura said.

"What do you mean?"

"There is more to this story than what you can see."

"Now, Laura," Belle said, "Don't go on about the dead. Let the poor man rest in peace."

"What do you mean?" I asked.

"I'm just saying that a man gets what's coming to him whether he wears a collar or not."

"What's that supposed to mean?"

"Oh, she's just mad because we made a donation to the building fund and now, we might not see anything come from it."

"You all donated?"

"Yes, dear, we needed to show our support. Now, it wasn't much, but we wanted to do our part. We were hoping we'd get to see the new sanctuary before we passed but now."

"It's not only that," Laura said, "you know that."

"I know no such thing. Anything you heard is only a rumor."

"Rumors about what?"

"They say the Pastor mismanaged the building fund."

"Oh?"

"Yes," Laura said.

"Oh, Laura," Belle said, "now you know that's only a rumor and you shouldn't be spreading that tale. Don't listen to her, Emma Louise, the Pastor was a good man."

"Well, just the same, we haven't heard back now, have we?"

"Heard back about what?"

"About our donation. We were supposed to get a letter or something, showing our donation and we haven't gotten anything."

"That don't mean a thing," Belle said. "They just lost track or something."

"We're not the only ones, Emma Louise. There're others as well. Rumor is the Pastor needed money and took it from the building fund. Now, everyone wants an accounting. Mark my word, once the man gets buried, we'll see what the accounting is down there."

"I don't believe it," Belle said, "Young Pastor Bennett would never do anything like that."

"I'm just saying…"

To be friendly I spent an hour more with them talking about other things. Aunt Laura and Belle made me a breakfast of eggs and freshly made baked biscuits. They put out several jars of home-canned preserves and I managed to stuff myself with several calorie-filled biscuits. Before I did any more damage to my cholesterol levels, I finally went out and dragged Blue away from his play friend and we left.

The sun had made its way higher up over the mountain and the temperature rose to a tolerable level, but I didn't pay much attention to it with my mind on the good pastor Bennett and his accounting practices.

***

Back at the studio, I got Blue settled in with a doggie biscuit and after shedding two layers I sat down at my computer to work on that slide show. With only a day until the Friday viewing, I had already cut it close.

Using a slide presentation program my photography system came with, I picked out a somber background design and made up a title page. When it came time to load photos I realized I hadn't copied any of the materials the church gave me so had to pause while I looked through the church folder for what I needed.

I spread the files from the folder out on a worktable and began to sift through the photos Candi had given me and the other materials prepared by the architecture firm. There was a bunch of renderings of the proposed church, and a plot map with dimensions and other information. One of the files was a Feasibility Study on the lakefront property in terms of value with several comparable examples and appraisals from around the lake. A second report was a Cost Analysis of building the church. Other reports included a Market Analysis of the area industries, an Environmental Impact study, and a Population

Growth study of the lake area showing the projections for the lake community's growth and whether that growth would be big enough to support taking on the debt to build the new church.

The renderings showed a tall, mostly glass building, standing snug against the lakeshore. The legend showed the dimensions for the building, 80 feet by 120 feet. A sizable building like that, 10,000 square feet, more if it had a basement, would run two or maybe three million, easy, depending on furniture and fixtures. Not including the land. I began to wonder more about the so-called building fund.

I scanned several photos and a rendering of the front of the building into my computer. The graphic artist that drew the rendering highlighted the glass structure as it reflected the blue water of the lake and the surrounding green of the forest. An inspirational summer vision of the church and a reminder of *Living Waters* and what it was meant to be.

I also scanned several photos of the Pastor at work, tending his flock, preaching, and sitting at a picnic table with members of what I gathered were members of a youth group. Young Candi and the Pastor appeared in several shots, together. Altogether I had about thirty slides. I figure with about 10 seconds per slide they'd have a loop every five minutes. Should be enough time to guide the good pastor into heaven. Of course, that depended on the accounting.

Chapter Eleven

Thursday Afternoon

I worked on the slide presentation until noon then getting hungry, I leashed Blue, and we went out. I passed the Fish & Game on my way and sticking my nose up against the plate glass window motioned to Jeff where I was headed. When he saw me, he held up a hand with three fingers, which I surmised indicated he'd be with me in three minutes. Instead of standing there like a puppy waiting for a treat, my invisible tail wagging vigorously, I headed over to the *Coffee Bean* and grabbed a table. I just hate the way some women fawn over some men.

I got one of May Shaw's famous grilled pimento cheese and avocado sandwiches, a fresh-baked doggy biscuit for Blue, and had just sat down with my coffee when the town attorney and brother to the Mayor, Randall Shaw, came in and walked right up to my table. Knowing I would be interrupted for a good while, I took a big bite of my sandwich and waited with my mouth full.

"What's this I hear about you looking into the Bennett case?"

Normally, with my mouth empty, I would have had something smart to say to Randall. Big like his brothers and well-dressed in a dark gray suit, he loomed over me like a storm cloud ready to burst.

"What's this I hear from Franklyn about you and this Bennett thing?

With my mouth full I could only shrug up at the man while I chewed.

"Don't play dumb, Emma, he told me all about it"

I nodded again.

"You should know, Emma, that we're doing business

with the Church. We're going to finance the construction loan for their new sanctuary."

When I raised my eyebrows he said, "It's a big project, maybe three million or so. Hard to say exactly since we don't have all the plans in, but I don't want you messing around in this and torpedoing the project."

I shook my head a couple of times, indicating I would never do such a thing.

"Yeah, I know you, Emma. You'll be off accusing everyone you see of murder, getting someone falsely arrested, and before we know it, muddying the waters enough to sink this whole deal for us."

I finally swallowed the last bit of avocado and cleared my throat, but before I could get a word out Randall said, "You just stay out of this, Emma, stop butting in where you're not wanted."

I was about to say something, but he quickly turned and went to the door. As he went out, Jeff came in.

"What did Randall want?" Jeff asked when he had picked up a cold roast beef sandwich and a sweet tea from the counter and sat down across from me.

With my mouth full again I shrugged.

"Was he talking to you?"

I nodded yes.

"About what?"

I held up one finger, and after I swallowed said, "He warned me about butting into the Bennett thing."

"What do they care?"

"Oh, they're going to finance the construction loan for the church's new building, and I guess he's afraid the project might fall through if I discover something that holds everything up."

"Like what?"

Like what indeed, I thought. If it was murder, then Pa could be in trouble. But if was suicide, then sad as that would be for the church, Pa would be in the clear. What was there to gain otherwise?

***

After lunch, I spent an hour in the studio putting the last of the Pastor William Bennett Memorial slide show together. It wasn't my best work, but it would do, especially since I wasn't charging.

I took Blue out for a quick walk to do his business, and then we drove over to *Living Waters* to deliver the slide show file and while there talk to Pastor John again.

Blue never tired of riding in the Jeep. I kept the passenger side window down so she could hang her head out and bark at people as we passed. I know it was dangerous, what with flying particles, especially on the unpaved roads, but when we were on the highway, I let her have her way. The only problem was on the cold days when I had to run the heat on full blast so I wouldn't freeze from the cold air flooding in through the open window.

I pulled into the church's parking lot but parked at the far end so Blue wouldn't be barking at everyone she saw. I rolled up Blue's window a notch so she wouldn't feel tempted to jump out and left her sitting in the passenger seat, hoping she wouldn't get bored and decide to tear up the upholstery to pass the time. I had just started across the lot when I saw Pastor John come out of the church office and climb into a big white SUV and drive off.

An assortment of people bustled about the small office and not a head turned when I went in. I waved at the one man I knew, Wendell Hawkins. When he saw me, he came over.

"I brought the slide show," I told him, holding up a thumb drive.

"Well, I appreciate that. I know the ladies in the Bereavement Committee will appreciate it too. I heard them arguing this morning about the music. Having the slides will give them an idea on what music to play. Come on back."

Hawkins led me back to what had been Pastor William Bennett's office, through the maze of people, all busy with the task of sending their pastor off to heaven.

"Emma," the man introduced me to a woman sitting at a desk outside the pastor's office, "this is Francis Bennett, Church Secretary. Ms. Shaw brought over the slides for tomorrow night."

"Wonderful," the thin woman said, getting to her feet to accept the thumb drive. "We were hoping we'd get it in time to arrange the music."

"Yes, sorry it took so long, I said, following her into an empty Pastor's office. "I'm afraid I was a little busier this week than I expected. Is Pastor John here?"

"No, no, he went to town," she explained, putting the thumb drive on the Pastor's desk, "something about the insurance."

"Insurance?" I asked.

Wendell Hawkins looked at Francis Bennett and she smiled, "Yes, there's always something to look after here. I'm surprised anyone can keep up with it all. And now with the Pastor gone, well, I just don't know."

I wanted to ask more about the insurance issue, but I didn't know if the good Francis would be willing to explain so I held back. Thinking of an alternate plan I said, "Say, Mr. Hawkins, guess who I have out in the Jeep?"

Out in the parking lot, I put the leash on Blue and let her out. She went right up to Hawkins, sniffing around his trouser legs, and I wondered if a dog could sniff out the scent of their own breed, or do all dogs smell interesting?

"Good, girl," the man said giving her back a good rub. "You got a pretty dog, Emma, where'd you get her?"

"I got her from Dan Walker last fall," I said, letting Blue lead us over to a grassy area from where you could see the lake, and away from any chance someone would hear us talking.

"Oh?" he said, seeming surprised, "I didn't know Dan was in the breeding business?"

"No, it was a gift."

"Say," Mr. Hawkins said, "wasn't it you that looked into his wife's murder?"

"Yes," I admitted, "it was a pretty sorry thing, for sure."

"I know, who would have believed it?"

"That brings up this whole matter with Young Pastor Bennett."

"What?"

"Whether it was murder or suicide."

"The Sheriff says it was murder, that's why he's looking for your Pa, sorry to say."

"It's okay, I know Pa wouldn't have anything to do with the good Pastor's death."

"But if not him then who?"

"Maybe it was suicide."

"I've been thinking about that Emma. I know the Pastor was stressed out, as they say, with a lot on his mind."

"Like what?"

"Well, we got this darn building project."

"Sounds like you're not in favor of it?"

"No, and quite a few in the parish don't want to see it go through."

"Why?"

"Too much money. The Pastor said he'd figured all the funding out, but plenty of us thought it too much of a good thing. Then when Clare backed out of her deal…"

"Wait, what?"

"Clare Bennett…she and the Pastor were working on a deal. You know Clare owns all the land down on the lake. Well, she agreed to donate the land to the church. With the land, the church could get a loan for the building, using the land as collateral. You know that property is worth a lot of money."

"And?"

"Well, most of us here are poor folk and we aren't used to borrowing, especially borrowing as much as it would take to build that new church, even if the land was free."

"I see, but if the deal is off, why are you all still planning to show the building project at the memorial service?"

"We always had two options."

"What do you mean?"

"Well in case Clare's land didn't pan out the Church was looking at a second site. We can buy the land behind the church and expand the church there."

"Do you have money for that?"

"Well, we didn't, but now with the Pastor dead, we might."

"How?"

"The Church had a life insurance policy on the Pastor."

I imagine my face looked kind of perplexed

"Yep, got it a year ago, the Church has been making the premium payments and is the beneficiary. It was Pastor John's idea, and the Elder Board agreed the Pastor's life was worth insuring so they got the policy. Oh, it's not a lot. Not enough for a big lakefront church but it's enough to build an expansion behind us. So, with the life insurance money, and no debt to carry, the Elders voted to move ahead with the expansion."

"On the land behind the church?"

"Right, I think we can get it at a good price, and we could add on and stretch out a little. It would be much cheaper that way than to build new down on the lake."

With all that running through my head, I said goodbye to Mr. Hawkins and putting Blue in the Jeep, went back to town.

I wondered about the whole premise of the insurance. Was that forward-thinking or what? I mean who thinks about insurance anyway, I know I don't.

***

The biggest insurance agency in town belonged to the Shaw family. Auto, health, medical, life, liability, fire, and or natural disaster, the Shaw Insurance agency had it all. They had health insurance at the lumber mill, but to hear it from anyone up there, it wasn't worth much. I wondered if the life insurance policy they sold the church was any different.

Located in the center of town around the square, I saw a car sitting out front of the insurance company's office, so I stopped in front of the studio. Leashing up Blue, we slowly walked up the sidewalk as Blue visited every tree along the way. About halfway there, I saw Pastor John come out of the insurance office, climb into a white SUV, and pull away.

Noting the sign on the door that said it was a dog-friendly building, I pushed open the door. "Patrick Shaw," I called out to the Shaw family member standing at a file cabinet when I entered the office with Blue. Patrick Shaw was older than me and played football with my brother, Early. There was a time when people thought he was a pretty good high school center, big and mean, but when he went off to college he switched to women as a major and since then had been married, at the last count I recalled, six times. There seemed to be an endless supply of women that thought taking a chance on Shaw's riches was worth the damage to their psyche.

"Emma, how the …"

"Ah, ah, ah …"

"Well, great to see you, just the same. Where've you been keeping your pretty little self?"

As far away from you as possible, I thought, but said, "Been keeping busy. You know with the photography studio and all."

"That's right," he smiled, moving across the room to meet me, trailing the brown aura of greed I see forming around all the Shaw men. "I've been keeping an eye on your construction. I've been meaning to drop in on you to talk about getting some insurance on your business."

"You think I need insurance?" I asked him, taking a step back, feeling safer, and let Blue drift between us where she growled up at the man.

"Every business needs insurance, Emma," he said, looking down at Blue. "At least some liability," he added, moving back a step. "For instance, in case that dog of yours bit someone. And now that you've improved that old building you really should increase your insurance there to cover the added value."

"How do you know what amount of insurance I have?"

"The bank required you to cover the value of the building when you financed it, and since the bank…"

"Since the bank is owned by the Shaws, then they arranged the insurance through you?"

"Something like that, Emma. We may have a monopoly on certain industries in town but we still charge below-market rates, so you won't get a better deal than through us."

"Well, okay, I'll think about it."

"You should because the worse time to get insurance is when you need it."

"Say, speaking of insurance, was that Pastor John, from *Living Waters,* just left out of here?"

"Sure was, do you know the Pastor?"

"We recently met, I did some work for them, you know for the memorial service tomorrow."

"Yeah, well, he came in to discuss a few things. We insure the church operation."

"Life insurance too?"

"Who told you that?"

"It doesn't appear to be a secret, Patrick, the church is open about its activities, everyone knows that they want to build a new church and they were careful about insuring their biggest asset at the time, the pastor. So, is that what Pastor John was here about, collecting on the life insurance?"

"Emma, I can't talk about a client's affairs with you. I don't think you represent the church."

"I heard there was a hold-up or something?"

"Look, Emma, you need to follow up with the church Elders if you want specific answers."

"Well, how about a general answer? Why would there be a hold up in the benefit coming through?"

"Well, in a case like this, it might not be as straightforward as you'd think."

"What do you mean?"

"Well, if you stop to think about it, Emma, there is a big difference in life insurance paying off on someone who is murdered and someone who commits suicide."

Chapter Twelve

Thursday Night

On the walk back to the studio, I continued to mull over the murder-suicide scenarios on the case. If poor pastor Bennett's death turned out to be murder, then the Church would collect on the insurance and the building project would go forward. But, and it was a big 'but' since I didn't know the particulars, but on the other hand, if the good pastor killed himself, then there would be no insurance money and likely no new church. I wondered just who benefited more in either scenario. I knew Pa would benefit more if the Sheriff would drop his murder case, but who else? And what if it was suicide? It didn't appear the church was a hundred percent in favor of the expensive expansion, anyway, so not collecting the insurance money wouldn't bother a good portion of the faithful followers.

I pushed open the front door of the studio and we went in. I filled Blue's bowl with fresh water, gave her a doggie treat for her good behavior while we were traveling about, then started upstairs to wash up. Somehow the whole afternoon made me feel dirty. It was probably from my time spent with Patrick Shaw, but to tell the truth, the whole affair began to make me feel like I'd brushed against a chimney and got soot all over me.

When I got to the top of the stairs, I smelled coffee.

"It took me a good part of an hour to figure out your fancy coffee maker," Pa said from the counter where he sat. "I finally remembered the order of the steps you explained to me once, and sure enough it spit out a cup."

"What are you doing here and where have you been?"

"Drinking coffee and hiding from Sheriff Banner."

"You can't hide forever, you know."

"I don't plan on it, just long enough for you to figure this whole thing out. So, have you come up with anything yet?"

It surprised me, him coming right down to the reason for his visit, besides getting a free cup of coffee. Since he became sober, he'd grown into quite a talker and it would have usually taken him a half hour to get to the reason for his visit. I guess being accused of murder will get you asking straighter questions.

"Not much I'm afraid."

"What did the Sheriff say?"

"He said he wanted to eliminate you from his shortlist of suspects."

"That should be a long list."

"Long list?"

"That's right. From what Clare tells me there should be other suspects on that list.."

"Like who?"

"That's what you are supposed to look into."

"Now, Pa…"

"Did you talk to Pastor John?"

"I did."

"And what did you think?"

"He may be a little opportunistic, but I don't see why he'd kill his brother."

"They never got along, you know."

"Says who?"

"Clare says they had an argument about church funds."

"I may have heard something about that."

"You need to keep talking to people."

"Speaking of people, can you tell me who was down in the basement when you and the Pastor argued?"

"Why?"

"I might want to see if their impression of the event corresponds with the Sheriff's."

"Well, Bessie Lawson was there, she's like the church treasurer, and Wendall Hawkins and his wife were there too. I think he told me once he was in charge of putting things up after events. Then Mr. and Mrs. Hollins were there because Clare told me she's in charge of social events and is always the last one to leave. And Joe and Wynona Rider were there. They're the ones to start this whole mess."

"What do you mean?"

"They were the ones who asked the Pastor about the sermon. I gather they had some personal issue, and the Pastor was trying to have a private chat with them, you know, to make them feel better."

"Why were you and Clare still there?"

"The Pastor asked Clare to stay to discuss a private matter."

"What kind of a private matter?"

"That was between the Pastor and Clare."

"The Pastor's dead, Pa, what difference does it make?"

"It's still Clare's business, Emma, that's the difference."

"By the way, where is Clare, her sister said she left town."

"You talked to Ruth?"

"I went over and we had a good visit. Why didn't you tell me that Clare had a deal with the church? Was that what the pastor wanted to talk to Clare about? About her backing out of the deal?"

"Who says she backed out?" That deal was set to go forward if they got their books in order."

Pa got up and started another Keurig cup through the machine. He stood watching it, looking in wonder, like it was magic or something. When done, he took his cup back to the island and sat.

"Clare lost some faith in the Pastor when she looked into the church budget." He said. "Apparently, a sizable amount of cash has disappeared from the building fund."

"How much?"

"She didn't know for sure, but it looked like several thousand dollars."

"That's quite a bit," I commented, thinking about that big new SUV Pastor John was driving.

"Yes, that's what the rift was between the Pastor and Clare. She said she would be withholding any more support for the church until a full audit was conducted. The pastor protested and held it against her. I think that's why he reacted so angrily Sunday night. You know, I think he thought God himself told him to build that new church."

"That's when you jumped in and had words?"

"Yes, that's when I spoke up, and he was lucky I didn't pop him one for the way he spoke to her. But Clare had told him if they could clean up the books, she'd go forward with the land donation."

"Well, I guess that's a dead deal then, now that the pastor is dead."

"Yep, he was the driving force behind that, but still, no one would wish that upon the man."

"By the way, what time did you leave the church that night and where did you go?"

"Does it matter?"

"Of course, the Sheriff needs your alibi to clear you. That way he can look for someone else. You do have an alibi for after you left?"

"I do, I went home and straight to bed."

"Pa, that's not an alibi," I told the man seeing a flicker of pink in his aura indicating he was lying about going home or going to bed."

"Man's word should be worth something."

"Not in a murder case, Pa, the Sheriff will want more to leave you out of this whole mess."

"Then you'd better get to the bottom of it then because that's all I've got."

I watched Pa and his aura settle into steady dim yellow,

beating calm. Serenity usually accompanied that color, although at the moment I didn't know what he had to be calm about.

"Where have you been since Monday?"

"What do you mean?"

"We went up to your house."

"We...?"

"Jeff and I, we went up there after dark."

"Why?"

"To ask you a few questions but you were gone and we noticed you left in a hurry."

"What makes you say that?'

"You left your Bible and took your shotgun. We saw the power was cut and wondered what happened."

"Oh, Jeff must have turned the power back on."

"You knew?"

"I went back after a while."

"Where did you go?"

"When the power went off in the house I took off after them."

"Who?"

"I don't know," he said, his aura flickering out in a color I don't believe I ever saw from Pa. "Probably some of those druggies that hide up there in the mountain. They've been breaking into places and I guess they thought mine was an easy target. They probably thought I was asleep and could take advantage of me. But I surprised them."

"Or maybe it was the Sheriff?"

"They didn't identify themselves."

"Did you give them a chance?"

"Either way, I ran them off."

"Ran them off or ran off?"

"What's the difference?"

"Pa, if you are evading arrest, it could come back hard on you."

"I just got to stay out of the Sheriff's way until you clear all this up."

"So, where've you been all week? I've called you a couple of times."

"I told you I had to get the corn in and that's kept me busy."

I hated seeing the muddier pink color of untruthfulness wicking out of his aura.

"I've been keeping an eye out for the Sheriff. I can see the lower town road from the upper field. I saw a sheriff cruiser yesterday afternoon, so I jumped down and dropped the picker and drove the tractor off the field and parked behind the trees. I waited an hour or so after the cruiser left out then I went back to harvesting. I got it all up now and Ben Jordan, down Lenore way, he's been pulling the wagons over to Oak Grove Mill. We should have cornmeal by winter, bagged and ready to send out."

By sending out Pa meant, distribute. He came up with the idea to raise corn for cornmeal that could be distributed through the area food banks. He and a bunch of retired farmers had put their land back into use with the goal of alleviating hunger in the Black Mountain communities. This would be their first harvest and they were all anxious to see the results of their efforts.

"The yield was down some, but the quality looked good. Harold Bruce, over to Farmington, said with the combined harvest over the six farms in the co-op, it wouldn't matter. We'd still get a good amount when added up."

Pa raised his cup and finished the last of his coffee.

"Well, I got to run."

"Where are you going?" I asked him as he got up and stretched his back out. "This might be a good time to see the Sheriff and straighten this mess up."

Pa looked at me and smiled. "No, Emma, that's why I have you."

"Pa, you need to talk to the Sheriff and explain your actions."

"I've got no actions to explain."

"What about that pistol you bought from Jeff?"

"Oh, did he tell you about that?"

"He did, he's worried too."

"What's it to anyone?"

"Pa, Pastor Bennett was killed by a small round bullet. Probably a handgun."

"That doesn't prove anything."

"Pa, it's just one more piece of evidence the sheriff will have against you."

"I bought it for a friend, I don't even have it anymore."

"What friend?"

"No need to get anyone else involved in this. You leave that alone. You just need to find out who killed Pastor Bennett. Until then I'm going to stay unavailable."

"You've been lucky until now, Pa, you can't hide from the sheriff forever."

"The day I can't hide from the Sheriff will be the day I'm in the grave and the man can find me from the inscription on my headstone."

"Now, Pa."

"Emma," he said, and coming to me gave me a stiff hug. He'd become more of a hugger, since going sober, but I still felt hardness in him, like he hadn't completely come over to the warm side. "If you want me to come out of hiding then you best get to the bottom of this thing."

Fitting the whole situation, Pa went down the steps and out the back door and disappeared. I wondered where he was going. Surely not back to the house. With the Sheriff's periodic visits, I doubted Pa would hang out there. Maybe he was staying over at Louise Looking Bird's place. Louise was my Pa's former mother-in-law. Louise and her family farmed and raised cattle on a big spread on a plateau east of the mountain. Some say her people came into the valley with the first white men, and together they drove the Catawba out. Brotherly love!

I went down the steps and found Blue at the back door, pawing away at it, like she wanted out to follow after Pa. I knew the man liked to brag about his skill in the forest. It was a well-known fact that Pa was one of the best men in the woods. But even with that, there were only so many places to hide in the mountain.

Chapter Thirteen

The Varsity Boys Soccer game started at seven, so I loaded Blue and my gear into the Jeep and drove over to the stadium. I found a secluded parking spot at the end of the visitor's gravel parking lot that provided enough distance from the field so that when she went to barking, she wouldn't disturb anyone. I cracked the windows to a level where she couldn't escape, and I made my way out to the fields. The stadium lights were just starting to take effect, so I got a few shots of the boys warming up.

I know most parents wanted shots of their sons playing in the game, but the fact was that some of the boys never played during the games. Like most coaches in competitive leagues, the Broncos coach played the best eleven players for most of the match and only one or two subs. The other boys on the team sat on the bench. I found if I got a few action shots of these boys during the warm-ups they sold about as well as the game-time shots of the regular starters. Parents never missed an opportunity to have something to remember their boys' playing days, first string or not.

The visiting team thoroughly outplayed the home team and in addition to demoralizing the players, it was bad for business. With the home team suitably embarrassed, the parents were not in a purchasing mood and many of the fliers I passed out after the game ended up littering the parking lot.

Suitably dejected about the missed sales opportunity, I went about the parking lot salvaging what I could of my advertising materials I used for marketing, whether football or JV girls' volleyball.

In the nearing darkness, with my eyes on the gravel parking lot, I stooped to snatch at a loose flyer as it scooted by me in the wind and missed. Caught in an unbalanced position, someone unexpectedly took advantage of the situation and pushed me over. I managed to get my left arm up to protect my face before I crashed into the gravel surface, preventing severe damage, but leaving me in an awkward spot from which to fight back at my assailant. When I reached around with my right arm, he grabbed hold of it and pushed it up behind my back, pinning me tightly.

I'm usually not caught so off guard like that. After basic training and my deployment, I felt I could take care of myself in any situation, but as I've found out, most assailants don't come at you directly. No, most try to sneak up on you from behind. This is why it's good to have a hero come to your rescue from time to time.

"Would you mind getting off me?" I spoke to the man on top of me. I figured it was a man by the weight of his knee in my back.

"I have to tell you something."

Since the man was set to tell me something, I figured it wasn't a random mugging, not that I had much of value to steal, although there was my thousand-dollar camera, sitting on the seat in the Jeep. Of course, Blue barking at the man would be a hindrance there. I was sorry I hadn't left the windows down a little lower.

"Like what?" I said through squished lips, now hearing Blue add a deep howl from the Jeep.

"You must stop the investigation of Pastor Bennett's death."

"What investigation?" I played dumb, hearing Blue's howls grow louder still. I wondered if anyone else could hear her.

"We know you are looking into the matter, and you need to stop."

I wanted to say something smart back, but could only think of, "What's it to you?" *original*, "You guilty of something?"

To make his point he ground his knee into my back and

pushed down on my head so I could feel the sharp rocks cut into my arm.

Just when he started to apply more weight on my head, Blue let out a growl and sprung through the air. Miraculously, she had gotten out of the Jeep. Blue to the rescue!

At the last second the guy threw up his right arm to protect his neck and Blue clamped down on the man's wrist and the two of them went crashing to the ground. Though not quite full-grown, Blue weighed in at a good seventy pounds and in a full-speed collision, packed quite a wallop. The man toppled over with a thud and the two wrestled for possession of the man's arm. The man managed to pull free from Blue's teeth and tumbled several feet away, where he rolled nimbly to his feet, losing his ski mask in the tussle.

"You need to get a hold of your dog!"

"I don't think so."

I don't know if he could see Blue and her snarling jaws and sharp teeth in the dark, but after feeling her wrath he must have had a good idea of what he was in for if he stayed around because he took off into the woods without saying more.

Blue didn't immediately run after him, pausing to bend down to sniff at me, no doubt checking to see if I was still alive. I gave her a pat on the head and said *good girl*, after which she licked my face, turned to where the man had been, let out a growl, and took off after him. I could hear the man crashing through the underbrush. Unfortunately, he must have parked a vehicle nearby because I heard a door bang shut and then an engine start. The sound of something driving away, and Blue howling after it, echoed in the forest.

I managed to sit up and cradled my arm to my chest. Several cuts and lacerations caused by the sharp rocks of the gravel lot bled from my arm. I counted my blessings for getting my arm up in time to protect my face. I didn't appreciate the heavy-handedness, but it appeared the stakes in the case had risen.

Blue came out of the woods and trotted over to me, panting from her effort, and jumping up on me, knocked me over again. I didn't mind. Using her as an assistant, I got to my feet and limped over to the Jeep. The passenger side door window was hanging out of the door frame. Apparently, the old window unit was no match for an angry Blue. *Good to know.*

Using my right hand, I got Blue in and started up the Jeep, and then labored into town driving straight to the hospital emergency room.

After I told them that Blue was my service dog, they let Blue accompany me inside. They put me in a wheelchair, and wheeled me into a stall.

Knowing that Pa couldn't be found, I hesitated when the admitting nurse asked if there was anyone to call. I could have called my sister-in-law, Becky, but she was so busy with her three boys at home. But it didn't matter because I really wanted Jeff anyway, and gave them his number. Never one to be called fast, Jeff surprised me and showed up a minute later.

"Where were you?" I asked the man who usually provided my bodyguard service.

"I was at the shop. I didn't know you were out for adventure tonight. What happened?"

With the admitting staff out of earshot, I said, "Someone mugged me in the school lot after the soccer match."

"I thought soccer was a non-contact sport?"

"Oh, so funny, Jeff, I always knew you were a funny man."

"Are you hurt bad?"

"Just my pride. I let some clown get the drop on me, but Blue chased him off."

"Good girl, Blue," he said and patted her on the rump.

"My hero," I said. "Better be careful, Jeff, Blue might be taking your place."

"You'd be in good hands, Emma, or should I say, *paws.*"

When all cleaned and bandaged up, Blue came over and sniffed at my gauze-covered arm. She looked sad and whimpered a bit, then growled a little. I expect that the last sound was a *just wait until I see that guy again* sound, directed at my mugger. After what seemed like an hour of paperwork we went out to the hospital parking lot.

"What happened to your car?" Jeff said when he saw the window hanging half out of the door frame.

"Blue squeezed through to get out when she saw the mugging. Luckily these cars aren't quite the tank they are advertised to be."

"Tell you what, why don't I buy you a late dinner, and tomorrow morning we'll run the Jeep over to the Whitakers' yard. They're bound to have a window kit on hand to replace the damage."

Suitably heartened by the mountain tradition of neighborly kindness and carbohydrates, we went across Main Street to the *Coffee Bean* for an adult beverage and something to eat.

I rewarded Blue for her bravery by snitching several of May Shaw's doggy biscuits for her.

I ordered a grilled pimento cheese sandwich, with May's homemade pimento cheese, along with a house chardonnay, and we retreated to the back of the dining room.

"Want to tell me what happened?" Jeff asked before he started in on his regular roast beef sandwich and a beer.

"You know, the usual, *I better mind my own business,* warning."

"The Pastor Bennett business?"

"That's the one," I saluted and drank down my wine in one long gulp.

"Did you recognize your assailant?"

"No, it was dark, but a big guy, about 220, with boney knees, wearing a ski mask."

"Could have been me."

"Could have been half the men in town."

"That reduces the pool to about a couple of thousand guys."

"He knew me."

"Oh?"

"Yep, told me to stop my investigation."

"Oh?"

"Well, this guy will be sporting a few tooth marks. Blue got a good bite onto his arm, right about the time he was pushing my head down into the gravel lot."

"Oh yeah? Maybe we should go back out to the scene of the crime. There might be some evidence out there."

"No, it's late out and the lot lights don't cast much light. We'd better wait until morning."

"You're sure?"

"Mama always told me that things always look better in the morning."

Of, course, *Mama wasn't always right.*

Chapter Fourteen

Friday Morning

After our late-night romantic dinner, which Jeff had to watch me manage with one hand, and three glasses of wine, he walked Blue and me back to the studio. Out front, the stoop light shone brightly on the doorway and Jeff leaned into me and gave me a hug. I liked the feel of his body. Not too boney or hard, but just the right amount of softness. Before Jeff, it'd been a while since anyone was gentle with me, caring like they meant it.

Jeff accompanied us inside and turning quickly, I couldn't help melting into his warm arms for another hug and slow kiss. After the catastrophic evening there was no place I would rather be than in his arms.

In the morning I assumed nothing more happened between us since I woke up with my clothes still on. After three glasses of wine the night before, I didn't remember getting into bed. Ah, Jeff, always the perfect gentleman. He did take my shoes and coat off before tucking me in. I laid there for a moment thinking about how it would have been if Jeff had stayed over, and my arm wasn't bandaged up like a mummy.

Blue bounded up on the bed and interrupted my daydream, signaling she was ready for her morning walk. I groaned at her and put the pillow over my head which she immediately snatched off and flipped onto the floor. She proceeded to attack the cushion with loud earsplitting bark and sharp teeth meant to rend material to pieces.

"Okay, okay," I told her and dragged myself off the bed, every muscle in my body screaming out in pain after the beating I took the night before. Since I didn't need to dress, I worked on my favorite moccasin boots with one hand and went down the stairs to the heated studio. On the back porch, I wrestled myself into my winter parka and leashing up the hero dog, threw my hood up and over my head. Holding the leash in my good right hand, we went out into the cold and drab gray morning. *Wonderful*, just what I needed.

Like most people, I preferred sunlight to clouds. Studies showed and I can confirm that I am just a whole lot happier under the warm sun. But winter has its time, and its time was coming. I could only hope for an extended fall.

I stood outside shivering while Blue finished her business, then retreated to the studio and back up the stairs to the kitchen.

I got the Keurig going and added extra cream and a spoon of chocolate to the cup before the coffee started dripping, completing the task with one hand as my left hand was still bandaged. After scooping a big cup of dry food into Blue's dish I took my coffee and was just checking my calendar on my phone when Jeff called up to me from downstairs.

"How are you this morning?" he asked, after coming up the steps and taking a seat at the counter.

"I'm fine," I told him, holding my mug in one hand, "and how did you get in here?"

"You always leave the back door open."

"I do?"

"Yep," he said as Blue padded over and begged for a scratch behind the ear. Jeff obliged the dog with a gentle rub, and I thought about asking for the same but instead said, "You want a coffee?"

"Sure," he said, smiling at me.

"Why are you looking at me like that? I asked him, starting another cup through the machine.

"What do you think?"

I looked down at myself and realized Jeff probably recognized my outfit from the night before, and if he recognized that, then he also recognized I hadn't had my morning clean-up.

"Oh, God," I said. "I'll be right back," I called out as I left the room for my bedroom.

I wondered how long a womanly, *I'll be right back,* was? Under certain circumstances could it go long enough to include a shower? I figured, under certain circumstances, it could.

I showered briefly, the task taking longer one-handed, but didn't wash my hair, which should have shaved 20 minutes off the clean-up task, but I gave it all back when the hot water hit my sore muscles and I lingered far longer than a womanly linger would take, my wounded hand up in the air away from the water stream, like the Statue of Liberty

I dried off as fast as I could and skipped the make-up routine, what routine I had anyway, and settled for face cream. I wiggled into clean jeans, shirt, and socks and hustled back out to the great room, expecting to see Jeff gone after the thirty-minute ordeal, but instead, I found him seated comfortably on my leather sofa in front of the fake plywood fireplace covering the hole in the wall. He looked comfortable sitting there. I could almost imagine him sitting there every morning like this, after getting up from a warm night sleeping in my bed, lounging together on a lazy morning. I wondered if he felt the same.

"This is going to be great," he said. "When you tear down this painted fireplace and they get the real one built. When is that happening anyway?"

"Mr. Williams said he's on it and promised before winter sets in."

"Isn't that what he said last winter?"

"He did, but I think he means it this time since I haven't paid him for the final work. He probably needs that money for the holidays.

"You want me to have a talk with the man?"

Jeff was always asking if I needed his help. I know he was only being polite and helpful in asking, but I resented the offers. I mean, I had gotten along quite well these last fifteen years, without his help. I took a certain pride in my independence. Why did he think I needed help? Why did I suddenly resent him for asking? Why was I having babbling thoughts like a high school teenager? Was it going to be this way every time I felt beholding to the man?

"No, that's okay, I spoke to him a few days ago and I think he's got it scheduled for next week."

"Don't worry," he said, "I wasn't going to rough him up, or anything."

"Good...he'll get to it."

"Speaking of roughing up, how are you feeling?"

"I'm pretty sore," I said, stretching my arms and rotating my neck, "but on the mend. I got a good night's sleep. Thanks for putting me to bed."

"You're welcome. So, shall we get started?"

"Started?"

"You know, I promised we'd take your Jeep over to the Whitakers to get the window looked at."

There it was again, more help! "Oh, I forgot."

"And then we need to take a look at the crime scene, you know, for evidence."

"Don't you have to work this morning?"

"I'm off until this afternoon."

Great, I thought, or was it? Did I want to get Jeff involved more than he already was? Why couldn't I just accept his help? What was wrong with me anyway? It must have been something to do with seeing Jeff so comfortable in front of my fake fireplace. What would I feel like if it was a real fireplace?

"Great," I said.

I grabbed my parka, hooked Blue up, then we went out and walked down the street to the Fish and Game Shop, where Jeff's truck was parked in front. We put Blue into the crew cab seat in the back and we climbed in front and drove over to the hospital parking lot. I got out and started up the Jeep with the busted-out window and followed Jeff north of town to Whitaker's salvage yard.

The Whitaker's yard overflowed with every imaginable vehicle. Side by side the old cars filled several rows. Most of the vehicle's engine hoods stood open, like yawning mouths at the dentist, just waiting for the drill bit to dislodge something attached. I hated the dentist!

I pulled into a parking area behind Jeff. When I got out of the Jeep the aroma of used motor oil hit me and I could hear Blue, barking from out of Jeff's truck. A group of men were gathered in the yard looking over a truck.

"What's wrong with her?" I asked Jeff.

"I don't know, as soon as we pulled up, she started barking. Better leave her in there."

I noticed one of the men was Zachary Bennett, another was Ben Ruffin from the service station. The last man was one of the Lawson boys. When we approached them, Mr. Whitaker left the group and came over, but the gathered men continued the examination of the truck.

"What's going on?" Jeff asked.

"The highway patrol dropped that truck off yesterday. Left over from an accident investigation. I'm going to sell it and some folk are interested in buying it. Truck like that always creates interest.

Jeff explained to Mr. Whitaker what needed to be done with my Jeep. When Mr. Whitaker advised he had just what I needed and he'd fix me up that morning for fifty bucks, I gave him the go-ahead. People in town swear the Whitakers can fix any vehicle and the farmers couldn't get through a season without them. Most of the old farm tractors and combines still in use owe their extended lives to the Whitakers.

"I've got a couple of Jeeps this year in the yard," the man said. "I'll pull the window out of one that was in a bad rear-ender a couple of months ago. It should fit perfectly."

"I bet you've got an inventory for about any model vehicle in town."

"I try to keep one for every model I see, you never know when you'll need something."

"Anything you don't have?"

"Not much, there's a lot of old-timers in the mountains that keep their vehicles far longer than normal vehicle life."

"What's the oldest car you've worked on?"

"I've got a couple of Studebakers I work on. Ewell Smith, over to Jonestown, he drives a 1950 Studebaker that breaks down every couple of months, but I've got a whole row of them cars so I always have a part to pull to fix it. I get people buying online for Studebaker parts as well. I'll get orders even from out in California sometimes."

"A 1950 Studebaker, that's pretty old."

"Ms. Bennett has an older one, a 1945 Studebaker. I think her daddy bought that right after the war and it's been in that family ever since. They never get rid of anything."

"Is that Zachary Bennett over there?"

"That's him. He stopped by to look at that truck. You'd think with all their money they could afford a new truck and not one that was in a wreck or fifty years old."

At that moment the meeting broke up and the men went in different directions. When the lot cleared of vehicles Blue finally quieted down.

I gave Mr. Whitaker the Jeep key and he said he'd drop it by the shop when he was finished. He said I could pay him upon delivery. When we left, we drove over to the stadium and I directed Jeff over to the parking spot and he looked at me, like wanting to know why in the world would I park so far away from everyone.

"I like to park out of the way because of Blue," I explained before he asked me about my parking priorities. "If she sees me, she gets to barking. This way she stays out of trouble."

"Lucky you."

I got out of the truck and pulled Blue out, unleashing her so she could roam about.

"I don't see much here on this gravel," Jeff said. "Is this about where it happened?"

"A little more over here," I directed Jeff over to an area closer to the tree line and where Blue was sniffing. "I like it here because Blue gets a little shade if the sun's still out."

We had our heads down looking for any sign of the attack when Jeff said, "Take a look at that, Blue's found something."

We went over and Blue was growling and pawing at a black wool ski mask.

"That must be what the guy was wearing. Blue and he got into it pretty good, and I bet he came out of the fight maskless, but it was too dark to see his face."

"Do you recognize it?" he said, picking it up and handing it to me.

"You mean black wool mask with eye holes? Oh yeah," I said, sticking the mask in my parka pocket, "besides the eye holes there must be a couple hundred of those in town."

"Where did you say you heard a vehicle startup?" Jeff asked.

"Through the woods. There's a path there."

Jeff led Blue over to the wood's edge and led her back and forth, Blue sniffing the ground. Within a minute Blue got a whiff of a scent and took off through the woods.

We trotted after the dog and in about fifty yards we came to the end of the tree line where a dirt road split the heavy forest. The road led out to the highway in one direction and back to town in the other. Blue stopped and moving in a circle, sniffed along the ground.

"He must have parked out here and driven off that way. A lot of people park out here when the stadium lot fills up. I wonder if anyone saw him? We could ask around."

"Sure," I said, reaching down and hugging my dog. "If we

had the manpower, we could interview everyone who came to the game, find out who parked along here, then find out if any of them saw another vehicle around the time I got mugged. That's what we would do if we were working with a real police department with enough manpower to interview a couple of hundred people."

"But we're not working with a real police department, right?"

"Right. The mayor would sweep the whole thing under a rug before he'd let a bit of bad publicity out that would hurt business in town."

We turned around and trudged back to Jeff's truck.

"You know," Jeff said as we drove away, "that dog of yours is quite a tracker."

"She's a beauty, that's for sure. I'm glad I got her after all."

"What do you mean?"

"Oh, you know, it's a lot of work having a dog in the middle of town. Out on the farm, we let the dogs run free but here in town I have to keep her locked up half the time."

"Blue seems happy enough. There could be worse things than being locked up with you."

I had to smile at that remark.

***

Jeff dropped me off and hustled to his shop. Back to business, I went into the studio, took off my parka, gave Blue a doggy treat, and went to my desk and computer to check the calendar of events for the day. I found that if I didn't check my schedule regularly, I'd miss something. The software program I bought for the studio included an integrated calendar that could send me new appointment messages and I found it a little like Christmas when I got a message that someone had booked an appointment. Happy day!

I could tell the staff at *Living Waters* were not football fans. No one in town would have dreamed of scheduling any event, even a viewing for a beloved pastor, opposite a Friday night high school football game. Luckily for them, they scheduled it for an early start, at 5:00. That would give most people the opportunity to get there early so after paying their respects, they could then hustle over to the game before the seven o'clock kickoff. Of course, for the hungry, that left little time for dinner, so I expected the faithful would overrun the concession stands and deplete the nacho and cheese inventory. I reminded myself to buy my own tray of chips and fake dip before the rush.

Overnight I received a couple of orders from the previous day's soccer match. Win or lose, grandparents had to have a photo of their aspiring athletes. With the overlapping fall seasons of football, soccer, and cross country, the demand seemed to stay steady each month.

Using an arm and a half I ran several poster-sized prints, a big favorite, a handful of 8 by 10's, and a bunch of 4 by 5's.

At noon Mr. Whitaker dropped my Jeep off and after inspecting his handy work I paid him.

He had one of his boys follow him over and once they drove off, I decided I was hungry and needed calories.

I woke Blue up from her mid-morning nap so we could take a noon walk, and when done we got in the Jeep and drove over to the Shaw Diner. I almost texted Jeff about going along but I didn't want to appear like I was constantly desperate for his company, although I pretty much was.

The Shaws ran the diner at the edge of town, a family operation since the thirties. Used to be the only place in town to get something to eat, a pack of cigarettes, and a tank of gas in one stop. But the changing times all but eliminated the tobacco run, gas was cheaper at a chain station off the interstate, and food was healthier at a number of close-by places, including at the *Coffee Bean*. But if you wanted a hearty salty lunch then Shaw's diner was still a good choice, and if you wanted to hear the most recent gossip, Shaw's was the only choice.

I parked in the rear of the building and Blue and I went around to the front and into the dog-friendly restaurant. Blue liked the diner as she always encountered a local hunter or farmer there for a big meal and more often than not, they had their dogs with them. It was a gathering place for locals, man, and beast alike.

"Emma," Callie Jones called out to me when she saw us come through the door, "where've you been girl?"

Once I set up shop, Callie became one of my best customers, a factor of the six boys she and her husband Ray brought into this world. Though the same age, she had started her motherhood right after high school, and now her offspring spread across several grades and sports age divisions from first grade to high school. I acknowledged a long time ago that the head start Callie had on me on making a family was one I would never catch up to. At the rate I was going I would be lucky to just get married.

"Hello, Callie," I said to the lady standing behind the counter, a red apron protecting her blue jeans, her dark hair up in a ponytail pinned to the top of her head and out of the way. Although her husband worked up at the mill, Callie worked at the diner during the morning and lunch hours to make the ends of the family budget meet. For many men in town, a job at the mill seemed to be the mother lode, but the reality was it didn't pay that well, and if you didn't have a secondary source of income, it would be hard to raise a family, especially a large family.

I took a seat at the counter and after Blue went up the aisle between booths saying hello to the canine customers, she came back and rested at my feet.

"What'll you have," Callie said, pouring coffee into a thick white ceramic cup that appeared mysteriously in front of me.

"I'll take the lunch special, hamburger, fries…" and in an effort to eat healthy added, "and an unsweetened ice tea."

"Who drinks unsweetened tea?"

Who indeed, "Okay, make it half-cut."

Callie called out the order to someone cooking in the kitchen on the other side of a narrow window.

The counter stools were all taken and Callie walked up and down the line refilling coffee cups, sweet tea glasses, and flirting with the men sitting there. A few truckers sat along the line, off the highway for a bite to eat or rest, but most were local men. Farmers, hunters, and the retired, all happy to be out of the cold for a hot meal and a look at the pretty Callie, who even after birthing half a football team, still looked high school pretty enough to stand up on the homecoming court, which of course she had.

"What happen to your arm?" she asked, seeing the big bandage.

"Fell down."

Someone behind the window called out "order up" and Callie put my very large plate of food in front of me and a napkin-wrapped bundle of utensils and ambled down the counter again.

The burger had a huge slice of cheese on it, the meat medium-well, and the fries were crisp and heavily salted, perfect. When Callie came back to my table she had to wait for me to finish chewing before I could answer her question I didn't hear.

"I said, wasn't that terrible about Pastor Bennett getting killed? I mean, who'd want to kill a pastor?"

Once I swallowed and drank some tea to wash down remnants of fries I said, "Some say it might have been suicide."

"I think I heard that and it wouldn't surprise me."

"Oh?"

"No ma'am, he came in for lunch once or twice a week

127

and I could tell, that here lately, he'd been under some pressure, like stressed out."

"Oh?"

"Yeah, just last week he apologized for the small tip he left. Said something about a tight budget, which surprised me. You know Ray and I belong to *Living Waters* and we tithe weekly like everyone and I know the weekly offering is in the thousands."

"Maybe it's that new church he wanted to build?"

"Could be. You know he's the one that started that whole thing, but lately, I think that maybe he bit off more than he could chew."

"You think?"

"Ray sits on the building committee, and he said the weekly meetings always got bogged down when the financing topic came up. He said the Pastor always told everyone that he and the Good Lord were taking care of the money and that we shouldn't worry about it, but he said he could tell, the Pastor worried about it. As well he should. I know we're a growing congregation, but a million-dollar sanctuary is a big haul, even for an already established parish."

Callie went off again to see to her other customers and left me with my burger. I had cut the thing in half and spread catsup on it from a pack of packaged condiments and spread some on my fries as well. I planned on keeping half the burger for later, but knowing I'd get hungry in the afternoon, I ate most of the second half as well, but saved a big wedge of the burger meat and dropped it to Blue. When I swiveled around to leave, the Mayor Franklyn Shaw was standing right in front of me.

"Emma, we got to talk."

Franklyn's three brothers trailed him. Mathew Shaw, who ran the lumber mill came next, then Randall Shaw, and then Dr. Miller Shaw, a thinner and somewhat nicer version when compared to the others.

"What about Franklyn?"

With the question, the dining room became noticeably quieter as everyone paused in mid-bite to hear what the Mayor was about to say. Knowing the gossip mill was probably already running hot enough, the Mayor suggested I come over to his office to discuss a matter of great importance.

I knew he wanted to talk to me about Pastor Bennett, so agreed and told him I'd drop in that afternoon.

"When?" he snarled at me.

Blue snarled back at the man.

"I've got some work in the studio and as soon as I'm free I'll be over."

I could tell he wanted to argue, but since we were standing in a public place he nodded and the foursome went up the aisle, like a tidal wave, and out the door.

I waved good-bye at Callie and left her a five-dollar tip, more for her boys than her, and Blue and I went to the register to pay and then out the door to the Jeep.

I worked in the studio for a good two hours and when my phone vibrated, I answered the mayor's call.

"Did you forget about our meeting?"

I had, actually, but said, "Just finishing up and on my way."

I took Blue out for a walk and tossed her a doggy treat. Even though Town Hall had an open-door policy with dogs, I knew the Mayor really didn't care for the four-legged citizens of the town. I didn't even think Blue liked the smell of Town Hall. The last time I had her over there, she squatted in the rotunda and peed, leaving a big mess.

When I entered the office reception area the Mayor's pretty second wife, Shelby, greeted me with a big "howdy stranger"!

"The mayor is expecting me," I told Shelby who wore an outfit more suited for a night out on the town as opposed to a workday.

"Emma," the mayor barked out at me when I went through his office door, "didn't I tell you to leave this Pastor Bennett thing alone?"

"What's it to you, Franklyn? When you wanted me to look into the Barbara Walker case you were all for it."

"That was different. Look, I know Randall talked to you about this. The bank is going to fund the construction and provide a long-term mortgage for the new sanctuary. We even cut a point off the going rate."

"That was generous of you."

"Generous has nothing to do with it. It's a long-term investment in the community."

"You mean, you'll have them on a leash for the next thirty years with a constant flow of interest payments. I suppose it's a variable rate as well?"

"What do you care?"

"I don't really, but it's just like the Shaws to provide a deal that will set them up with a debt that will be hard to maintain. And then what? Will you foreclose and sell the property to a developer at a huge profit?"

"You always think the worse of the family, Emma, that's just business as usual."

"As usual for the Shaws, almost verges on predatory lending."

"No one's holding a gun to their heads."

"Look," I said, getting a pang of guilt from the gun to the head reference, "Sheriff Banner is off base on this thing and it could affect the project and your loan."

"What's wrong with the Sheriff's case?"

"Oh, he can't wait to pin it on Pa. Now, you know my Pa wouldn't have anything to do with this."

"That's why you need to get your Pa in here to clear all this up. Once the Sheriff gets beyond this he can get after the real killer."

"Maybe there isn't a killer," I said.

"What do you mean?"

"There's a few folks around say it could have been a suicide?"

"What's he got to be suicidal about? He was a family man with a growing parish."

I didn't want to go into the rumors about the good pastor, so I said, "People are just saying the building project was getting to him, stressing him out. If the Sheriff wasn't so fixated on Pa, he'd have to investigate further and talk to a few different people. He'd see there might be another angle on this thing."

"You really think so?"

"Look, Franklyn, I'm just getting into this, but I wouldn't be surprised if it turned out a suicide."

"So, what? Murder or suicide, the church told me they are going forward with the project."

"If it's suicide it will bury your loan."

"What are you talking about?"

"He didn't tell me right out, but you need to talk to Patrick Shaw about the insurance policy the church had on the Pastor. It might be that in the case of suicide the policy won't pay out. No murder, no payout, no building."

"What do they need insurance money for? They have a deal with Clare Bennett for the land on the lake. We're taking that as collateral to secure the building loan."

"Clare backed out of the deal. There's no land!"

The Mayor's eyes grew big and his mouth hung open. There wasn't much in town that the Shaws didn't know about, but this looked like a surprise to the man.

"Where'd you hear that?"

"It's just something I found out."

"You talk to her?"

"No, not really. It seems she's out of town and no one knows where."

To get the meeting over with I said, "Franklyn, you've got

to get the Sheriff on the right track. The sooner we know what's going on down at the *Living Waters* the sooner you'll know about your loan."

"I'll talk to Banner. I've got a few questions about this investigation myself."

I left the mayor with his hand reaching for his phone and heard him tell Shelby to get Sheriff Banner on the line. It looked like the Sheriff was running a sloppy investigation and I was reminded about his initial review at the crime scene so since I was out I decided to go over and visit with Mr. Gilmore, the long-time Funeral Home director and as someone with the only experience, the town's sometime medical examiner. I was hoping the man could shed some light on the matter.

Chapter Fifteen

Friday Afternoon

Gilmore's funeral home sat at the end of town, surrounded by lush grass and trees. Being the only funeral home in town it saw a good amount of business. They treated the dead and the living well and the locals rewarded Gilmore with a steady business, no matter which church you attended when alive.

"Emma Louise," the old man greeted me when he saw me standing at the back door of his treatment room, "where've you been keeping yourself?"

I was beginning to wonder why everyone had that comment. As far as I was concerned my whereabouts were as plain as anything, I'd been working.

"Oh, here and there," I said.

"I haven't seen you since Barbara Walker died."

"That long?" I answered him, noting a bright purple aura about him, signifying a spiritual person, unlike what you might suspect in a mortician. I expect most people think of the trade as dark and morbid, but with Gilmore, it was a Godly mission to send his clients off to eternity looking their best.

"What happened to your arm?"

"I fell."

"Well," he paused, and concluding that I was probably just clumsy, he asked, "you here because of young Pastor Bennett's death?"

"You think that's the only reason I'd come by here?"

"Well…"

"You're right, that's why I'm here, about Pastor Bennett."

"A real shame," he said, turning and leading the way into his lab. A wall with four stainless steel doors took up one side

133

of the room and he went to the opposite side where he sat behind his desk, "the Pastor dying like that, so young."

"I know what you mean," I said, sitting on a metal chair across from him, "a lot like Early, too young."

"What's that old song, *Only the Good Die Young?*"

"Billy Joel…great song, sad topic."

A moment of silence hung over us, heavy like fog over the lake, during which memories of Early and his premature departure from our world came back to me. Afterward, I asked Gilmore, "What do you think happened to the Pastor?"

"It's hard to say, Emma."

"The Sheriff says it was murder."

"So, I hear."

"He's been out looking for Pa."

"So, I hear."

"People down at Living Waters say the pastor was under stress, maybe depressed.

"So, I hear."

"Some say it could have been suicide."

"I heard."

"Mr. Gilmore, are you going to give me anything on this? What do you think of the suicide angle?"

"It's possible. There's no rail around the fountain. The pastor could have fallen in if he was standing nearby if he did it.

"Any evidence on the man's body that would point to suicide?"

"It's inconclusive."

"What, the suicide theory?"

"The Sheriff might be jumping the gun on this."

"Really?"

"There's little evidence to support either theory."

"Wouldn't there be evidence of a self-inflicted gunshot wound?"

"Normally, yes, but the gunshot residue is never

conclusive and, in this case, we got the body soaking all night as well. That would wash off any evidence.

"Wouldn't there be trace evidence in the water?"

"You'd expect it I think, but when the cleaning committee saw the Pastor down in the water, they tried to get him out, but you know he was a big man. When they couldn't lift him out of the water, they being all elderly ladies, they drained the fountain to get at him. So, the water in the Baptismal Fount washed down the drain."

"No trace evidence?"

"Well, if the Sheriff had roped off the area and shut the church down for the State to get in there and do a thorough forensic search, then they might have found something. But he didn't and by now any trace evidence is long gone down the pipes of that busy church."

"Why didn't the sheriff think about that? He should have known about the water-destroying evidence. He shouldn't rule out suicide at this point and not jump to a murder conclusion and an unlikely suspect. *Like Pa.*"

"Like most things, Emma, a man can only see what he wants to see."

"That's no way to run an investigation."

"You don't get to be Sheriff because of what you know, Emma. You get to be Sheriff because of *who* you know."

Frustrated with my visit with Gilmore, I got back to the shop without even remembering the drive, but I had to snap out of it. I still had Young Pastor Bennett's viewing and I needed to get ready for the football game at 7:00. Like most people, I'd be making a beeline for the stadium as soon as I paid my respects and wouldn't have time to run by the studio in between.

When I opened the door of the shop, Blue was waiting for me, holding her leash in her mouth. I almost told her to forget our afternoon walk. I didn't have time, and I wasn't in the mood, but with her big brown eyes looking at me I quickly gave in, so I leashed her up. The things we do for our children.

Giant white oak trees bordered both sides of Mill Row, from the juncture of Main Street down to the lake. At over a hundred years old they dwarfed the street, spreading their branches out and above, creating a brilliant rainbow kaleidoscope of red, yellow, and brown leaves in the crisp fall air.

For several weeks the fall foliage drove tourists into town to view the mountain wonderland of color, but the season's prime viewing window was over. In some of the trees, limbs already stretched skeleton-like over the street, a carcass of the changing season. The Bed and Breakfast inns and bedroom rental operations would soon turn to holiday tourists and winter sports enthusiasts, and the town would brace for another season of business. Oh, happy day!

***

The current sanctuary at Living Waters could only hold about two hundred faithful worshipers. Bursting at the seams for ordinary services, at a quarter to five a line of people outside already stretched a hundred or more, showing a testament to the young Pastor's personality.

I arrived early enough to help set up the slide show. I wore a thick long sleeve black sweater to hide my bandaged arm, and black jogger pants. I hoped my get-up was not too casual for the solemn event, but with the game coming up I didn't want to take the time to change wardrobes. This way I could pull a sweatshirt on and change into a pair of running shoes at the stadium and be ready for the warm-ups.

After setting up the slides and starting the five-minute video loop, I joined Pastor John and the church staff down at the front of the nave as they held vigil over the open casket for a private moment before the crowd came through. Mr. Hawkins was there, and I recognized others from the cleaning crew. Candi was there and holding a handkerchief up to her nose, she spent a good amount of time wiping at tears.

I didn't know her, but a woman dressed in black with two small children stood up front among a small group of mourners. A tall teen draped his arm around the woman's shoulder. I suspected the woman was the pastor's wife. When they approached the casket, she had to lift the children, one at a time, so they could look in at their father. I don't know why people practiced the morbid tradition, especially for children's sake. I wondered how many little guys over the years had been scarred for life by the ordeal.

I took up a position at the rear and kept several rows of people between me and the family. I kept my head down, as much as possible, shifting my feet, uncomfortable with my own faith. Twin projectors broadcast the slide show of the pastor's life on blank white walls on either side of the altar area. The man's continence, larger than life, broadcast down on the group, like God himself over his flock. When Mr. Hawkins saw me, he winked at me and gave me a thumbs-up.

The doors opened, and the long procession started in, led by a man blowing a bagpipe. The solemn, *Amazing Grace,* echoed off the walls. I'd forgotten that the Bennetts, like the Shaws, came over originally from Scotland.

The size of the crowd startled me, and I felt small under the man's spell, strong even after death.

I took up a position in the last row, near the side exit, where I could make a quick and hopefully unseen escape when the time came. A great number of the Shaw family tree made their appearance and they too seemed to position themselves at the rear. The Mayor and his wife Shelby came in near the head of the line. The faithful of the Pastor's congregation took seats and settled in for the evening. A recorded version of the tune, *A Mighty Fortress is Our God*, was piped in, taking the place of the bagpipes.

When a moment of silence followed the end of the hymn,

Pastor John took the pulpit. I don't know what I expected. Maybe a eulogy praising his brother or maybe a few words on the topic of death itself. Maybe something along the lines of... though the faithful are leaderless a leader will come forth? That kind of thing.

What we got was, "He will wipe every tear from their eyes. There will be no more death or mourning or crying or pain, for the old order of things has passed away." Perhaps signaling, *there was a new sheriff in town.*

I didn't catch the rest of Pastor John's message as I was trying to make my escape, and as I had predicted, many of the crowd, after a quick look at the man in repose and paying their respects to the widow, didn't even sit down, making their way up the aisle and out the doors, me following close behind. I hoped the Good Lord wasn't watching our great escape.

Chapter Sixteen

Friday Night

Even after all the years away, I marveled at Friday night football in Black Mountain. More than a tradition, the Friday night event bordered on reverence, matching the Sunday church faithful in attendance and fervor.

I tried to make it early to the games, and since the school system was paying me I wanted to make sure they got their money's worth. It didn't cost me anything for the extra, with all digital shots, just a little time.

I also enjoyed the time on the field. The high school itself only brought back gloomy memories of my time there. My high school circle of friends was rather small and even they abandoned me when rumors of my aura reading cast me as the local teen witch. At the time, I dreamt of having the power of a *Carrie,* to set fire to the school, but my ancestral gifts were limited in scope and even with the clearest view of a person's aura, my interpretation could be less than accurate.

My brother Early's second son, Johnny, played on the team. The boy played linebacker like his dad and Becky, his mom, said he already had several offers of scholarships. I had a feeling he was an easy bet to end up down at State, to join his older brother, and where his father played.

The game against county rival, Buncombe, began under a cloud-filled sky that promised cold and rain before the night ended. The crowd didn't notice the falling temperature as the Broncos and Cavaliers battled up and down the field with scoring at a premium, and I shot the action with one-and-a-half good arms. A last-minute interception by Johnny sealed the hard fought 7 – 0 win. As the fans left the stadium, both satisfied and cold, rain began to fall, but I doubted anyone really noticed.

"Did you get a picture of Johnny making that interception?" Becky asked me. When I looked up from packing my gear, I saw her standing under an umbrella held up by a tall good-looking man I'd never met before.

"I did," I said, rain dripping off the red state cap covering my head. "I was moving down the line with the defense and I knew something big would happen. I'll send you a copy."

When she didn't say anything more, I introduced myself. "Hello, I'm Emma Shaw."

"I'm sorry, Emma, this here's Drew Carter."

"Drew, nice to meet you."

"Likewise," he said then added, "I knew your brother the Chief."

"Oh?"

"Yes, ma'am, ran into him a couple of times."

"Oh?"

"Yes, Ma'am, he helped me out of some trouble a while back."

"Oh, well…"

"Speaking of trouble," Becky interrupted, "what's this I heard about you getting mugged?"

"It wasn't much to worry about."

"Just the same, why didn't you tell me?"

"I don't know," I said as we walked to my Jeep in the rain, huddled under the loan umbrella, "Jeff came and took care of me."

"Oh yeah?"

"Ah, yes," I said, putting gear in the back seat and fending off Blue as she tried to escape, "he was right across the street so I got the emergency room staff to call him."

"Well, just you remember you got family here who care about you, don't shut us out."

Was that what I was doing? I didn't think so. The business was dominating my life right at the moment and then the case with Pa and all. How people ever found time to run a business and have a life was a mystery to me. Besides, it looked like she had Drew to keep her busy enough.

Becky and her man walked off and I climbed in the cab and started up the engine.

When I felt a tap on my shoulder I about jumped through the roof of the Jeep. Pa was sitting in the back seat with Blue.

"You scared the ...you know what out of me! What are you doing here?"

"I came to watch the game," he said, scratching behind one of Blue's ears. "You know I wouldn't miss one of Johnny's games."

"You watched the game from here?"

"No, I was over on the visitor's side, out of sight, but I could see him play."

"You know the Sheriff is still looking for you?"

"I know, I've been keeping out of sight, from him and that big dopey son of his."

"Have you been staying at the farm?"

"No, they've been staking that out, I've been hold up somewhere else."

"Where?"

"Now, better you don't know, so if you are ever asked you can honestly say you don't know."

"That's a bit mysterious, isn't it?"

"No, I'm just being careful, and since we are on the subject, what's going on with the investigation? What have you found out?"

I turned around in my seat and faced the man, looking him over in the dim glare of the parking lot lights. From what I could tell, he looked to be in good shape, except for the rainwater dripping from him. Freshly shaved cheeks and clean clothes added to his bright aura, a light blue in the dark of night. The fact was, he looked better than ever.

"I haven't turned up anything concrete about the pastor," I told him, then I filled him in on what I found out up until then, but so as not to worry him, I didn't include my mugging.

"So, Gilmore didn't rule out suicide?"

"No, he said there was just nothing conclusive on that."

"Well, that's something. I mean, I'd hate it for those folks in the congregation, but just the same it would get me off the hook."

"There's more here than I can put my finger on, Pa. Do you still think staying away is helping your cause?"

"My sitting in a jail cell wouldn't help any. If it wasn't suicide, and it wasn't me who killed the good Pastor, then someone else is out there with blood on their hands."

"Yeah but who?"

"If you find out the why, that might lead you to the who."

"I guess, but just the same, it might let the Sheriff concentrate on finding another suspect if you come on in and give him your alibi."

"No, if the Sheriff had me locked up, he'd throw the key away and sit back and wait on the trial. This way he's at least going about looking for clues. If he had me in one place he'd stop altogether."

"But once the sheriff confirms your alibi, he'd let you go."

"Maybe."

"So, where were you after that Sunday argument with the pastor?"

"That's my business."

"Pa...who were you with?"

"You leave that be, Emma, it's got nothing to do with this."

"But pa..."

"Emma Louise, I already told you, now you need to move on."

I waited, watching him in the gloom, wondering why he wouldn't come clean about his alibi. I trusted him but wasn't so sure the Sheriff would. "So, what are you going to do now?"

"Well," he said opening the back door and stepping out in the rain, "until you solve this thing I'm staying out of sight!" With that, he disappeared in the dreary night. Blue put her nose up to the window and whimpered. I felt like doing the same. Since I'd been home Pa and I had forged a closer father/daughter relationship. Trying to catch up on the *together* time we missed during his drinking days and during the time I had vowed never to return home. Never say never.

I pulled the Jeep around and headed for town. The rain let up, turning to a light mist, and I turned the wipers off. I passed the *Coffee Bean* and saw a bunch of people gathered at the *Bean* to have a celebratory after-the-game victory cookie. May Shaw made the best oatmeal raisin cookies anywhere. They were as big around as a dinner plate and just as thick.

I could see the crowd through the street-side windows. The place was jumping, and I heard the laughter from the place, even out in the Jeep, making me think I should join the crowd. I just couldn't get Pa out of my head. I was beginning to wonder about his alibi and just who was he protecting. The next time I saw him, I was going to ask him straight out. I'd like to see him try to lie to me.

Needing a pick-me-up, I parked and put Blue up with a doggy treat and made my way back to the *Bean.* When I passed the one alleyway downtown between buildings, a lone figure stepped out on the sidewalk blocking my way. Tall and broad he herded me into the alley and out of sight of anyone out on the street.

The man, whom I assumed was a man based on his size, hovered over me, and glared out through the eye holes of a ski mask, making me shiver like I was caught out in the cold without a coat. "What's this all about?"

"I was about to ask you the same. What's it to you about the Pastor's death?"

"I'm looking into it."

"Why?" the man asked, stepping closer and forcing me

up against the outside brick wall of the downtown emporium, his face so close to mine I could smell his bad breath.

"The Sheriff thinks my Pa might have something to do with it."

"Now, look, your need to drop this little investigation of yours and leave things be."

"Or what?"

At that, the man stood back and turned to look out toward the street. When I followed his eyes and looked that way, I saw Jeff walk across the alleyway opening.

"Jeff!" I called out.

"Emma," he answered, turning, and seeing me he rushed into the space, "what are you doing in here".

It was then I realized I was alone. "He was right here."

"Who," he asked, looking around.

"I don't know, some guy, he cornered me in here and was asking about my looking into the Pastor's death."

"Who was it?"

"I don't know, he was wearing a mask."

Jeff took a couple of steps in the direction away from the street, like he was going to take off in that direction but seeing me wobbly on my feet he stopped. "Are you okay?"

"I'm fine. Just a little shook up. Where'd you come from?"

"I saw you park and followed after you."

"My hero!"

With my heartbeat settling down to a normal range, Jeff guided me up the walk to the *Bean* where I ordered several glasses of wine, for medicinal purposes. After getting the scary encounter buried in my subconscious, Jeff walked me back to the studio and up the stairs to my bedroom. I assumed nothing happened between us, again, since I woke up fully dressed the next morning.

Chapter Seventeen

Saturday Morning Graveside

Through my bedroom window I could see the morning had broken clear in a brilliant Carolina blue sky. Rain from the evening before left a swollen Swannanoa River.

Blue jumped up on my bed and tried to peel the covers off me. We engaged in a brief scuffle for a quilt my mama made me that I took to college and had been carrying with me wherever I called home. Somehow, both the quilt and I had returned to Black Mountain. To avoid damaging the heirloom, I gave in and let Blue win the tug-a-war.

Still shaken from the previous night's alleyway encounter, I forced myself up and took Blue for her morning walk. When back I made a cup of coffee, opened my phone, and stared at my calendar, wondering if I could muster up the energy to work through everything crammed into the scheduled ten hours of daylight. I only made it halfway through my first cup when the studio door below opened and Sue Ellen Shaw called up that she had arrived for work. Blue charged down the steps to greet the pretty girl and I could hear her shouting at the dog to stay down and behave.

"Looks like we have a busy day ahead of us," Sue Ellen called up. "Do you want me to load last night's photos?"

"Go ahead and I'll be down in a minute. We've got the Bailey family coming in first thing, then the Johnsons, and then Bonnie Stewart and her brood."

"I rushed into the bathroom. With my arm feeling okay I cut the bandage off. I took a quick shower and shampooed my hair. With the busy morning I wouldn't get a chance to clean up before Pastor Bennett's graveside service, so needed to be ready to dash over there. In addition to that, I would have to sneak out to coach my youth football game at ten o'clock.

After dressing in black, both convenient for a game and appropriate for a funeral, I went downstairs to get the camera and computer in position for the first family shoot. It seemed like just about everyone in town was getting their holiday cards early this year.

When I went into the studio I saw that Sue Ellen wasn't alone.

"Ms. Shaw," Sue Ellen introduced, "you remember my boyfriend, Tim McBride. He said he can help us out on Saturdays."

"Tim, how are you?" I asked the good-looking boy, not having met him one on one, but certainly heard enough of him from Sue Ellen. According to her, he was the best thing to land on this earth since *'sliced bread'*. It looked like Blue agreed because she sat at his feet while he scratched behind one of her ears.

"Sue Ellen said you all needed help. I hope you don't mind I came on in, you know, without an interview or anything?"

"If Sue Ellen recommends you then that's good enough for me."

"The best thing, Ms. Shaw, is Tim is great with kids."

"He is?"

"Yes, ma'am, Tim's got three younger brothers and sisters, so he's used to them."

That might have been the best recommendation he could have come with because that wasn't my strong suit.

"Can you stand on your head?" I asked the boy.

"I can if you need me to."

"Tim's athletic, he plays on the football team."

"Are you Tom McBride's boy?"

"Yes, ma'am, Pa and Chief Early played together. He always used to talk about those days."

"Used to?"

"Yes, ma'am, he died two summers ago."

"Oh, I'm sorry."

"It's okay, it's been a while."

"Tim's father had that football brain thing."

"CTE?"

"Encephalopathy," Tim said. "He had it pretty bad."

I wondered how the boy could play football with a history of CTE in his family. I asked him, "don't you worry about that?"

"Well, I know Pa would want me to keep playing, so I watch out for myself on the field. You know, I don't lead with my head on any blocks. Plus, equipment is a lot better than it used to be, back when Pa and the Chief played."

With time ticking away, we barely had time to set up the main studio before the Baily family stormed in. Six runaway kids under the age of ten took over the shop and chased Blue into hiding upstairs. After we wrestled the group into a sitting, I fired off as many shots as I could get. The whole affair took an hour, and I was lucky to get eight or nine good shots.

While Sue Ellen showed Mrs. Baily the digital results on the big monitor and the package options, Mr. Baily took the kids out back and walked down to the river.

No sooner had the place calmed down than the Johnsons came in with three boys under the age of five and pandemonium started up again. When Mr. Johnson threaten his boys with bodily harm, they settled in for some fine family shots that would make any holiday card shine.

While Sue Ellen showed Mrs. Johnson the results of everyone's efforts, Mr. Johnson took his boys down the walk to the Fish and Game store. I put my hands together in prayer for Jeff, grabbed my gear, and I rushed out to coach my little league football game. I was halfway to the field when I realized I left Blue at home. I said a little prayer for her as well. If the Stewarts and their four little girls got there before I got back, I didn't know what Blue would do.

***

By noon I could barely bend over, my back sore from stooping and cajoling little monsters to smile. Sore like I had worked two shifts at the mill, but I didn't have time to rest because Pastor Bennett's funeral was next on the agenda, next like the nail awaiting the hammer.

A fast-moving tributary of the Swannanoa River bordered the *Living Waters* cemetery, sweeping westward toward a sunset, carrying souls to infinity. Lush green grass, its color stubborn against the season, welcomed visitors to the peaceful ground. A white fence guarded the area, keeping the sleeping safe from teenagers out for a spooky adventure.

A line of cars backed a half-mile down the road. Mourners walked silently toward the hollowed grounds, their heads bent, their faces hidden under hats or behind scarves.

A small tent protected the immediate family. A cold breeze, intent on holding the faithful hostage to thoughts of the doomed life of the present against the afterlife of an uncertain realm in the future, whipped across the area. Even the clear sky above was unable to lift the spirits of the gathered.

Pastor John stood at the head of his brother's casket, a Bible in hand, reading. I only caught the last of his words, "John 3:16...For God so loved the world that he gave his Son, that whoever believes in him shall not perish but have eternal life."

I heard several laments of "Amen" from the gathered, following the Pastor's words, and I heard crying among the faithful. The loudest from young Candi, dressed in black, holding a handkerchief to her face, beneath a black veil, being a bit dramatic to my way of thinking.

At the end of the service, the crowd quickly retreated to the church basement for refreshments and warmth. I went over to the drink table and picked up a solo cup of sweet tea and took a big gulp.

"Nice of you to come by," Mr. Hawkins said when he came up to me.

"Sure thing, I wanted to pay my respects."

"And thanks for the slide show," he said, and then like it was a clip from a Saturday matinee he added, "I think everyone enjoyed it."

Looking around the crowded activity room I saw Candi again and went over to talk to her. A group of similar-aged young ladies surrounded her.

"Sorry about the Pastor," I said again, unable to thik of anything else. I mean what do you say to people after a funeral?

"I still can't believe he's gone," she said. "It's like I expect him to show up down here and make everyone feel better."

On the opposite end of the hall, a group of well-wishers had lined up to pay their respects to the widow and her children. I measured how long I'd have to stand in line, but I had a busy afternoon ahead of me so didn't join the group. Eventually, I'd have to talk to Pastor Bennett's new widow. I needed to ask her if she knew of anyone who would want to kill her husband.

***

The rest of the day went by in a blur. We had two more studio sessions in the afternoon, and I had a under 12 football game to shoot. Taken together I made more off the youth games then anything so couldn't pass them up. By the time the game ended, I had to drag myself back to the studio where Blue was waiting with her leash in her mouth.

Leaves from the trees along Mill Row covered the road in a layer of red, yellow, and brown. The fall spectacular season was coming to an end, its remnants a reminder of the season of life itself. Death or birth are transitions we all face during our short stay in this world. At the moment the only question for me was who ended the good pastor's stay too soon?

After Blue romped through the leaves we went back to the shop.

Sue Allen and Tim were sitting heavy in their chairs, and I could tell it had been a long day for them.

"I don't know what they are paying you here, but it is probably not enough."

"Do we get paid?" Tim asked.

"Don't worry," Sue Ellen told him as she stood up and collected her things, "I do the books around this place, and I'll tell you when payday is."

Alone for the first time all day, I went up the steps to the apartment an gave Blue her dinner, a scoop of dried dog food. She didn't seem to mind, not a picky eater. I marveled at a dog's requirements for happiness. A warm place to sleep, a simple meal, and five or six walks a day seemed to be all she needed. Come to think of it, that would almost satisfy me too.

I needed a shower but asked myself, what for? So instead, I went to the end of the room and collapsed onto the sofa, the only real piece of furniture in the place. Two old camp chairs sat opposite and a table I made out of four cement blocks and three planks of left-over wood. The rest of the room looked unoccupied. The periwinkle gray walls stood barren, even with twenty or so gallery-quality framed photographs in the studio below, calling out to be displayed. I never liked putting up my own work. I put my stuff out downstairs for marketing purposes, but I hadn't gotten around to putting up anything upstairs like I hadn't yet fully committed to the place. I wondered what a psychologist would say about that.

Blue came over and jumped onto my lap, reminding me of my commitment to her.

"Not now," I told her. "You just went out."

Reminded of commitment, I took out my phone and texted Jeff.

"You free tonight?"

Moments later, I sat looking at the little screen, thinking what is taking the man so long to respond. I mean doesn't he keep his phone in hand, just waiting for me to text him? After a very long minute, he texted back,

"What's up? Another caper?"

Funny, funny.

"No," I texted, *"just dinner."*

"Are you buying?"

"My treat.

"One hour!" was his last text back.

Looks like I did need that shower after all.

When I first got back to town I made it a point to visit with Pa on Saturday nights, but lately, Jeff had become my go-to alternative. It seemed more than not, Pa was always busy on Saturday nights. *What was up with that?*

It took longer than I anticipated, to get ready, counting the ten minutes I took staring at my closet. It should have taken a minute as there weren't many options in there. I decided I needed to visit Miller's clothing shop and add a pair of slacks to my wardrobe, maybe something in another color besides black. I could also use another blouse. My selection of flannel plaid shirts and old college tee shirts was limited. I settled on a clean pair of jeans and a State sweatshirt, hoping Jeff would see the attire as support for the alma mater. I hooked up Blue and went out, locking the shop behind us.

From the sidewalk, I could see Jeff through the window sitting at a workbench, fiddling with something. The Carson Fish and Game shop had been a fixture in downtown Black Mountain for a century or more and the Carsons were known across the foothills of the Blue Ridge as the best gunsmiths in the state. Jeff and his brothers had stayed in town to carry on the family tradition although to hear him talk about it, they didn't make any money in the store. He said most of their income came from gun and knife shows and selling antique firearms online.

"How are you?" he asked when Blue and I went into the shop. "After last night?"

"Never better," I lied, not wanting to go into the whole thing. "We were so busy today that I really haven't had a chance to think about it."

Moving close I could see Jeff was working on some mechanism of an old revolver. He had parts and small tools spread out on a velvet mat that covered the wooden workbench top.

"What are you working on?" I asked him as Blue jogged up to him and tried climbing in his lap. The smell of Gun oil lingered in the air.

"I'm changing out the trigger mechanism of this old Colt Navy Revolver," he explained holding Blue up and away from his work area. "Calvary officers carried them in the Civil War, and they were also used during the cowboy days out West."

"Do people still use them?"

"If they are maintained they'll work as good as new. Bud Brown brought this one in for me to look at it. He said it misfired the other day and he about blew his foot off."

"How much repair work do you do?"

"A good amount," he said, pushing Blue down onto the floor, "if you keep up with the maintenance on a pistol or rifle it will last forever. Families up here have old guns handed down for a generation or more. I'd do more if I could get it. I'm thinking about adding it to our website and maybe putting out the word on Instagram. It's only been a sideline up to now, but I can see the potential."

"So, did you have a busy day?"

"Fall hunters came by for ammo and supplies this morning," he said, "and tourists crashed the place all afternoon looking for souvenirs, so I can't complain."

"What's the hottest tourist item?"

"We sell a ton of the Daniel Boone pocketknives to the men," he said, making a note in an account ledger. With Blue out of the way he closed the ledger, "and the women like our '*I'm Game*' tees. You know, the play on words, written across the chest area."

"Cute."

"I know, it's a little crude," he said, getting up and moving to a clothes rack and pulling a beige tee shirt off and showing me the gag saying, plastered across the chest area of the shirt, *I'm Game*, "but we sell a bunch of them. You know what they say?"

"The customer is always right?"

"That's it. Besides, we need to sell whatever we can to keep the books balanced in this place. The side stuff we sell keeps our accounts in the black. I don't know what we'd do without the cash flow," he said, going over to his desk and retrieving his account book. "People can get less expensive fishing equipment at the big box stores, and men don't buy shotguns like they used to. Now all the young people want are those assault-style rifles."

"You don't sell those, right?"

"No," he said, going over to a file cabinet and thumbing through to a section. When he found the correct place, he inserted the book and slammed the file drawer closed, locking it with a push lock."

"Say," I said, remembering something. "do you always lock up your account ledger?"

"Got to," he said, placing the *I'm Game* tee shirt back on the rack where he pulled it. "If we ever had a fire, it's the only record of who in town owes us money. That file cabinet is supposed to be fireproof. I hope we never have to find out if that's true."

"Well, let me take you to dinner, you can take your mind off business for a while."

"I can think of a few other things that would take my mind off business."

"I'm sure you could, but let's try a roast beef sandwich first."

Jeff locked up his place with a big brass key and with Blue leading the way we walked up the sidewalk to the *Bean*.

"So," Jeff asked me when we got to the *Bean*, "what's this meal going to cost me?"

"Don't worry," I said, "you won't have to rough anyone up." At least I didn't think he would.

Chapter Eighteen

Saturday Night Caper

"You want to do what?" Jeff asked me when I told him what I planned and why I needed his help.

"Keep it down!" I told him, looking around the *Bean's* crowded dining room, hoping no one heard me when I explained what I needed Jeff to do. The aroma of freshly baked bread mixed with a wood fire filled the space.

"After last night I figure I must be getting close to something."

"Like what?"

"I'm not sure, but something, so I need you to help me break into the *Living Waters Church* office."

"Why?"

"I'm thinking it may have been Pastor John who cornered me last night."

"What makes you say that?"

"Just something about the way he talked. You know, sounded familiar. Besides, there's something going on over there with the church finances and I think it has some bearing on Pastor Bennett's death."

"You don't think it's suicide anymore?"

"I haven't given up on that, but whichever it is, the church's account books could shed light on it."

"You can't just ask around?"

"I have but the answers aren't conclusive, at least not enough to get Pa off the hook."

"How do you know where the church keeps its books?"

"They keep them in a file cabinet like the one you have in your shop."

"How…"

"I saw it when I met with Pastor John. I remembered just a while ago when I saw you put away your ledger. The church's cabinet is just like yours. It's got one of the push locks too. I saw Pastor John put a big ledger in the top drawer of the office cabinet."

"Even if you get in the office, how are you going to open the file cabinet if it's locked? Unless you break in."

"No, I wouldn't want to let anyone know someone was snooping."

"Then how…"

"You could get in by picking the lock."

"So, you know how to pick a lock?"

"You can use a couple of paper clips."

"Emma, you watch too much television. It's a lot harder than it looks in the movies. And even if you had the tools I think breaking and entering is against the law."

"Only if we get caught."

"There you go with that 'we' thing again."

"Wait…how do you know it's harder than it looks?"

Jeff had just taken a big bite out of his roast beef sandwich. During the half minute he chewed away, he stared at me, like he was evaluating what it was going to cost him if he joined me on another midnight caper.

"How do you know it's harder than it looks?" I repeated.

When finished chewing, and after he took a sip of his beer, he said, "Okay, Emma, we lost the key to one of our gun safes a couple of years ago. I messed with it one weekend and figured out how to pick that lock. It took a while to get in, but luckily there are videos on the internet that show you step by step. I've got a few tools that make it easy, and I've gotten to the point I can pick some locks quickly. I've used the tools a few other times to get into other gun safes. A lot of old-timers will die without telling anyone where they hid the key to their gun safes. You know, the nearest locksmith is over in Morgan. Most people around here never lock their doors or cars. Only their gun safes."

156

"So, you could pick the church's file cabinet lock?"

"Well…"

"Jeff!"

"Okay, okay, if it's the same style, probably I could."

"And if it's not?"

"Most of these locks all operate on the same mechanisms, pins, and cylinders, once you learn to pick one lock you can pick any old lock."

"Old locks?"

"Yeah, newer locks have added safety features that are harder to get around."

"And if the church file cabinet has an old lock?"

"It should be easy enough, but Emma, this is serious stuff here, breaking and entering."

"I know it's a lot to ask Jeff, but it's Pa's life we're talking about."

"He would do everyone a favor if he'd just come in and talk to the sheriff."

"I know, but in the meantime, I've got to see what I can do. Now, if you don't want to do this, I understand. Maybe you can show me how to do it and I can go by myself."

Jeff smiled at me. I knew I put him in a tight position. He knew I would never think he'd let me go alone. It was actually very unfair of me to ask, knowing he wouldn't refuse.

"Can I at least get another beer?"

"Later."

***

After agreeing to help me we left the *Bean* and walked back up the sidewalk. Jeff stopped at the Fish and Game shop to gather a few tools and I took Blue back to the studio and sent her to bed. I know she wanted to go along to help but as long as Jeff was with me I didn't think I'd need her and her sharp teeth for backup.

Living Waters Church sat on a seldom used road but not chancing someone going by and recognizing my Jeep, I parked off the road about a half-mile away and made Jeff walk. We circled around the building and came up from behind. Years of rough use scarred the rear door of the church and even to my untrained eye, it looked flimsy. Jeff had the same reaction and didn't have to pick that lock as he lifted the door handle and using his weight, shouldered the door open. The back door led to a hall that took us to the sanctuary. Using a penlight, Jeff led the way across the sanctuary and by the baptismal fount. As we passed, I looked down at the empty pool like fountain at floor level, wondering how many church goers over the years had actually fallen in. At the end of the room we found another locked door.

The lock on the door looked solid but Jeff knelt down and took a look at it. He took two long slim pieces of metal from a pouch he carried and inserted them in a specific way into the keyhole opening and turned, pushed, and twisted back and forth until the lock clicked. He took a pair of needle-nose pliers and clamping down on the two metal pins at once, he turned them over and the door opened.

"Wow," I said, "just like in the movies."

The door opened to a hall that led to the side of the Church that housed the office. We found a door, unlocked, in a likely location and when we opened it, we found ourselves in the church office area.

I led Jeff to the pastor's office and we found that door locked.

"Use a credit card," I suggested to Jeff.

"I told you, you watch too much television."

"I don't even own a television."

"Well, I've never used a credit card before so let me take a look at this."

Jeff knelt at the door and after examining the lock with the glow from his penlight, he got up and took a step back. He pushed me to one side and put his finger up to his lips, indicating I should be quiet. Putting his shoulder to the door and grabbing hold of the doorknob, he lifted and put his weight into the door, and it popped open.

"Wow, that's great!" I said.

"With this old lock, even *you* could have pushed it open."

With the door ajar, we got into the former Pastor William Bennett's office and now the current office of Pastor John Bennett.

The file cabinet sat against the wall at the far end of the room.

Jeff used his penlight to work his way across the room and when he got to the cabinet he said, "Well, we won't need to pick this lock."

"Why not?"

"It's not locked."

I moved around him and seeing the cabinet unlocked I pulled open the top drawer, but I didn't see any financial books or ledgers. Just to make sure I looked into the other file cabinet drawers as well.

"I don't see any account books," I said, surprised.

"Looks like someone beat us to it."

"Who?"

"Someone who had access to the file cabinet."

"That could be anyone."

"No, this cabinet wasn't broken into, it was opened with a key. Someone with a key got in there and took the financial files if they were there."

"They were there."

"Then someone took them."

"Who?"

"I don't know, you're the detective, I'm just the lock guy."

At that moment bright lights flashed across the room, and we ducked to the floor.

"Oh, oh," I whispered, that must be one of the Sheriff's deputies. How did they know we were here?"

"They couldn't know, so there must be a security system that links with the Sheriff's Department. We must have tripped something at the back door. Let's get out of here."

Retracing our steps, we were halfway across the sanctuary when we saw a light beam from a flashlight coming from the rear entrance of the church. When I looked back, I saw another beam coming up the hall from the direction of the office we just left.

We quickly hid as best we could. The two sheriff deputies met in the middle of the sanctuary, under the steeple.

"This is a waste of time," one said.

The other one said, "Dispatch said the alarm went off fifteen minutes ago."

"Well, there's no one here now," the man said, and I recognized the voice of Ross Banner.

"The back door was forced open."

"Well, it doesn't look like anything is missing. Whoever got in saw there wasn't anything worth taking and must have left. We'll get the church staff to check in the morning, in the meantime let's go get something to eat, I'm starving."

"You're always starving. Doesn't your old man feed you?"

"Not that old miser. I have to buy my own food."

We waited until we saw the flashing sheriff cruiser's lights go off and heard the vehicle drive down the road before we took a deep breath. The space in the baptismal fount was big enough to hide both of us from a cursory search, although a careful look would have surely found us at the bottom of the dry pool, entwined in each other's arms.

"Ah," I said, pushing out at Jeff's chest, trying to get some breathing room between us, "I think they're gone."

"We'd better wait another few minutes," Jeff said, pulling me closer, "they might come back."

"No, Jeff, they are not coming back."

"How do you know for sure?"

"Jeff!"

"Okay, okay," he said, releasing his hold on me, "but you still owe me a beer."

***

On the way back to town Jeff and I went over the results of our midnight caper, zero.

"Someone wants to keep the church financial records hidden," Jeff said as I drove.

"Someone?" I asked back.

"How many people have access to those and who has the most to lose if the records get out?"

"I don't know," I said.

"Don't you?"

I paused before continuing, knowing the number of people who could gain something if those records didn't come out would make up a very short list. "Pastor John?" I asked.

"That's who I'd put my money on."

"You think Pastor John would kill his own brother?"

"I didn't say that. I said he looks guilty for taking the records."

"You mean maybe the two things are not related?" I asked.

"Could be like you first figured," Jeff explained. "Pastor William Bennett might have committed suicide, for all the reasons we've discussed, and now that he's out of the way, Pastor John can take advantage of the situation and cover his financial shenanigans. You said he appeared quite upbeat about everything, right?"

"He was almost giddy, the first time I spoke with him."

"There you go!"

I didn't know where I was going, actually, but I did know

next time I spoke with Pastor John, I would put it to him direct, and see if he could lie to me about killing his brother.

Chapter Nineteen

Sunday

Folks in the mountains take the Lord's Day of rest seriously. Even the Shaw Mill is closed on Sundays. But recently, with tourists flocking through town during the four seasons, most of the businesses on Main Street met the Lord halfway and stayed closed on Sunday morning but managed to get their shops open by one o'clock to catch a late-rising paying customer on their way out of town after a weekend get-a-away.

Local parishes made further accommodations to the reality of the business world by moving service times back earlier to give everyone time to get home for a quick lunch before opening businesses.

Sunday morning usually found Pa preaching at his Sunday school class. Pa kept up the Sunday ritual and treated it as a calling, studying the weekly passages and preparing to speak on the word of God. Of course, with him being on the lam I doubted he'd make it to his Sunday morning duties this week. I was wrong.

After my night of breaking and entering, Jeff left me at the door of the studio. He didn't get his beer, but I promised him a rain check. When I awoke in the morning I found Blue staring me in the face.

"What?" I asked her, expecting an answer.

"Woof," came the expected response.

I pulled myself from under the covers, noting a decrease in the pain in my arm from my recent brush with death. Shivering, I looked for something to put on and settled on my long robe and parka. I slipped into my Ma's furry slippers and took Blue out for her morning ritual.

When we got back, I longed to return to the warm covers

of my bed. With Pa dodging the law I supposed he'd be absent this week from his Bible study duties. Still, in order to show support, and make it look like I really didn't know anything about his sudden disappearance from the town landscape, I decided it would be better if I attended and then look surprised along with everyone else about Pa not showing up to teach. Besides, I might pick up some more gossip about *Living Waters*. Nothing like competition to swell the rumor mill.

Since Blue gets me up at the crack of dawn, I had time to spare and decided to load the previous day's shots on the website, on the chance I'd make a Sunday afternoon sale. It always takes me longer to get the photos downloaded and up on the site hence I have the teenager take care of most of those duties, but after getting my morning coffee I sat down at the computer and worked my way through the process.

By the time I saved all my work and published the updated files, my extra time ran out causing me to rush to get ready for church. Foregoing another shower, having just taken one the night before, I dressed in my Sunday black, combed out my hair and tied it with a rubber band, and left Blue at the door, whining. I didn't hesitate though. The taking Blue to Sunday services experiment ended after the very first try. I don't know if it was the choir, or the pitch of the church organ, but whatever it was, Blue spent the hour of services howling from the Jeep in the church parking lot, like she was calling out to God herself. The stares I got from the other God-fearing people in the congregation that morning convinced me that from that morning forward, Blue would be spending the day of rest, resting in her studio bed.

I climbed into the cold Jeep, started it up, and turned on the heater. The short ride to the church was over before the engine generated heat for my legs, so I froze as the blower blew cold air at me and all I could think about was Blue sleeping warm under my covers back at my apartment. I wondered how unusual it was that visions of my warm bed contained a dog and not some good-looking guy, like Jeff.

Cars and trucks parked along the road a good hundred yards back from the church. Late, not for the first time, I got out and trudged my way to meeting knowing I'd probably missed the Sunday school lesson for the week. I had only reached the edge of the parking lot when I saw two sheriff deputy cruisers and a crowd gathered at the Sunday school entrance. Deputy Ross Banner and a small contingent of other deputies gathered in a gaggle and I wondered what brought them all out.

"What's going on?" I asked the first person I came up to, a man in Pa's Sunday school class, although my stomach began to churn with worry.

"Your Pa came to Sunday school and the Sheriff showed up to arrest him," the man said, recognizing me.

"What for?" I asked as if I didn't know.

"They said for murdering young Pastor Bennett."

It wasn't surprising that the Sheriff wanted to arrest Pa, what was a surprise was why Pa thought he could just show up and not be discovered. Sheriff Banner may be deliberate, but he wasn't dumb. I couldn't wait to find out what Pa was thinking when he decided to show up for Sunday school.

"Logan saw them coming and he took off out the back of the church and up into the mountain."

"Did they follow him?"

"Not yet," the man said, "I think they are trying to get organized. You know, I don't have to tell you it will be hard to run down your Pa once he gets up in that mountain. Every minute that they wait is another hour Logan can put between them."

I left the man and went up to Ross Banner.

"What's going on?"

"We got a tip that your Pa was here this morning so we came over to check it out."

"A tip from who?"

"Someone called our 911 center. We got here ten minutes ago but it took us a while to find your pa's Sunday school classroom and by the time we found it he'd already made his escape."

"I'm sorry to hear that," I said.

"I just bet you are," the Sheriff's son said. "What brings you out here? Did you know your pa was going to be here?"

"No, how would I know?"

"Pretty coincidental, you showing up like this."

"Nothing coincidental about it, Ross, I've been coming down here to Pa's church since I moved back."

Just then another Sheriff cruiser came into the lot and after stopping the Sheriff got out of the vehicle, dressed in Sunday clothes, not his uniform.

"Did you catch him?" the Sheriff said, joining our little group.

"No, someone must have tipped him and he took off before we could get to him."

"I wonder how that happened?"

"I can't figure it."

"You don't think it had anything to do with you all storming into the parking lot here with your lights flashing and tires squealing? Did you turn on your sirens to boot?"

Ross Banner turned his head away from his father, avoiding eye contact.

"What are you doing here?" the Sheriff asked me, seeing me standing there among the uniforms.

"I came to go to meeting."

"I think that's a bit of a coincidence," Ross Banner said.

"Well," the Sheriff said, looking directly at me, "is it a coincidence?"

"I've been coming here since moving back to town, Sheriff, I've got my own faith to look after. You look like you were in church his morning."

"That's right, and I don't appreciate being called out here

in the middle of the service."

"I didn't call you."

"Yeah, but your Pa is the reason. When are you going to get him to come in?"

"Knowing my pa, Sheriff, if he's up in that mountain and you want to talk to him, you're going to have to go up and find him."

"Logan Shaw?"

"She's right, Pa…"

"Call me Sheriff you…"

"Sheriff, sheriff, then, and she's right. Why don't we put a team together and track him down?"

"Why? I'll tell you why, because we wouldn't find him if we had a map. Everyone knows Logan Shaw knows this mountain like the back of his hand."

"He's just a man, Pa, and any man can be found if we put a big enough team together."

"This is your second chance at catching him, Son, and so far, he's outsmarted you."

I wondered when the first time happened.

"Give me enough men this time and I'll catch him."

"I don't know, I've heard tales from back in his liquor running days, they said he was like a ghost in these hills."

"That was a long time ago, Pa, I don't reckon he'd be getting on like he did back in the day."

The Sheriff ignored his boy and looked at me again, "Okay, what's it going to be?"

"What do you mean?" I asked.

"Are you going to help us out on this deal with your pa? Or are you going to make me hunt him down?"

"Why are you even bothering with him anyway? You know he didn't have anything to do with Young Pastor Bennett's death."

"Yeah, yeah, you've said that before, but he's still the only suspect I got, and unless you've come up with someone else…"

When I didn't offer anyone else he said, "Just like I thought, no one else with a motive, means, or opportunity."

"Look, Sheriff…"

"No, Emma, you look, now I've slow-played this thing because Logan is a Shaw, but I can't ignore the facts. Your pa needs to come on in or I will have to go up and look for him."

"But Sheriff…"

"No, I gave you a chance to figure this out, and you can't because there is only one explanation. Now if your pa wants to come on in and provide us with his alibi, then we can move on, but if not then he stays the number one suspect. The only question I have is are you going to help us track him down?"

"I couldn't do that, Sheriff, even if I could, that's my Pa out there."

"Then you are aiding and abetting!"

"I am not. I didn't know Pa was coming in today. I'd hardly say he was trying to evade arrest if he came in to go to Sunday school. For all we know, Pa might not even know you are looking for him. Has anyone in the Sheriff's office actually spoken with him?"

"We can't find him."

"Okay, but that's no excuse to say he is evading arrest. For all you know, Pa is just out hunting."

"Why'd he run off?"

"Who says he ran off?"

"He wasn't here when Ross got here."

"Maybe Sunday school was over, and he just left."

"Before service?"

"Plenty of people leave right after Sunday school, Sheriff, you know that. That's why they have a back door to the place."

"Oh, that's enough! Now, I've listened to plenty of your reasoning, and I've got one last thing to say. If your Pa doesn't come in by tomorrow afternoon, I'm getting an old fashion posse together and we'll go look for the man. I think twenty men and some dogs should do the trick."

"Sheriff," Jeff spoke up, just coming into the circle to hear the last of the conversation, "Sheriff, if you send that many men to look for Logan Shaw, then you'd better take along more than one body bag, Logan is not about to be taken easily."

"What do you know about it?" the Sheriff asked Jeff.

"I know what my Pa used to say about Logan Shaw. Pa served with Logan in Vietnam, along with a few other men in town, including Lawrence Shaw. They'd all tell you the same, Sheriff."

"What would they tell me?"

"They'd say… *"when you go hunting mountain lion, better expect to get clawed."*

***

"Where'd you come from?" I asked Jeff after our conversation with the Sheriff ended.

"I was in the shop working on some orders when I saw the Sheriff fly down Main Street. I took a guess he was heading here."

"That's pretty good deductive reasoning, Jeff."

"That and somehow I get this weird feeling at the back of my neck when you are about to step into trouble."

"Well, whatever it is, I'm glad you showed up."

"Oh, oh…"

"That's right, Mister, you've stepped into it now. We're going to take a hike."

"Don't tell me…"

"That's right, as soon as we pick up Blue, we are going for a walk in the woods."

***

The Smoky Mountains form a lower range of the Blue

169

Ridge Mountains. The Cherokee named the area, Shaconage which means "*land of the blue smoke*". Traditional Cherokee life was steeped in myth and mystery. The Cherokee Shaman's ability to see visions has never been limited to seeing auras, as many shamans possess the ability to see the connection between the spiritual world and the natural world.

Though Pa was only part Cherokee, this ability to be one with nature was powerful within him which made him one with the forest. If we were going to find him, we were going to need help.

"You're going to do what?"

"I need to stop at the studio to pick up Blue," I told Jeff. "Pa is so good in the woods we're going to need her help. Ask anyone."

"No, I know your Pa is a woodsman, Emma, but do you think Blue can find him?"

"There's something between Blue and Pa, Jeff, she's one with the forest so she naturally has a connection to Pa. We need to get on out to Pa's house. I'm sure he'd stop there before heading up into the mountain. Once we get Blue up there, she should be able to catch Pa's scent. Do you remember the other night when we were up there? I think Blue had his scent but lost it and came back."

"So, you think Blue can lead us right to your Pa?"

"No, not right to him, just in the general area. Once we get close Pa will come in and meet us."

"What if he doesn't want to be found?"

***

While at the studio Jeff entertained Blue and took her for a quick walk, while I got some stuff together for our adventure and put on some hiking clothes. I loaded everything into a small pack with other gear, camping gear – not photography gear – and when he came back, I handed it to Jeff to carry. I knew I'd get an argument from Jeff if I insisted on carrying the load. Jeff, being the gentleman, would of course insist and then I'd make the case for a woman being just as capable of carrying a load as a man. In the end, he'd win the argument, just because I'd grow tired of the back and forth. So, just to avoid expending the energy I'd need for the hike, I just handed him the bag and put Blue in the Jeep for the ride up to Pa's house. Jeff only smiled.

Pa's house sat about a mile up the mountain from the church, at the edge of the thick Pisgah National Forest. Even during the light of day, a path could quickly fade into shadow and many a fella had been known to get lost in the darkness.

I went into the house and while there I fetched one of Pa's dirty shirts out of his laundry basket. Going outside I showed it to Blue. She immediately yanked it out of my hand and Jeff, and I spent a minute wrestling Blue for possession. When finally organized, I led Blue over to the trailhead and she took off, her nose to the ground, dragging me behind her. It took a mile or so but Blue finally settled down into a walk and Jeff and I caught our breath as we made our way deeper and deeper into the forest.

"You sure this is going to work?"

"Sure, I am," I said, maybe not thoroughly convinced but sure enough to add, "Blue has got this!"

After another hour of steady climbing, the trail leveled off some and following a shallow rise we found ourselves on the ridgeline along Black Mountain.

"Momma used to come up here on this trail," I told Jeff when we stopped for a drink of water. "She liked to get away from things, time to time. The thing was, living and raising two kids in the mountains proved more trouble than she figured. I think she may have suffered a bit of depression. That's why she took to drink. Then when she got God, well, without the liquor crutch, she was on her own. Nowadays, you could probably get a pill for it. Back then you went for walks."

I poured some water into Blue's water bowl that I had made Jeff carry up the mountain and she lapped up all of it. After our respite, we headed off again stopping after another hour to eat lunch.

"Well, "Jeff said, sitting down on a fallen log and swinging the pack off his back. "Let's see what you made me lug up here to eat."

"I made some peanut butter and jelly sandwiches."

"That's your idea of a lunch?"

"What could be better, protein, carbs, and grains. A perfect meal."

"Yeah, if you're in kindergarten."

"Don't worry I put a few granola bars in there too."

"Wonderful…"

I gave Blue a doggy biscuit, but I could see she wanted a granola bar.

With lunch completed, we washed everything down with water and started out again. An hour later we noticed the thick forest thinning out and knew we were reaching the apex of the ridgeline. Even though we hadn't seen any sign of Pa, Blue was still pulling at her lead, still on his scent. With the afternoon approaching, I was beginning to wonder if I had miscalculated on just where my Pa was holed up. I hadn't figured we'd be up there after dark, but if we didn't come upon my pa soon, it would be late by the time we headed back down to town.

Then just as suddenly as she had taken up the trail, Blue stopped. A wide stream, only a few inches deep, flowed across the trail. We watched the dog walk left up the stream then turn around and go right, her nose down to the ground. I figured she'd lost the scent so took her across to see if she could pick it up on the other side, but she looked as lost as ever. She finally stopped altogether and looking up at me barked out and wagged her tail.

"I guess this is it," I said to Jeff.

"What?"

"The trail's end."

"I don't see your pa."

"No, but Blue's lost the scent."

"So..."

"So, now we wait."

"Why don't you take Blue up the bank a little way, and see if she can pick up the trail again."

"No," I said, coming back across the stream and settling down on a soft bank of grass, "this is an old Cherokee trick."

"What?"

"Crossing a stream like this. I expected to see it before but we hadn't come to any water yet so this is the first opportunity he had."

"For what?"

"He went in the water here alright but he probably went up a distance before he climbed out of the stream. Probably onto those rocks up there. Up on the rocks he could skip across for a hundred feet or more without ever putting a foot on the ground. No dog, not even Blue, could track a man across rock like that and he could have come down anywhere. No, we'll just have to wait now."

"Wait for what?"

"Wait for Pa. He's not far off. I figure he's up higher on the ridge, watching us now. He can see back down the trail, from where we came. As soon as he sees we weren't followed he'll come down."

"You sure about all this?"

"I'm sure enough to get some coffee going."

"Where are you going to get coffee up here?"

"In your pack. You carried it up here."

"You made me carry coffee up here?"

"Coffee and a pot and cups to boot! Give me that pack and gather some wood. I expect Pa could use a cup about now."

Once Jeff gathered a bundle of sticks together, I got a fire going in a shallow hole ringed with large rocks. Using the water from the steam, I filled an old camp percolator and set it on the fire to boil. After three minutes I put in the coffee strainer with grounds and put it back on the fire. A minute more it started to perk and we had coffee a minute after that.

Pa must have smelled the coffee because it didn't take him long to come out of the woods, trailing his orange aura of vitality behind him.

"That smells good," Pa said coming into our little camp.

"I knew you'd show up if I put a pot on. How are you fixed for supplies?"

"Not too good," he said, coming to the fire and squatting down. He had on his fall season camouflage hunting gear, his good boots, and heavy coat, and toted his bow, not his shotgun. I noticed his quiver carried a dozen arrows with broadhead tips. Apparently, Pa was stealth-hunting and not out to make a lot of noise. I didn't let the fresh blood on his hands and arms bother me. "I stopped at the house but was in a hurry. I stumbled on a buck though. He was down here drinking when I came around the bend and I got off a shot through his heart. He took off on a dead run for about fifty yards upstream and I followed him. I was dressing him out when I smelled the coffee. Once I saw it was you, I made sure you weren't followed before I came down."

"Well, Jeff packed up a few things. Some more coffee and sugar, a box of instant oatmeal. That's about all I had in my pantry. It should last you a couple of days."

"Thanks, a couple of days is all I need."

"What are you going to do with that buck?" Jeff asked.

"I got him field dressed and it's cold enough to preserve the meat. I might start a fire and dry some. Here," he said, taking a hunk of meat out of a pouch on his coat and tossing me a thick piece of venison," put that on a spit and we'll have a bite for dinner."

"Don't know if I'd be settling in for a long stay, Logan. The Sheriff was talking about putting a team together to come up and find you."

"Sheriff Banner? Ha, it'd be a cold day in summer before the Sheriff could track me up here."

"Pa, the Sheriff sounded serious. That's why we came looking for you. You need to come on down and straighten this whole thing out."

"I told you, Emma, I can't do that."

"Look Pa, this isn't a cut-and-dry case. I've got nothing so far in my investigation and it's looking more and more like it might take a while before I turn up anything concrete. It sure would make it easier if you came out and told the Sheriff about your alibi. That way he could check you off his list and we could all concentrate on finding out who killed young Pastor Bennett. With the Sheriff set on you as the prime suspect, he's just wasting time and energy and the trail might go cold on the real killer."

Jeff hadn't said much during the conversation. I got the feeling he wasn't as sure of my Pa as I was. He knew that a man lugging a bow and quiver of broad point arrows around was a man to be respected, no matter who he was.

"What's your take on this, Jeff?" Pa asked, looking up at him.

"Well, Sir," Jeff said, squatting at the fire, directly across from Pa, "I might have to agree with Emma on this." Fixing the deer meat to a straight stick and using the rocks in the pit, he got our dinner situated over a hot spot. "Look," he clarified, "we both know the Sheriff is pretty much a fool. But even a fool might get lucky and find you up here if he brings enough men along. He could flush you out eventually."

"Banner? Ha! Besides, where's he going to get enough men? I don't see that happening in Black Mountain."

"Remember, Pa, the Sheriff can pull from Morgan. He might not find any men in town that would join up with him but the men down in Morgan don't know you. I imagine he could put a team together if he put out a call. You might be a legend in Black Mountain, Pa, but to men in Morgan, you'd just be another person of interest."

"You're probably right about that but I figure he'll take at least two days to get a crew together. That's two days more that you'll have to work this case. Two days to find out who killed Pastor Bennett. Until then, I'm not showing my face in Black Mountain."

"And after?"

"The Sheriff might see what it means to hunt a man."

"Pa, that doesn't sound like you. In fact, I think that sounds like a man who has lost his faith. Here," I told him, pulling his Bible from my coat pocket where I put it after taking it from his house. "You might need this."

Pa took the Bible. He stared at it a good minute before saying anything. Holding it in his palm, like he was weighing it, he said, "I still have faith, Emma, and I have faith in you."

In the late afternoon light, I watched Pa's aura beat into a lavender range, the color of a spiritual person, at one with their surroundings and at peace with themselves. There, with the Bible in his hands, I saw relief come into Pa's shoulders and for the first time since we found him, he looked like the pa I loved.

We spent an hour or so going over the case and eating off the spit, after which Jeff and I started the hike back. It was downhill from there, but it still took three hours. By the time we got back down to Pa's house, it was well past dark, and we were both dead tired. Even Blue looked beat as we three came out of the woods and climbed into my Jeep for the drive down to town.

At the studio door, Jeff smiled weakly at me and went up the walk to his shop and his truck.

I let Blue in and gave her some fresh water. She'd already had a hunk of leftover deer meat so I knew she didn't need a dinner bowl of chow, but I gave her a doggy bone. She picked it up and went off to her corner bed and flopped down, saving the bone for later.

I followed after her and climbed into my bed, barely managing to shake my boots off. The next thing I knew it was morning, Monday morning, and I had things to do!

Chapter Twenty

Monday

Next to the Day of Rest, Mondays may be my slowest day of the week, business-wise. I usually spend a good bit of the morning filling orders from the weekend games but actual customers in the shop are rare. I had my weekly Boy's middle school soccer game at 3:00 but until then just computer work.

After taking Blue for her morning ritual, I fixed a cup of coffee and two slices of whole-wheat toast. In addition to finding out who killed Pastor William Bennett, I was determined to start eating better.

I had been working at my desk for about two hours when Mayor Shaw came in.

"Your Pa gave himself up."

"What…when?"

"He came in an hour ago. He said he heard the Sheriff was getting a posse together and came down to save the town the trouble. I wonder where he heard that?"

"I don't know, you know how news spreads in this town. Where is he?"

"He's down in a basement cell over in Town Hall. He'll have an arraignment hearing sometime during the next couple of days."

"Then what?"

"Depending on bail and all, he'll be held over at the county lockup in Morgan until a trial is set."

***

"What do you mean I can't speak with him?" I asked the town magistrate, Bartholomew Shaw, when I showed up in his office in Town Hall.

"Emma, your Pa hasn't been arraigned yet, so I can't let you talk to him."

"Look, Bartholomew, you know this is crazy, Pa couldn't be guilty of this, you know him, he's family."

"My hands are tied, Emma. After we get through the charges and all I might be able to let him out on bail but until I hear what he has to say in court, I've got to keep him locked up."

"But why?"

"Because he might be guilty. In his youth, your Pa ran liquor through the hills around Black Mountain. To say he was on a collision course with the law is an understatement. He got lucky when he went off to Vietnam."

It was a much-needed detour in Pa's spiral of descent that promised a hard time and a short life. When Mama came into his life, he changed some, but the demon liquor still chased him. I was away at college when Ma and Pa did a one-eighty, and they left those hard days of liquor behind them and picked up on the harder days of Christ. I asked him once what brought about the change and he told me he got God.

So, you just couldn't convince me that Pa had killed anyone.

"Look, Bartholomew, the jail is down ten feet in solid rock, I couldn't get Pa out of there with a jackhammer. Let me talk to him and find out what's going on here."

"Emma, it isn't even our jurisdiction anymore. The Sheriff runs the jail as part of his contract with the town."

"Bartholomew, the town is the Shaw family. You mean to tell me you're going to let Sheriff Banner tell you how to run this town?"

I knew this last bit would do the trick. Bartholomew Shaw thought about it for half a second before he gave in saying, "Okay, Emma, but just because you all are family of a sort. Now, I'll let you in to see him but after the arraignment, the

179

Sheriff will have him transferred to the county lockup and we won't have jurisdiction after that, so you better get busy."

"What do you mean?"

"Don't be smart, Emma, we all know you are working on this case. We don't want to see Logan go down for this but unless you come up with something, there won't be much we can do about it, even if he is kind of family!"

You had to descend a long stone staircase to get to the Black Mountain jail, housed in the basement of Town Hall. It was well suited for the purpose. Back when the Town Hall was built I understood the jail got quite a bit of use as the town was known for revelry, especially after payday. Located below street level, it ran along the back wall of the building, with squat barred windows about eight inches high, that faced out onto the rear parking lot and a picnic shelter you could rent for family reunions.

Several tons of concrete foundation and solid granite walls prevented any possibility of escape from the jail and the Shaw family took great pride in that.

Although he complained about it, Ross Banner, playing jailer, led me down a narrow stone staircase to the basement below and down a narrow passageway to a wide room with a bank of five eight-foot cells. An array of fluorescent lights centered in the hall cast bright light into every corner of the room and I couldn't imagine anyone getting any sleep down there if they stayed at night. Pa was in the far cell. The only one occupied.

"Hello, Emma Louise," Pa said when he saw me standing outside his cell. One-inch, painted black, round, floor-to-ceiling bars separated us, but Pa came over just the same, and reaching through the six-inch separation he squeezed my hand.

"Pa, why in the world didn't you provide the Sheriff with your alibi for the night the pastor was killed? You told me you had one."

"That's my business."

"Pa, what's going on?"

When the man didn't say anything back I knew why.

"Who are you protecting in all this?"

"What do you mean?"

"You heard me, Pa, who are you protecting? You wouldn't be in this bind unless there was someone you needed to protect. Just who?" I asked him, and then I knew. Just to make sure I asked him right out, "Are you protecting Clare Bennett? Is she your alibi?"

Pa's aura came out in full force. I expect he knew I could see it clear enough. Pa never fully understood my aura reading thing. He knew it had something to do with my birth mama and our Cherokee ancestors, but he never knew how it all worked.

"Okay, okay," he said, his aura beating yellow with emotion but no lie, "its' Clare. I was with Clare that night."

"I knew it! So, what's going on? Tell the Sheriff about Clare and let's get you out of here."

"I can't do that."

"Why not?"

"I've got to protect Clare's reputation. She's a God-fearing lady and I won't be the one to muddy her name."

"Pa, these are different times. I don't think you need to worry about that. Plenty of people have out-of-marriage relations nowadays and don't think anything about it."

"Well, I think about it and so does Clare. I think she's a bit embarrassed about it. I mean here we are, taking up at our age. So, that's why you got to solve this thing. Find out who killed Pastor Bennett. Get me out of this mess."

"Pa, if Clare cares about you, she shouldn't be worried about how this looks."

"Look, Clare's got reason to worry. She doesn't know me and right now I'm just a question mark in her story and I want to be more."

I couldn't get my head around what Pa had got himself into and there were too many loose ends.

"Pa, what about that handgun you bought? When the Sheriff finds out about that, he'll have even more reason to keep you locked up down here."

"Look, Clare knew I was a hunter and had been in the military, so she asked me about getting a gun. She said she'd gotten several warnings about her decision on the new sanctuary since she told young Pastor Bennett she could back out of the deal. There're some crazy people down at that church, Emma, and Clare's sorry she ever started going down there, but now she's stuck in the middle of this thing. That's why she left town."

"Where'd she go?"

"Now, Emma, you're my baby girl but don't expect me to be showing all my cards. I've got to respect Clare's privacy, and you got to respect mine."

"Pa, do you understand your leaving yourself open to being considered guilty? Jeff says that come tomorrow or the day after, the Sheriff will get the information on that gun you bought. When that comes in the Sheriff will have what he needs to nail you and you could find yourself bused over to the county jail.

"I'm not worried, Emma Louise. I know you'll find out who killed Pastor Bennett before then."

Great, nothing like a little pressure.

Chapter Twenty-One

Monday Afternoon

After seeing Pa, I went back to the studio and tried to do some work but after the best part of an hour, I knew it wasn't happening. Feeling terrible about failing to get Pa out of the mess he was in, I started to get ready for the boys' middle school soccer game I needed to shoot

I grabbed my gear, hooked up Blue, and we drove over to the fields, thankful for having something other than Pa to think about.

Like the last few days I had, the match was fairly exciting, ending in a seven-to-seven draw. I got some great photos of ten different players scoring and the mob of players celebrating each goal. Out in the parking lot after the game, I passed out every flyer I had. I imagined I'd do quite a bit of overnight business, especially when those parents who couldn't get to the game found out their son scored a goal.

I loaded the photos onto the hard drive and when Sue Ellen came in I told her to post them on the website and check for orders. With things in hand at the studio, I got Blue on her leash and walked up to the Game Shop to see Jeff.

"I heard about your Pa, Emma," Jeff said when I dragged myself into his shop, the little bell over the doorway announcing my entry, "sorry he's in such a mess."

"Thanks, I needed to talk with someone about all this, do you have time?"

"Let me get Bobby to work the counter, he's in the back."

After Jeff's brother took over the sales duties, we went up the walk to the *Bean* for an early dinner.

I wasn't very hungry, but I forced myself to get one of May's nighttime soup specials and even though it wasn't a weekend, I also glass of chardonnay. Jeff got his regular roast beef sandwich and a beer. Blue got a doggy bone from the doggy jar.

"I wonder why your Pa turned himself in?" Jeff said as we sat down at a table near the dining room fireplace.

"He didn't want anyone to get hurt."

"Did he give the Sheriff his alibi?"

"No."

"Why not?"

"He's covering up for someone."

"Who?"

"I can't tell you. I promised Pa I'd keep it to myself but he's innocent like I've said all along. I just have to find a way to prove it."

"By finding the guilty guy?"

I nodded my head.

"Well," he said, between bites and gulps, "you could start with, Pastor John. He's the only one who could have taken those account books. He must be hiding something."

I enjoyed the respite with Jeff. A warm fire burned bright out of the big fireplace. Blue curled up, asleep at my feet.

We stayed for another hour and just enjoyed each other's company. But when the place began to fill up, thoughts of my Pa in jail crept back into my head and the spell was broken. I needed to face the truth, I was a terrible detective. Getting up we both headed back up the street. Jeff walked me to my place and gave me a big hug. Well, at least one good thing happened.

Chapter Twenty-Two

Tuesday Morning

Mama always said things looked better in the morning. I don't know about that. It seemed most mornings looked the same for me, Blue staring at me with her leash in her mouth. I dragged myself out of the bed and shivered from head to toe. Blue went ahead of me down to the back door and clawed at it like it might open on its own. After putting clothes on and leashing the unbearably happy in the morning dog, we went out into surprisingly fair weather. A few clouds floated in patches of blue sky on the horizon. With the sun coming up the daybreak color of blazing pink rivaled one's imagination.

Back in the kitchen, I fixed a cup of coffee and toasted two pieces of raisin bread.

A quick look at my calendar showed a clear day ahead up until 3:00 PM when I had to shoot a middle school girls' soccer game. The games, which are always high-scoring affairs with little defense, are not well attended. Most parents in the mountains are at work at three o'clock in the afternoon, so you don't expect a big crowd. Not like on Saturdays when parents crowd each sideline of even an eight-year-old game, acting like the battle on the small pitch was the World Cup.

Since I needed to concentrate on getting my Pa out of jail and I had the time, I decided to drive out and visit with Pastor John and get to the bottom of what was going on with Clare and Pa.

I put Blue in the Jeep and we drove down to *Living Waters*. I took a chance on catching Pastor John there. After the emotion of Young Pastor Bennett's sendoff Saturday and Sunday services, I figured things at the church would have settled down and it would be Tuesday business as usual at the church, and that he'd be around, doing things, you know, like destroying evidence.

I drove down Lake Road to *Living Waters* and parked at the rear of the deserted church lot. It was a shady spot, cast by a span of tall spruce trees someone planted years ago, judging by their height and the width of their trunks. After opening the windows an inch or so, I locked Blue up, even though she whimpered a bit.

I was about to start the walk to the church when I looked out toward the lake and saw a Studebaker across the road from the church. I didn't see anyone in the immediate area but remembering what Mr. Whitaker had said about those cars, it could have only been one or two families, and only one family had permission to be down there. I put my curiosity aside and walked to the church office.

The Pastor's big white SUV, conspicuous in its size, sat in a spot with a sign overlooking the area that read, *"Reserved for the Pastor"*.

"Anyone home?" I called out after I entered the deserted office area.

"Back here!" came the reply, and I followed the sound back to the Pastor's office.

"Emma Shaw," Pastor John greeted me from where he sat behind his desk when he saw me standing in the doorway. "Come on in. I'm glad you dropped by. I wanted to thank you for the slide show, I think everyone appreciated it."

I found myself saying, "The pleasure was mine," like I had just delivered a pizza and not provided a photo eulogy of a beloved departed pastor.

"Sorry about your father," the pastor said, coming around to serious stuff. "I know it must be hard. Do you know why he did it?"

"Did what?"

"Why…why he killed Pastor Bennett?"

"Who said he killed him?"

"I thought that was why he was arrested?"

"He may have been arrested for that, Pastor John, but last I checked, a man is innocent until proven guilty."

"I didn't mean anything about it, Emma, it's just all that I've heard. People say your Pa and the Pastor had an argument and the Sheriff..."

"I know what the Sheriff thinks and he's wrong. My Pa wouldn't kill anyone, not over some gospel verse in a man's sermon."

"I understood it was more than that?"

"More like how?"

"Well, Emma, I don't think this is the place to be discussing your father's motives for his actions."

"My Pa didn't have any motives."

"Oh, no?"

"No."

"Well, I heard Clare Bennett and your Pa are somewhat of a couple."

"What if they are?"

"Look, I guess this will come out eventually if it gets to trial and all, but Clare Bennett backed out of a generous land donation she promised the church."

"What's that got to do with my Pa?"

"Your Pa talked her into backing out of the land deal."

"Says who?"

"Look, we were in a meeting, right here in the office, when Clare told Pastor Bennett that she wasn't going to donate the land to the church. Said she changed her mind."

"Why?"

"She said it was unseemly to spend so much money on a building when there were people who didn't have enough to eat right here in town. She said the church's treasure could be put to better use than one man's vanity to build a church for his own glorification."

"She said that?" I asked, surprised that any woman in

town would be so outspoken. But it worried me a little that Clare was spouting off social injustice comments that appeared to mimic Pa's so directly like that whole cornmeal to feed the hungry project he had started.

"She said that," Pastor John confirmed. "Now, I know he overreacted, Pastor Bennett. He said some hurtful things to Clare. The man, bless him, was consumed by the building project, but he didn't deserve to be killed."

"It could have been suicide?"

"The Sheriff says since there was no gun found at the scene then it must have been murder."

"Someone could have taken the gun to make it look like murder."

"What would be the benefit of that?"

"Oh, I don't know, Pastor John, I hear in the case of suicide a life insurance policy wouldn't payout, whereas if the man was murdered, well, that's another story."

Up until then, I think Pastor John thought he was winning the game between us, but after my life insurance comment, he realized he was in for a scrap.

"What do you know about the Pastor's life insurance? Have you been talking to Patrick Shaw?"

"What difference does it make? And for that matter, what difference does it make if you don't get a big payout if the deal for the new sanctuary is off." And thinking a little more critically I asked, "Unless there's some other reason you need the money? So, what's up, Pastor John, are you having trouble balancing the church account books?"

Up until then, Pastor John's aura had remained hidden. I've encountered that from time to time, with people who are able to hide their feelings, but after my statement, his aura throbbed out in a massive brown-red hue, indicating anger.

Tired with the dance around I came right out and asked him, "Did you take the gun Pastor Bennett used to kill himself, to make it look like murder, so the church could claim the life insurance benefit and use it to cover up a shortage in the church's books?"

"I didn't do any such thing," the man said, and his aura didn't fade into the pink glow of untruthfulness, much to my surprise. "Where did you get that idea?"

"I've got eyes and ears, I've spoken with a few people. I know the pastor was under stress here."

"That would be convenient for you, wouldn't it? It seems if you can prove it was suicide it gets your pa off the hook."

"It's no secret I'm looking into this for my Pa's sake. He didn't kill Pastor Bennett and he doesn't deserve to be locked up for another person's crime. Now, if you know something that will help clear up this matter you need to come on out with it."

"Emma, I don't have to air out the Pastor's family laundry in public, and I certainly don't have to explain our finances to you. If we were ever asked in front of a judge, I'd be forthcoming but I'm not beholding to you to let you drag the church and Pastor through the mud of public opinion. So, if you are going to continue investigating this then at least grant me the courtesy to leave me out of it. I didn't have anything to do with my brother's death."

I could see from Pastor John's aura that he hadn't been lying to me on anything. Still, there was something going on in the church finances. I wanted to ask him about the missing church books, but I didn't know how to explain how I knew about the books being missing. I certainly couldn't explain it to the Sheriff, and from the way it was looking, Pastor John may be the wrong Pastor to be looking at in all this anyway.

Chapter Twenty-Three

Tuesday Noon

People call me dense but it's more. I'm always thinking three steps ahead and don't process details right away. Although he came right out and said it, I didn't catch Pastor John's sub conscious meaning about dragging the church through the mud, until I was halfway to town.

Taking the clue, I turned off the road and stopped, and looked up the good Pastor William Bennett on a search engine on my phone. The Pastor had a wide presence in cyberspace, and I found his address listed on a religious site although his name popped up on other social media platforms as well.

I didn't need to plug it into the GPS app because I knew exactly where the Bennett's home would be. I had to reverse my route and drive back toward the church but veered off on Lake Road where a new residential development of big two-story brick façade homes was built. Many of the homes in the Shaw Real Estate Lakeside Development, bordered the lake. Whereas most of the town's traditional families lived in grand old residences off Main Street, a good deal of the town's growing upper-middle class found homes in the new development including Pastor Bennett and his family.

I'd run through the neighborhood several times when out with Blue. A patchwork of trails created a perimeter trail around the lake, but with about twenty-five miles of shoreline, I had yet to circle the whole lake in one run, tackling shorter stretches at a time.

I found the Bennett address at the far end of the development on a heavily wooded lot to the rear and an open pretty view of the lake to the south. I pulled around a circular drive and stopped at the front of the two-story colonial.

Since Blue had been penned up for a good hour, I hooked her up to her lead, and let her jump down and sniff her way toward the water's edge. I led her to a grove of pine trees so she could take care of business and from there I heard kids laughing.

With Blue in hand, I made my way toward the sounds. Over the last year, I found that Blue made for a great icebreaker, especially around kids. Out on open land, Blue lost the territorial instinct and accepted any piece of property as communal and any child under the age of eight as a long-lost relative.

With a plan in mind, I bent down and unhooked Blue's leash. She looked up at me one time, like asking for my permission, and after I nodded at her, signifying okay, she took off in the direction of the children's voices.

With the lake water getting colder by the day as winter approached, I didn't expect the Bennett children would be swimming and found them instead, playing on an elaborate wooden jungle gym set, built about twenty paces from the lake's edge.

"Hello," I called out while still some distance away.

I recognized Mrs. Bennett from the funeral services. Dressed in a gray jumpsuit she sat on the sand with her youngest and looked like they had been building a castle out of the coarse lake sand when Blue stormed in among them.

"Blue," I called out, "come on back here!"

I tried to look like a mildly distraught dog owner in pursuit of a runaway pet but never one to pretend, I wasn't sure how my charade went over.

"So sorry about that," I apologized, hustling in among them and hooking Blue up to her leash. "She just took off when she heard your kids laughing."

"It's okay," the attractive woman said, her two children swarming around Blue, "no harm done. The children just love dogs. We've been wanting to get one for some time but held off until little Abigail could walk about with a little more confidence. You know, they can toddle over without much of a push."

"Well, that's probably a good idea, Blue here can be like that bull in a China shop."

"Is that her name, Blue?"

"Yes, Bluebonnet, actually, but Blue for short. I think she might be embarrassed if I called her by her full name in public. You know she has a reputation to maintain."

"You're Emma Shaw, aren't you?"

"Yes, and you're Mrs. Bennett."

"I am and this is Abigail and Ariel."

"Nice to meet you all."

"I saw you at the funeral services. The church staff says you put together the slide show of William."

"Yes, ma'am, and if I may, my condolences about the Pastor."

"Thank you, and I must apologize, William and I discussed you several times."

"Oh yeah?"

"Yes, yes, we so wanted to go down to your studio for a family sitting but we could just not find the time. You know the weekends can be so busy for a pastor's family.

"I'm sorry I never met the Pastor."

"You were related, you know."

"No, I didn't know."

"Yes, William's great-grandfather and your pa's great grandmother were sister and brother."

"I didn't know, although I know the Bennett's and the Shaw's go back a long way."

"Yes, they do. Is that why you are here, about your Pa?" she asked, getting up and moving off, away from her children who had gone back to playing. "You know, I don't believe the Sheriff's theory. I don't see why your Pa would have a grudge big enough that he'd kill William."

"How did you know about the Sheriff's theory?"

"Pastor John came by one day to ask me about William's missing Bible and mentioned it then."

"I'm glad you feel that way, Mrs. Bennett..."

"Call me Martha."

"I'd like that, Martha, that was my aunt's name."

"As was my mother's as well. It goes back quite a few generations."

"So, since we both agree my Pa wouldn't have a reason to kill the good pastor, do you have any idea who might?"

"No, I don't, but it wasn't your father."

"I agree, so you must know how I feel, about Pa getting locked up for something he didn't do?"

"The Sheriff locked up your father? I didn't know. We've been staying out here mostly, staying away from the church and town, so I hadn't heard."

"Yes, ma'am, he's to be arraigned on a murder charge, and unless I can come up with some compelling evidence, I'm afraid he'll be shipped out to a county facility and held for trial."

"That's ridiculous."

"Yes, ma'am, that's why I came out here."

"So, you're looking for evidence to implicate someone else?"

"That, or, and forgive me," I said, looking to make sure the kids were out of hearing range, "I'm looking for some evidence that your husband may have committed suicide."

"No, William may have been many things, but he wasn't a quitter. He'd never take his own life. You know, William and I didn't always lead the Christian life. He was quite a hell-raiser back when we met, back in college. Bad boy image if you can imagine. Always scheming to get rich. And he fell into drugs for a spell. I left him several times. I know what they say about enabling, but I always expected the best of William, even though he disappointed me many times.

"After a long separation, he told me he wanted me back. He said he had changed, that he found his calling, and he was clean. I didn't believe him, but he showed me. If anything, he went overboard with the anti-drug message. Especially to the youth.

"He was serving in Hickory with his brother, John, and seemed to have licked the demons of his past and really settled in on his mission. We had several good years there, Emma, and then came here. But old habits are hard to break, even when the eyes of the Lord are upon you."

"What do you mean?"

Mrs. Martha Bennett paused before answering. She was looking down at her playing children. I wondered what she was thinking. Here she was, with two small children and a dead husband. What was her plan for the future? Did anyone have a plan for that? If it was me, I might think of suicide.

"Men are weak, Emma," she finally said, in a whisper, "and William was only a man."

Then she said, speaking louder, "I'm afraid I can't help you with this, Emma, I think we'd better let Sheriff Banner complete his investigation. If he asks me, I'll tell the Sheriff your Pa couldn't have had anything to do with William's death, but for the sake of the children, I can't put us through anything more. We've been through enough."

***

Though sparsely attended, I always enjoyed the middle school girls' soccer games. I also found out pretty quickly that the sales of photos to the parents of the girls in middle school turned out to be my most consistent cash flow stream, so I never missed a game.

As predicted the two girls' teams battled all match with the home team getting a final score with time about to run out to win the game, 9 to 8. The losing coach argued with the referee for more time but the youth official said the league rules didn't provide for additional time so that was the match.

Both teams seemed happy enough with the outcome and even though there were few spectators in attendance, I went out to the parking lot and passed out flyers. After I harassed the last car out of the lot I turned around and saw the field was empty and I was the last one there.

With night approaching, and the opportunity before me, I went over and let Blue out and we went over to the soccer field. A perimeter fence surrounded the area but in between stretched out about three acres of open space. I reached down and released Blue's collar. For the second time that day, she paused and looked up at me.

"Go on," I told her. Turning about, she sniffed in the air and then took off.

In the fading light, Blue was a streak of black, racing from one end of the field to another. Filled with the urge, I started out on a slow jog, following the fence line as it circled the middle school athletic fields. I used to be a regular runner, forcing myself out for long morning runs, before my knees started to bother me. But I can still get out and jog for an hour or so when the urge hits.

Running used to be an anecdote to an occasional bout of depression I encountered when I lived away from Black Mountain. A counselor suggested more exercise for the mild malady instead of eating, and I tried it. I never ran as a sport growing up. It seemed to me that running in the mountains was about as good a run as you could get. Early and I would always find ourselves running through the woods, chasing something, or being chased. It seemed like I'd always been running, running from something real or imagined.

After the hour ended at sunset, I rounded Blue up, and we headed back to town. I flicked on the Jeep headlights, casting a dim light in the darkness. Alone in the quiet of the Jeep, I recalled the long day and wondered again about the darkness of Martha Bennett's comment about having already *been through enough.*

Chapter Twenty-Four

Wednesday

On Wednesday morning Blue greeted me with wide eyes and a thumping tail. I was beginning to see the value in installing one of those pet doors, you know the ones that flap open at will, so Blue could let herself in and out. I heard they could be trouble though, like when a possum or raccoon decided to use it to get in the house. I didn't know which was worse.

Once cleaned up and both of us fed I went down to the studio and looked at my calendar. I had my weekly football practice in the afternoon and the photography studio management system had booked a noon shoot for a holiday sitting for the Campbell family. I knew Lucy Campbell. She went Pa's church and attended his Sunday school class. I could only imagine she was coming in with grandkids, old as she was.

With time to spare, I decided to get organized. This running around without a plan was too hard on my nerves and my psyche.

I took out a stack of 3x5 cards. Back when I was looking into Early's murder, I learned that the random accusation method proved unreliable. When I investigated Barbara Walker's death it proved wrong most of the time. I accused so many different people in that case that when people saw me walking down the street they turned and walked the other way lest I accuse them of a crime they didn't commit. I needed a better way to get my thoughts in order, a tool to get my facts straight.

Over the past few days my amateur investigation had turned up an assortment of information, much I was sure to classify as irrelevant, but still a good deal. If you added in the fact I'd been mugged twice and warned off the case, I figured I was making progress. Someone surely thought I was getting close to something.

At the top of each card, I wrote down the name of someone I considered a suspect. I also wrote motive, opportunity, and means down the left side of the card with a couple of lines between the words.

As a starter, I just assumed Young Pastor Bennett was murdered and didn't commit suicide. Although the suicide verdict would get Pa off quicker, from what folks told me about Young Pastor William Bennett, he wasn't a likely candidate for suicide. His wife, Martha, shored that up with her comments that the Pastor wouldn't have taken the easy way out. Plus, there was no physical evidence of suicide either. As much as I hated to admit it, it seemed the Sheriff was right on that matter.

I put Pastor John on the first card. I wrote two motives down for him, money and power then checked off opportunity. Pastor John was certainly in proximity to his brother so that checked off and he was big enough, a good match for the guy that mugged me as well. Of course, as Jeff said, there were probably a hundred men in town who could fit the size description.

I wasn't so sure about the means but in Black Mountain, if you didn't already have one, anyone could get their hands on a gun. Maybe I needed to make out a card for everyone in town? Of course, if the motive didn't check out for Pastor John, then means didn't matter.

Since the land was at the root of the whole thing, I made up a card for Thomas Shaw. He was equally big, and money was definitely involved so the motive could be confirmed. I'd have to check on his alibi for that night. If he didn't have one, then I'd have to find the means. Unless everyone in town bought a handgun from Jeff I began to see how means for every potential suspect was going to be hard to prove. I'd have to ask Jeff. What were the chances that the killer bought the weapon from the Fish and Game Shop?

I didn't understand what was going on with the insurance thing, but Patrick Shaw was big and strong, and he fit the bill for my mugger friend. He had a reason to not pay out the insurance benefit, but for that to happen the Pastor would have to have committed suicide. In my scenario, suicide was off the table. Did that mean Patrick Shaw was off the table as well? Probably, I always liked the suicide scenario, even though no one agreed with me, but Patrick Shaw had really nothing to gain either way.

I put Sheriff Banner's name on a card. I had absolutely no reason to, but until I checked off motive, opportunity, and means, he stayed on there. I knew he wasn't likely to have been the mugger in the parking lot, but that son of his could have played that role. To my way of thinking that made him a suspect. It may have been purely spite, but I didn't like the fact that the Sheriff was so quick to accuse Pa. That alone was enough, so he deserved a card of his own.

I wrote Candi Peoples on top of a card. There was something going on between the Pastor and that girl with the come-hither look. No one had said anything specifically but I thought the Pastor and the wayward teen were more than just mentor and mentee. I don't know how I'd prove it, with everyone so tight-lipped about it, including the new widow, but Candi deserved a card of her own until I got to the bottom of the Pastor and her.

On the last card I wrote at the top, *Suspect Q*, which stood for someone I didn't even suspect yet. Especially since I thought my encounter in the alley was by a different person than the guy who jumped me in the parking lot. I didn't know why I deserved so much attention. I hoped I'd get a break and stubble onto something soon. If not, then it was back to square one and Pa was in trouble.

***

I spent the rest of the morning getting ready for the Campbell appointment and it was a good thing because they came in ten minutes early, dragging four little boys, ranging in age from two to five, the predicted grandchildren.

"Where'd you dig this crew up?" I asked the older woman. I could see that I needed to adjust the studio appointment scheduler. In addition to all the other information we gather in the pre-appointment questionnaire, we should also add a field that lets you know ahead of time, what the gender and age are of the kids coming in. That way we could be prepared. You know we might be able to arrange for a sheriff's deputy to be on-premises for crowd control.

"Those two are Jesse's boys," matriarch Mrs. Campbell pointed to the two older boys who made a beeline to the big chest where I kept toys for just such an occasion, "and these two devils are Miranda's," she said as she held the hands of the two youngest. "I've got to keep a handle on them, or they'll tear up the place."

I've yet to develop the mothering instinct. I know it's there, somewhere, deep inside. I feel it getting out, from time to time, but I don't encourage it. It would just be my luck if I ever had kids, I'd have a bunch of boys that I would have to ride herd over for the first thirty or forty years of their lives.

When Blue heard the ruckus, she came into the room and the older boys went over to her, and hugs, kisses, and slobber were exchanged. Even the two youngest joined in and a big kumbaya moment happened.

"That's some dog you have there, Emma Louise," Mr. Campbell said. "I can tell she's a real nurturing type. A real mother. She must get that from you."

I could have agreed with the man, but in reality, it would have been a lie. In the relationship between Blue and me, I think Blue is the mother.

With Blue riding shotgun, the Campbell family sitting went on without incident. When the session was over, Mr. Campbell offered to buy Blue. I turned him down but let him and the boys take the dog for a walk down by the river.

With the boys out, and confident that even if one of the boys fell in the water, Blue would save him, I got Mrs. Campbell to sit down in front of the computer monitor. We went through the digital pics and she picked out the holiday shot she wanted, and while she was at it, she ordered a bunch of other prints of the boys in wonderful smiling poses. It was smart of her to take advantage of the opportunity. By my look at those grandsons, this might be the only time this year she would be able to get them to sit long enough to take a picture.

After completing the order, the Campbell's left and I went upstairs and made a late lunch, a bowl of raisin-bran cereal. I didn't have a lot of time to spare because I had to get my gear ready for the football practice.

Practice started under a clear cold afternoon, but the players heated up quickly. The team was on a winning streak, and I think the boys felt it, practicing hard. My mantra had always been if you practice hard, you'll play hard. I think the boys all bought into it. There's nothing like winning.

***

Once a week Pa tried to drag me along to Swannanoa Baptist Wednesday night services, but I figured once a week Sunday morning salvation was plenty for me. If once a week wasn't going to get me through the gates of Heaven I kind of doubted twice would do it either.

For many communities, the Wednesday night service provided a social option for a congregation's youth. While Sunday services with prayers for redemption held sway over an adult congregation, the Wednesday night service provided the youth with the opportunity to mingle in a casual atmosphere and worship on a stage unfamiliar to most adults. I had heard *Living Waters* had a large Wednesday night youth service. Probably more because of the charismatic Pastor Bennett than anything. With Candi Peoples on my mind, I decided to visit the Wednesday night affair after practice, and not tell Pa.

I took Blue out for a quick walk and put her up with a bowl of food and fresh water and drove down to *Living Waters*. My ulterior motive of course was to find out more about bad boy Pastor Bennett. If he didn't commit suicide, then who did he make mad enough to kill him?

The administration of the Wednesday night service for *Living Waters* was turned over to the youth of the parish who spoke from the word of God and directed the evening. The service played to an overflow crowd that filled the church parking lot and I was left to park under a grove of trees about a hundred yards away at the back of a line behind other late arrivals. After hoofing it to the church I found a loud crowd, mostly standing, swaying to a heavenly choir verging on rock and roll. The only thing missing was the stench of marijuana in the air.

A small corner of the sanctuary was carved out for a band. I remembered from the set of drawings I saw that the proposed new sanctuary contained a prominent stage and band area right in front of the pews. In the current church, the youth had to be satisfied with a smaller performance platform. A drumming teenager sat on a raised platform and several other teens grouped around him playing acoustic and electric guitars, while a duo consisting of a tall good-looking boy and a cute young girl, belted out a cover of *"Come Alive"*, a Lauren Daigle top Christian hit. The thumping beat goaded the faithful in the pews to sway and clap along with the song and the female singer shouted encouragement, *"Come Alive!"* between lines of lyrics.

I marveled that the pews were packed equally with teens and parents. When the set ended the sanctuary buzzed but quieted when Pastor John took the stage and addressed the faithful.

I'm as much a fan of the good word of the Lord as anyone, but the Pastor's remarks receded to the background as the musical group's lead singer approached me. Finally, at rest and able to push her long blond hair up and back over her head, I got a look at the smiling face of Candi Peoples, still radiant from the reception of the adoring crowd. Fitted out in a black leotard, much too revealing to be considered churchgoing, she wiped her sweaty face with a hand towel as our eyes met in recognition.

"Enjoy the show?" she asked me. Her singing partner accompanied her, like standing guard, tall and broad, with brooding eyes, he draped an arm around Candi's shoulder, somehow familiar, but didn't say anything.

"I sure did. I didn't know the church had such a vibrant youth service."

"It was Pastor Bennett's idea. You know, a way to get the youth more involved. He always said the future of the church was in the hands of today's youth."

"From what I saw, the church is in good hands."

"Well, thank you," she said, after which she and the boy went off and sat among a group of youth. I could see her talking to her friends and she pointed at me from across the room while they all had a good laugh, I supposed at my expense. You know, the Ghost Whisperer.

"She puts on quite a show." Pa's friend, Mr. Hawkins, said coming up to me.

"Top rate. A little raw for Christian worship for me, I guess, and as much as I hate to admit it, I'm a little old fashion. So, how does the parish think about it?"

"Well, the church is divided. There is always pushback when something new comes along. For us, the Sunday morning hours are still the domain of the old, but Wednesday evening is set aside for the youth."

"I see some older folks here."

"Yes, not all the parents have gone over to the *rock side*. I don't blame them for tagging along with their kids. I'd want to keep a tight lead on my teenage boy or girl until I was comfortable with the new rage."

"How about you, Mr. Hawkins?"

"There are many paths to Heaven, Emma, many routes. We can only pray that they are not too difficult for most."

"Was Pastor Bennett's path difficult?"

The man paused a good minute. With Pastor John preaching in the background Hawkins signaled for me to follow him out into the atrium.

"Pastor William led a wayward life before coming here, Emma. I was on the elder committee that reviewed his application before we hired him. After he got the call, he put in five good years as youth director and associate pastor over in Hickory. He came with a good recommendation, and we liked what he said in his interview. We were trying to get the youth more involved, so we tried to see his new ideas as an opportunity to build up our numbers. Most of the old churches in town are stuck back in the fifties. We knew to move ahead we would need someone to lead the youth. He seemed to be the right choice at the time."

"At the time?"

"Yes, sort of like the Frankenstein tale. It didn't take him long to gather a loyal following of old and young alike. The numbers exploded and the church tithe swelled. With all the numbers up the Pastor started pushing for the new Sanctuary. Before we knew it, he had pretty much claimed the church as his own and there wasn't much we could do to stem his influence. Most of the long-serving elders were voted out and replaced by his closest followers. A lot of old-timers left the church after that but others like me, well, we decided to ride it out and hope for the best."

"Anyone hate it enough to maybe kill the Pastor to stop it?"

"There may be a few in the parish with a temper, but I can't think of anyone who would take that route."

"And now, with Pastor John at the helm?"

"He's only there temporarily, the Elders gave him a six-month contract. He'll have to show he can be a leader of the flock before he'll get hired full-time. Right now, I think the parish is still divided on whether Pastor John is the man to lead the faithful forward."

"And the church expansion?"

"That's up in the air, too. A good percentage of the parish want to dump the whole project, but the youth and their supporters want the expansion to go forward."

"Yes, I can see the young people would like a big stage."

"Yes, I'm afraid Pastor William catered to the youth, some more than others."

"Would you like to explain that?"

"No, Emma, I wouldn't. The Pastor is gone to his rest. The final verdict of his time on earth will be decided in heaven and not here."

I mulled over the cryptic comment from Mr. Hawkins on the long walk to my car. As with most of us, young Pastor Bennett appeared to have had a checkered past. I wondered if the past had come back to haunt him, or was it just a case of old habits being hard to break?

I had just reached out to grasp the door handle of the Jeep when someone came out of the dark and drove me into the Jeep's hood. My head snapped back and forward, and I would have done a face plant into the heavy metal but managed to get my arm up in time to cushion the blow.

I bounced off the hood and fell to the ground on my back. Someone tall and big stood above me, straddling my body, looking down, his face covered with a ski mask.

"What's with the ski masks?" I said to the guy, assuming it was a guy, as big as he looked. "Is there a website you can go to, you know, *activewear for muggers?*"

"I was told you had a smart mouth," he said in a soft voice, making it hard to tell if he was young or old.

"Who are you?" I asked, calculating the chances he'd answer at zero, but I asked anyway as I maneuvered into a better position.

"A friend with some advice."

"Oh yeah," I responded while bringing my leg up into a coiled position, "what?"

"You need to stop this investigation of yours."

I didn't need to respond to that. Shooting my leg up and driving my foot toward his groin area, I caught the guy unprepared, and he doubled over in pain, falling on top of me, crushing the wind from my lungs. He rolled off and got to his feet. I tensed in anticipation the man might set himself up for a kick, using my head as a soccer ball, but he took a couple of deep breaths and limped off into the woods.

I weighed the effort it would take to run after him, but it was dark in the forest, and to tell the truth, I just didn't feel like it. The idea of my head being used as a bouncing ball didn't sit well with me right then, but without backup, like Blue or Jeff, I might be outmanned if I caught up to the guy. As I struggled to a sitting position, I thought about what I would tell Jeff about my misadventure and what his response might be. In no scenario did I imagine his words would be encouraging.

Chapter Twenty-Five

Thursday

Thursday morning arrived on the heels of a cold snap. The mercury outside must have plunged into the teens. After waking up I slowly took account of all the aching bones and muscles in my body. I'm always amazed at how only a little actual body contact in a fight can later result in a host of aches and pains.

I struggled into my thickest long-johns and heaviest denim. Out in the kitchen area, I could feel a cold breeze. Apparently, the quarter inch fake fireplace was no match for a fall freeze.

Blue stood at the top of the steps with her lead in her mouth and I avoided eye contact with her until I got a K-cup going. Hunkered down in my coat I took her out for a short walk, promising a longer walk later. Making only a brief tour of her favorite outdoor spots we finished, and I limped back inside, grabbed my cup of coffee, and sat down at my desk.

I spent the morning going through the files of photographs stored on the auxiliary drive. Mixed in with the action photos I sell outright to doting parents, I store some of my more artistic shots. In most of these, you don't even see the athlete's face or uniform number. What you see are silhouettes of boys or girls in action, spectacular sunsets a background to blurred shots of athletes on grass fields, dirt in the air, sweat drops splashed across an image, stadium lights creating beams of brilliance, or casting dark shadow, and the mystery of sport.

I store the best of these in my personal file. These are the shots I save for matting and framing. Shots I'll put up at exhibits of my work or on my personal website where a portfolio of my best is on display for those interested in following the career of Emma Shaw, photojournalist.

I had my elbows on the desk reviewing slides when my phone vibrated indicating a text message.

"Lunch?" it read.

"When?" I texted Jeff back.

"Now!"

Having lost myself in my work, I'd lost track of the time. I got up and went into the half-bath and splashed cold water on my face, combed out my hair, and took stock of my looks after another mugging. The short respite from worrying about the factors surrounding Pastor William's death did me good, but I couldn't ignore somebody was trying to warn me off the case. Three muggings in a week? That had to be some kind of record.

I hooked up Blue and we went out the door, turned left, and I hobbled down the walk, still stiff from the beating I took the night before. Sitting at my computer for three hours didn't help my aching muscles. Jeff stood out in front of his shop, waiting. In spite of the cold, he only wore a plaid flannel shirt, rolled up at the sleeves, over jeans and no coat. He told me once that the cold never bothered him. After a year back in town and two winters, I saw that for myself.

"Where's your coat? It's freezing out here."

"It's practically still summer," he said and added, "and why are you limping?"

"If you buy me coffee I'll tell you."

In deference to me, he didn't say more, and we slowly walked to the *Bean*.

A small crowd scattered about the room and logs blazed away in the fireplace. The aroma of fresh-baked cookies filled the air. After getting fresh chicken salad sandwiches and hot coffee we found a table near the hearth and settled in. Blue curled up close to my feet and went to sleep.

"So, what happened?" Jeff asked me.

"Oh, you know," I explained between bites, "playing

detective can be dangerous."

"Like how?"

"People always warning you about sticking your nose where it shouldn't be."

"Tell me."

So, I did and when finished I felt better. I wasn't sure if it was the venting or the chicken salad.

"Why didn't you tell me you were going over to *Living Waters*, I would have gone along with you."

"I didn't know I needed a bodyguard in a church parking lot. If I did, I would have taken Blue along."

"After the last mugging, I think it should have been apparent that you need to stay away from dark parking lots. Looks like you are getting close to something, so you'd better be extra careful. Do you think the muggings are connected?"

"I don't think so, but it was dark, and the guy wore a mask."

So, now you have, three different suspects?"

"You tell me."

"For the same murder? You know, we've only got one dead body."

With Pa getting arraigned that afternoon I had things to do. As Jeff finished his coffee and I worked on the second half of my sandwich, I filled him in on the rest of my suspicions.

"Has the aura thing you do helped you any?"

Jeff knew about my ability to see auras and he also knew how unreliable it could be.

"Well, I got enough of a look at Pastor John's to almost check him off the list but there is still that thing with the insurance."

"In other words, you've got a way to go?"

"Yep...I do."

Just then Joanie Shaw came in and seeing us she walked over and said, "Well, well, well, you two seem cozy."

I looked up at Joanie and I'm sure it surprised Jeff when

I invited her to sit down and join us.

"Don't mind if I do," she said taking a third chair at the table, between Jeff and me.

After an awkward minute during which she sat ogling Jeff I said, So Joanie, I might know a friend of yours, Candi Peoples?"

"Candi…she'd no friend."

"I thought she said she hangs out with you at the brewery?"

"I may have seen her there, but we are not friends."

"Oh, I saw her the other day and she said you all were friends."

"She sings at the brewery from time to time, she and that ratty band of hers, but I wouldn't call her a friend."

"Competition then?"

"Candi? No way, I mean she may be young and cute, but it would take more than that to be any real competition for me."

On the chance I'd get some more on Pastor William I said, "She seemed to have a crush on young Pastor Bennett."

"Crush? Well, it'd be hard to say who had the crush on who. It was sad seeing the way the Pastor just pandered to that teenager, like some groupie."

"What do you mean?"

"I'm not sure what she had on him but she made it count."

"Now what do you mean?"

"Where do you think she got the money for that brand-new truck she drives?"

"Pastor Bennett get that for her?"

"Maybe not right out but she managed to buy it with something, and it didn't come from working anywhere."

"I thought she worked in the church office?"

"Sure, a lot of folks do but most are volunteers."

"How about the band?"

"That band? No way, they play for tips at the most."

"How about Pastor William?"

"Oh now, the Pastor got his all right. How do you think he could afford that lakeside house?"

"I'm sure the Parish provided for living arrangements."

"Oh, sure, the parish house if you call staying in a one-bedroom shack living. It may have suited an itinerant preacher a hundred years ago, but Pastor William expected more and he got it."

"How do you know all this? Do you attend *Living Waters*?"

"Me? No, my sister Bonnie does, she and her flock. She's got a couple of teenagers that just love it over there so Bonnie keeps me up to date with the local gossip. Why the interest?"

When I didn't answer she concluded the obvious.

"Oh, that's right," she said, turning her full attention to me, "I heard you were looking into the Pastor's death. Playing detective again, are we?"

"I've got to," I explained to Joanie, although it galled me to have to explain anything I do to her. "The Sheriff is trying to pin this on my Pa, and I know he didn't have anything to do with it."

"Well, good luck," she said getting up and as she did, she pulled at her short skirt, "I hope that vision thing you do comes in handy with this. I mean, that's what you use on your little investigations, isn't it?"

Joanie knew enough about my aura reading ability to know that it was a special gift. Too special, she decided, for the lowly me to possess.

Jeff didn't say a word during the whole conversation with Joanie but after she left, he asked, "What did you think of all that?"

"That's just Joanie being Joanie. She hasn't changed much since high school."

"No, I mean all that about the Pastor."

"Oh, you mean the proposition that the good Pastor

skimmed money off the collection plate to keep a pretty young mistress on the side?"

"Yeah, that."

"I hope it's not true."

***

Up until then, I didn't want to look too closely at the extracurricular activities of the young Pastor Bennett. I needed to face it though. Between the rumors of the man's nightlife, his widow's reticent willingness to discuss the man, and Joanie's, for what they were worth, observations, the Pastor was not coming up to a pastor's standard. I needed to start asking direct questions instead of beating around the bush as I had been. I needed to let the auras of these suspects either clear them so I can check them off my list or let them condemn them so I could dig deeper.

***

Pa's arraignment started at 1:00 pm in the Town Hall's main conference room which served double duty for Town Council meetings and court proceedings. It even looked like a courtroom. Magistrate, Bartholomew Shaw presided.

When they brought Pa into the room in handcuffs, he looked at me, like asking if I'd found out who killed Pastor Bennett. I shook my head, no...no, your good-for-nothing daughter failed miserably in solving the case and getting you out of jail. He looked down and turned his head away from me.

There was some legal talk back and forth between the magistrate and Sheriff Banner. The town attorney, Randall Shaw said a few words. At some point, Bartholomew looked at me over the rim of his reading glasses, like wondering when I was going to speak up and save my Pa. When I didn't he shook his head sadly and went on with the proceedings. Even Randall Shaw looked over to me, expecting me to stand and say they had it wrong. When I didn't, he too shook his head sadly and turned away. The only one in the courtroom that didn't look sad was Sheriff Banner. After explaining the charges, he sat back and smiled through the whole thing.

There was a flurry of activity from the front of the room and then they were hauling Pa up and out a side door. I figured this was when they'd cart him off to the county jail and who knew where after that? If I ever felt lower than that moment, I don't know when. I don't think I ever felt worst, even after mama died.

Anticipating their route, I ran out of the chamber and turned right down the hallway and intercepted the group. Sheriff Banner led the way with two deputies on either side of Pa as they moved toward the back door. I tried to jump between them to get at Pa, but Ross Banner stuck his big right arm out and shoved me away.

"Stay out of this, Emma," the Sheriff said to me, "save it for the county court."

I pushed Ross Banner's arm away from me and said, "You know Pa's innocent, you can't hold him for this."

"You had your chance, Emma. Until a court tells me otherwise, your pa's going to jail."

I probably should have said more and should have protested louder, but after my brief outburst, I realized something. When I pushed Ross Banner's right arm away from me, I felt a heavy bandage beneath his uniform arm sleeve.

"I'm okay, Emma Louise," Pa said to me, "you go on with the case. I know you can fix this."

The two deputies led Pa out of Town Hall and down to the back lot where two Sheriff cruisers sat, running. They loaded Pa into the back of one and with lights flashing they drove off.

I watched the little motorcade take my Pa away and I felt deep regret for letting him down. I also wondered about the bandage I felt under Ross Banner's shirt. Right at the wrist area where Blue had bitten that guy who mugged me in the parking lot the other night after that game.

Chapter Twenty-Six

Thursday Afternoon

With teams traveling to away games some weeks and hosting home games other weeks, I always had to stay on top of my schedule otherwise I'd miss an important shoot. Sue Ellen kept my calendar up to date with school events, which was great. What wasn't so great was not looking at my calendar carefully. I knew I had a school athletic event to shoot somewhere that afternoon, I just wasn't sure where.

Even though I could still see in my mind the sad face of Pa as they carted him away, I had no time to fret. With the usual three o'clock starting time for most weekday school events approaching, I needed to get back to the studio and gather my gear together. A quick look at my calendar reminded me that the afternoon event was a cross-country meet and not a football or soccer match. I should have remembered because of all the events I shoot, cross country has the fewest meets during the year. Somehow the idea of running for miles and miles didn't sit well with most high school students.

My own running career was off and on. When I was younger I could run great distances with ease. As I got older the challenge of distance running became more difficult. Now I was lucky to get out two or three times a week and if I had a week full of games to shoot, I might not get out at all.

The one good thing about shooting a cross-country meet was I could take Blue along. Since we weren't tied to a field or stadium, we got to get out and run right along with the runners, stopping every so often to capture the images of the runners in the struggle against time and heart, with Blue barking encouragement as runners passed.

The Black Mountain High School meets were held at the

edge of Lake Nebo, on a trail cut by the Cherokee long ago. As the runners competed, Blue and I spent the good part of an hour running alongside them, in the footsteps of my ancestors who called the Valley of the Three Forks, home.

***

By the time I got back to town from the cross-country meet, I was tired and hungry. I fed Blue and with some time to spare I loaded the new photos on the website. When Sue Ellen came in she could start on the orders but in the meantime, the afternoon pics of the meet were up for viewing.

With a break from business duties, I looked up a website on my phone. When I was done I texted Jeff.

"Dinner?"

"When?" he texted back after a minute.

"Now?"

"Thirty minutes," he answered.

"I'm hungry," I wrote.

"Fifteen," he answered.

"Real hungry!"

"Five minutes."

"I'm on my way," I ended the text stream.

Putting a leash on Blue we went out and walked down the street to the Fish and Game shop.

Jeff came out of the door and asked, "What's the hurry?"

"I want to get there before the crowd."

"Where?"

"The Black Brew."

"Is it the weekend?"

"No, but they've got a band playing tonight and I want to get there before they go on."

"Why?"

"Because I want to ask their singer a couple of questions."

215

***

The Black Brew Brewery opened off Main Street that spring. The owners had renovated an old textile mill that had closed twenty years before and sat empty for lack of interest. With the micro-brewery industry sweeping across the state, a local trio of third-generation moonshine runners decided to go into a legitimate business and got the county Alcohol Board to agree to support the new wave. I'm sure the Board figured it better if the young men brewed their alcohol in a legal setup, where each glass of brew could be taxed, as opposed to some forest hideaway beyond the grasp of state revenue.

Since its opening, the brewery had attracted quite a following. In addition to several IPAs they brewed on-premises, they also brought in a sampling of beer from other breweries in the mountains. The packed weekend parking lot I'd often noticed attested to their success.

I led Blue with her leash, and we went in the dog-friendly place with the aroma of fried food. As we made our way through the semi-crowded dining room, we passed several men seated at the bar laughing out loud as an attractive women bartender tried to pour beer from a tap. As we passed Blue barked out at the men and I had to rein her in before she bit one of them.

"Better get hold of that dog, sister," one of the men who looked familiar said as we hustled by them.

We found a booth out of the way in the back. A wooden table caddy housed several condiment bottles, napkins, a menu for food, and a menu for beer. The rough-hewn tabletops matched the overhead exposed beams. The HVAC ductwork was painted black and receded into the tall ceiling unnoticed. Peanut shells covered the wooden floor, a result of the baskets of free peanuts they placed on every table and which servers refilled when they got half empty. Jeff grabbed up a handful before he even sat down.

A waitress in jeans and a tight-fitting black tee shirt with *BLACK BREW* printed in white across her chest came to our table with a bowl of water for Blue, and to take our order. We ordered a house-brand IPA but we told the server we wanted to study the menu before ordering.

"Did you recognize that man at the bar," Jeff asked me as I looked over the menu.

"I thought one of them looked familiar," I said looking over to the still laughing men and the obviously perturbed bartender.

"One of the Lawson boys."

"Oh, well I guess they'll let anyone in here."

When the server came back with our beer, we ordered the Mountain Burger Special, two four ounce patties, slaw, and chili. I also asked her about the band.

"They come on at eight o'clock."

"When do they arrive to set up?"

"They'll come dragging in anytime now. They get a free dinner with the gig, so they come early to eat."

"Who's playing?" Jeff asked.

"Reckless Love," the young lady answered.

"Who?"

"They're a local group," she said, "The band's not much but the singers are pretty good."

"Reckless Love?" Jeff asked me after the server left.

"Candi Peoples sings in that group. She can really belt it out."

"Candi Peoples?"

"I checked the *Black Brew's* website and saw they are on tonight. You know, it's an off night. A chance to give new bands some stage time. If I can get to her before the band goes on, I have a few questions I'd like to ask her."

"And here I thought you just wanted to spend time with me."

"That's always on my schedule, Jeff, and tonight I get a

bonus if I can get Candi alone."

On cue, the front doors of the place opened, and band members started in, carrying equipment, including the good-looking guy singer I saw at the church the night before. The Black Brew's one-foot-high stage hugged an eight-by-twelve corner of the room. A house speaker system bookended the space, an assortment of microphones stood scattered about, and an array of spotlights hung from a truss above the front of the stage. Candi Peoples came in last, dressed in performance black, carrying only a big red bag, her hair spread out like wings in her wake, *angel or devil's wings*? I asked myself.

We sat and drank as the group started setting up. When it looked like Candi entered her "I'm bored" portion of the process, I went over and invited her and the other singer to our table.

"Do you know Jeff Carson," I introduced?

"Sure," Candi said, squatting momentarily to pat Blue on the head, "I'm Candi and this is Tucker."

"Good to meet you."

"Your family runs the Fish and Game Shop in town, right?"

"For the last hundred years or so."

"Pa goes there," Candi said.

"Is your daddy, Wade Peoples," Jeff asked the girl, "lives down Bath House Road?"

"Sure is."

"Wait," I said, seeing her aura beat in a steady washed-out rainbow color, "Didn't you say your family lived over in Morgan?"

"My mama and I do, but my daddy lives here. He works up at the mill. He and my mama have been divorced since I was young."

I wanted to point out to the girl that she was still young, as far as I was concerned, but knowing people's conception of time varied with age, I decided it wasn't worth getting into.

"How long have you been singing with the band?" Jeff asked the duo.

And giving an answer that confirmed my last thought on her age, she said, "Oh, like forever, since last fall."

"Forever?" I repeated.

"I know, right, but it's been fun. We played over in Asheville last week. Even got paid."

"No," I said, playing along. "You all must make good money. I mean, enough anyway, to buy that new truck of yours."

"Oh no," she said. "We never get that kind of money. They just paid enough for our gas."

"Well, how did you get enough for that big new truck?"

"Oh, well, we needed a good truck to pull our trailer with all the equipment."

"I didn't ask you why you needed the truck, Candi, I asked you how you paid for it?"

"What are you, my mother?"

"No, and if I were I'd have something to say about the way you dress."

"Well, who the heck are you?"

"I'm the person that's investigating Pastor William's murder."

With my statement the girl changed her tune, "I got nothing to say about that."

"How about you, Tucker, do you have anything to say?"

"He doesn't have anything to say either," Candi said for Tucker who had still not uttered a word.

"Oh, well if that's the way you want it. I guess we can have the Sheriff ask you a few questions."

"Why would the Sheriff want to ask me anything?"

"Oh, I don't know," and since I really didn't know where I was headed with my questions I said, "maybe because I've been up to see Martha Bennett, and we had a good talk about the Pastor, and you!"

"I don't know what that witch said to you about me, but the Pastor and I were only friends."

"The pastor didn't help you pay for that truck?" I asked, surprised at the tenor of her response.

"No, the pastor did not. What gave you that idea?"

I waited for her aura to bleach into the pink hue of untruthfulness, but it didn't.

"Something I heard around. Someone killed Pastor William and I'm just following up on a lead."

"Well, you got it wrong," Candi continued. "The Pastor helped me get clean and my daddy rewarded me by getting me that truck. He bought it on time and I'm helping to make the payments. Whenever we get a little more than expenses, we pay a little on the truck, but my daddy got the deal for us. He signed for it. He used to play in a band when he was young, and he knows how much I want this. He believes in me, unlike my mama. He says I can make it in the music world if I just keep my eye on the prize."

When her aura didn't blink pink, I had to believe her.

"How about you Tucker?" I asked the boy, reminding myself of his size.

"He doesn't know anything," Candi spoke for Tucker again.

"You have anything to do with the Pastor's murder?"

"No," he spoke, finally, his aura vibrating a steady magenta hue, a sign of a creative soul, not a liar, "what makes you think that?"

"Someone jumped me out in the church parking lot last night. It could have been you."

I expected him to deny it but he said, "Okay, it was me."

"You don't have to tell her nothing, Tucker," Candi said, "she's not the law or anything."

"No, it's okay."

"Why did you jump me?" I asked him.

"Mom said you'd been asking around about Dad."

"Who's your dad?"

"Pastor William was my dad."

After a long minute, during which I backtracked in my mind and tried to remember if I ever heard there was a third child in the William Bennett family I said, "You're Martha and Pastor William's son?" I asked, now recognizing the boy who stood along Martha Bennett's side at the funeral.

"Mom and Dad had me back when they were in college. I was a mistake, I guess. Mom wanted to have me, but Dad didn't. Mom says he was kind of a mess back then, drinking and drugs. He flunked out his sophomore year and he and Mom broke up. Mom raised me by herself for ten years. They tried to work it out a couple of times, but he messed it up each go-round. About six years ago they got back together again when Dad got the calling. It seemed to work out that time and they got married and had little Abigail and Amelia afterward."

"Why am I just hearing about this?"

"With Dad's position and all they didn't talk about it. I suppose it wasn't a good example for the youth of the church."

"But everyone can see you're theirs."

"People know I was their son, but not that I was born out of wedlock."

"I tell him it doesn't matter," Candi said after Tucker's explanation. "Plenty of young folk face that situation today. His Mom and Dad were funny about it. Most times it was like Tucker didn't even exist to them."

"Anyway," Tucker said, "I know Mom didn't want you snooping too deep into their past and this getting out, so with you looking into Dad's murder, you were bound to uncover all this, so I thought I'd scare you off. Get you to stop. For Mom's sake. I guess I wasn't thinking straight. When Candi told me you were snooping around I just..."

"Don't worry about it," I told him. "No harm done. I can see you were just trying to help out and I appreciate you telling me the truth about it."

Ruben D. Gonzales

"You know," Candi said, looking down at me, as they got up to leave, "the Pastor helped me a lot. I know there are some who say it was more, but there wasn't. I don't know what you heard, but there was nothing between the Pastor and me. I mean, the man was old, like my daddy's age, and he had kids."

I felt a bit foolish, sitting there, having just accused a young girl and boy of committing murder. I wanted to get up and leave right then, but our burgers came and Jeff wouldn't have it.

As much as I hated it, Jeff made me stay until he finished his meal and a second beer and then he extended our visit there and made me sit through the band's first set of popular soft rock covers. Candi belted out lyrics like she knew what she was doing. I only wish I could have said the same about me being a detective.

Chapter Twenty-Seven

Friday

I didn't think it possible but the next morning's temperature sank lower than the day before. Blue sat at the side of the bed, her leash hanging from her mouth, looking at me. I still hadn't figured out how the dog managed to pull the leash from the hook where I kept it at the back door. I tried to roll over and hide from her, but she walked around to the other side and growled.

"Okay, okay," I told her, "I'm awake – I'm awake!"

In a cost-saving plan, I didn't install an HVAC system in the second-floor apartment. The mountain summers are cool enough that air conditioning is not needed, and I figured with a good fireplace I could get by in the winter without pumped in heat in the upstairs space. There was electric baseboard heat in the studio business space below, so I hoped I'd get some heat rising from down there to temper the cold upstairs. The hole in the wall where the fireplace was supposed to be had tipped the scales on my calculations and I was reminded of this every morning as arctic air flowed through the cracks around the make-believe fireplace.

Knowing the cold spell would greet me I had slept in my long johns and stuffed my jeans and sweatshirt down under the covers, so they'd be warm from my body heat when I put them on before I got out of bed. Growing up, Early and I learned about cold mornings as Pa heated the old house with a wood-burning stove and if you didn't bank it right, you'd wake up to ice-cold floors. If I didn't see that fireplace finished by year's end, I might have to buy an electric blanket for the long winter ahead.

I put my parka on, threw my hood up and over my head, and went out into the cold. The morning sun peaked over the mountain horizon, greeting me. Blue paused in her morning ritual to sniff at the cold air. I didn't know a lot about the climate change that was gripping the planet but here on the mountain, the winters appeared to be starting sooner and lasting longer.

I led Blue down Mill Row about a block. From the lower road I looked up at the back of the buildings on Main Street and could see the Fish and Game shop's rear entrance. Jeff's truck sat at the back door, an indication he was getting off to an early day. With hunting season in full swing, I was sure the early morning hunters were standing in line waiting to get into the shop to pick up ammo so they could kill things.

With Blue in tow, I scrambled up a short bank and walked around to the front of the shop.

"Good morning!" I called out when I went in.

Jeff stood at the counter writing something down in an account book.

"You're up early," Jeff said, looking up.

"Blue gets me up every morning before I'm ready."

"Yep, dogs can do that."

"You've opened earlier than usual yourself."

"Hunting season! I've already sold a day's worth of shells and more to come."

"Say, since we're both up early, want to get some breakfast?"

"I can't, I've got to mind the shop, Bobby won't be in until later."

"Oh, I was wanting to talk to you about last night."

"What about?

"You know," I started to say and as usual, I had to squeeze the words out, like trying to spit out a piece of my liver, "I wanted to apologize about, you know, about the way I acted to Candi and her friend."

"There's nothing to apologize for."

"I don't know, I felt came on kind of strong."

"I think you were right on, Emma, there's something going on down there at the church. I just can't put my finger on it."

"I'm glad you think so. I've been worrying I'm on a wild goose chase with only my pa in my sights."

"Look, I've got a pot of coffee on. Do you want to sit awhile and have a cup?"

After two cups of coffee, I left Jeff with a shop full of customers and walked back to my studio. I topped off Blue's water bowl and gave her a scoop of dry dog food. I thought about making myself a cup of coffee but already hyped up I figured I'd probably have a heart attack if I added more caffeine to my veins.

Going back over to my desk I grabbed my 3 by 5 cards and spread them out. I took out Pastor John's card. Although he was still hiding something, I'd seen his aura clear enough to know he didn't kill his brother. I never believed it anyhow but there was something there he wasn't telling me. Whether or not it circled back to Pastor Willian I didn't know. In the meantime, I moved his card to the bottom of the stack.

Next, I took out Candi People's card. Although it was the "sexy" option, you know, family man and a man of God, falling for a young pretty thing, like a plot for a romance novel, Candi never faltered in her declaration that she and Pastor William's friendship was only that, friendship. I didn't exactly know how Martha Bennett fit into the picture, if at all. Maybe she was just jealous of the Pastor spending time away from the family. I was glad the good pastor was innocent of any hanky-panky, that's all the parish needed to hear. I mean wasn't getting murdered enough? I pulled Candi's card out and put it aside.

Thomas Shaw was next on my list. I needed to speak with the man and get a look at his aura. The aura colors I saw were not always conclusive, but they did enable me to narrow the field. I was sure Thomas knew all about the land when I spoke with him before and why else would he have gone right out to the church after we met if he wasn't forthcoming, like he was hiding something. Yes, I needed to talk with him as soon as possible. I didn't completely understand where the man fit in the whole puzzle, but he fit somewhere.

I worked in the studio the rest of the morning. I had prints to print and orders to fill. I wrapped up an order of 5 by 7s for a customer over in Morgan and planned out the timing so I could drop them at the post office after getting lunch.

"Hungry?" I texted Jeff.

After a minute he texted back.

"Starved"

"Diner?" I texted him.

"When?" he texted back.

"We'll pick you up in five."

"Waiting."

A man of few words. I liked that about Jeff. Nothing more boring than a man going on about himself.

I put Blue in the Jeep and we drove down the block where Jeff was waiting out in front of his shop. I pulled to a stop in the street and he jump off the curb and came around and got in.

"Well, now, this is service. Are you buying too?"

"I guess, you got the tab last night."

"I didn't think you noticed."

"I did, just forgot to thank you, you know, other things on my mind."

"Like murder?"

"Like that."

The noise level from the crowd in Shaw's diner approached diesel truck decibels and the smell in the place was a combination of diesel and fried food. I could tell Blue didn't like the loud chatter. Many of the town's businessmen, those whose shops could afford to close at lunchtime, jammed into the diner for heavy food and town gossip.

We found two stools at the counter and an old high school classmate, Polly O'Brien, worked her way down the counter and asked us what we wanted to drink. Jeff order sweet tea and I ordered coffee.

"Emma," Polly said, coming back to put our drinks in front of us. "I've got to call you and make an appointment for a family holiday card."

"I've got an appointment maker on my website, Polly. You can go on there and see what's available anytime: blackmountainphoto.com. I should have several spots open this weekend."

"Great, I've been trying to get Buddy and the kids together at the same time so we could drop by."

"How many kids do you have?"

"We've got four, from eight to fourteen, Beau is the oldest, then Bobby, Ben, and Brock."

"All boys?"

"Yep, that's why it's been so hard to get them together. They are all playing something, and Buddy is always coaching someone on Saturday mornings."

"Well, take a look, I'm open late on Saturdays, I'm sure we can find you a spot."

"How about you?"

"What about me?"

"You got any kids?"

"No, Polly, I'm not even married."

"I didn't mean anything," she said, looking at Jeff.

"That's okay, Polly," and without thinking I said, "I guess the right man hasn't come along yet."

"Okay – so what will you have?"

We both ordered the lunch special that consisted of combinations of one or two all-beef patties, different cheeses, fries, and a choice of different desserts.

"So," Jeff asked while we waited for our food, "what is your definition of the right man?"

I couldn't believe Jeff put me on the spot right there in the diner. I looked around self-consciously, thinking of my answer, hoping no one was listening.

"Someone trustworthy, brave, and loyal."

"Are we talking about a man or a dog?"

"A man with those characteristics is a start."

"How about a fella that can rough someone up?"

"That comes in handy, once in a while."

Just in time to save me from further embarrassment our food came, and I spent the next ten minutes stuffing my face hoping Jeff would change the subject.

I was finishing the last of my fries when Mayor Franklyn came up behind us.

"Are you two dating or something? Franklyn asked. "Seems like every time I turn around you two are together?"

Normally I would have said something smart back at the mayor, especially since Jeff and I had been on that discussion thread, but I paused in half chew when I saw that Thomas Shaw was with the mayor.

"Well, Franklyn, it's nice of you to be so interested in our relationship, but we're not ready to send out wedding invitations just yet."

"You let me know."

"You'll be one of the firsts, you and all the Shaw family."

"Good, we like to keep up with our own."

"Speaking of own…what brings you and Thomas Shaw out?"

"Just business, Emma, just business."

"Would this have anything to do with the *Living Waters* land deal?"

"As a matter of fact, it does, why?"

"Oh, well, Thomas told me the other day that he really didn't know about *the Living Waters* land. He didn't mention you were involved."

"Thomas, what have you been telling Emma here?"

Normally the mayor wouldn't air out Shaw family laundry in public, but I guess the topic kind of surprised him.

"I didn't tell her anything," Thomas said.

"He didn't, Franklyn, but obviously there's something going on between the Shaws and the church."

"I told you, we are going to finance the construction. That's all."

I wanted to ask more but I could tell from his steady aura that Franklyn was telling the truth. Whatever Thomas Shaw was involved in, the mayor was unaware of it. That was pretty informative.

"Look, Franklyn, I have a few things to ask you about the land by the lake. Why don't I meet you at your office and we can discuss my concerns."

"Concerns?"

"Yes, now or later in your office?"

The mayor took a look around the diner which had become noticeably quieter since our conversation started.

"Okay, we're heading there now. Come over after you finish your lunch."

Once the Mayor left, I got back to my hamburger and Jeff asked, "What was that all about?"

I filled Jeff in on my latest suspicions on Thomas Shaw and the *Living Waters* land as we finished our lunch and then we drove back to town. I parked midway between our two businesses. Jeff got out and went back to his shop and I went up the walk to the studio and put blue inside with a doggy bone.

Since we were going to be talking about the land down by the lake, I went over to my desk and picked up the church folder that contained all the photos and renderings of the *Living Waters Church* expansion project. I remembered there was quite a bit of information in there, besides the photos of the pastor in action and I thought it might come in handy when I confronted Thomas Shaw about what was happening.

When I turned over the church folder on my desk the contents came sliding out. One file had the photos of parish activities with Pastor William in full work mode. The second file had the renderings of the Church to be, if it ever happened. The third file contained reports from the architectural firm that prepared the preliminary plans and the renderings of the new church. The second to last thing in the folder was an envelope containing a plot of the area, including the dimensions of each lot lake up to the other side of the church. At the bottom of the folder, I saw the sticky note that I noticed before, which Clare Bennett had written, *"Emma, everything you need is in the file...C. Bennett."*

I put the note and other reports aside and took a good look at the plot plan for the area around the church. The plot noted lot size, zoning designation, value, and ownership.

More than interested, I went around my desk and sat down at my computer. I brought up the Secretary of State's Corporation division website and its corporation search engine. I plugged in the Limited Liability Company's name for the owner of the land right behind the *Church of Living Waters*. When the file came up, I opened and read through the latest annual report for the company.

When finished I printed out a copy of the report, folded up the plot map, and tucked both into a pocket of my jacket, Then headed out the door, and ran across the street to Town Hall.

Chapter Twenty-Eight

When I entered Town Hall, the big door made a bang that echoed in the near-empty building. As befitting a small town, the less activity among the halls of town government, the less change, and the more the ruling fathers liked it. As far as the Shaws were concerned, less change meant their authoritative position in the community remained unchanged as well.

I found Thomas and Franklyn Shaw sitting when I entered the room, both slouched comfortably in leather chairs, worn by years of large Shaw men. When they saw me, they both struggled up to greet me, a practiced southern tradition I'm sure they hesitated before granting me. The duo towered over me, making me feel even smaller when compared to their combined girth. Their heaviness settled on my shoulders like dead weight.

"Now, what's this all about?" the mayor asked as he sat back down and left me standing like I was reporting to the principal at school.

"As I said, I've got something to ask you both about the *Living Waters* land and how it's gotten my Pa in trouble."

"We told you, Emma," the Mayor said, "it's strictly a business deal. Sure, the bank is going to make a buck, why wouldn't it? It's not a charity. Plenty of town people work in the bank and their jobs depend on the bank making a profit."

"I'm not talking about the bank's bottom line, Franklyn," I told the man, annoyed again at how anytime someone complained to the Shaws they always made a point about how the workforce in town owes their employment to the Shaw family, in one way or another. "I'm talking about Thomas here and his wheeling-dealing buying up land around the church."

"What land?"

"The land behind the *Living Waters* Church. Look at

231

this," I told him, taking out the plot map showing the area in question."

"What's this?"

"It's a plot of the area around the church."

"So?"

"Do you see who owns the land right behind the Church?"

"It's an LLC, *B&B Real Estate, LLC*".

"Would you like to know who the registered agent is, for B&B, LLC"?

"Who?"

"Thomas Shaw!"

"Thomas," the Mayor said, turning and looking at the man, "what's this about?"

Thomas Shaw hesitated before answering. It probably surprised him that I dug up the details on the B&B, LLC. It probably never occurred to him that I would even know there was a website with public access to that type of information, and now the head of the Shaw family was asking what he'd been up to behind his back.

Thomas Shaw pulled himself up and out of the deep chair and straightening his coat said, "Okay, I helped a group form an LLC and brokered a deal to buy the land behind the church."

"Why?" Franklyn asked.

"Because they needed help."

"Is that the only reason?" I asked him.

"That and the commission. You know, Franklyn, seeing as how you don't pay me to run that office, I got to make a sale every now and then to feed the family."

"How come you kept it a secret?" Franklyn asked.

"I'm only the agent. It's the member's business what they do or how they do it."

I took a good look at the man's aura as it flickered out and asked, "Does this have anything to do with the Church expansion."

"I don't know," he said, his aura not showing he was lying. "I formed that LLC a while back, but just as the agent, I don't have an ownership interest."

"But you brokered the land deal, right? It seems to me the land is at the center of the Pastor's murder. You didn't have anything to do with that, did you?"

"I did the land deal, but I had nothing to do with the Pastor's murder," he said, and his steady aura showed me he was telling the truth, "and I don't have any idea what John Bennett is up to."

"Bennett?" I asked, starting to put the puzzle together. "Pastor Bennett is the "B" in the LLC? He's the one buying up that land?"

"He's been buying up a bit at a time, but bought the biggest piece from the Porter's about a year ago when the sisters moved away."

"But why?" Franklyn asked.

"I don't know," Thomas Shaw said again, his aura confirming he didn't know. "Maybe he's investing."

"I know why," I told them. "The church is planning to expand and build so that property is all of a sudden worth more than it was before. John Bennett stands to make a profit."

"I thought the Church wanted to build down by the lake?" the Mayor asked.

"They were," I told him, "but that deal was based on Clare Bennett giving the church the land. With that land off the table, I figure John Bennett will push the church to buy the B and B land for the new sanctuary."

"How are they going to buy that land?" Franklyn asked.

"Clare Bennett was going to give them the land down by the lake and we were going to lend them the money to build with the land as collateral. They don't have any money to buy anything."

"The church had life insurance on Young Pastor Bennett and when that benefit comes through, they'll have the money."

"That's awfully convenient," the Mayor said.

"Isn't it now?" I agreed. "Maybe convenient enough to set all this up as a murder?"

"What do you mean?"

"That's why Bennett's been accusing Pa of murder. If it was murder then the Church gets the money and when they buy the land, the LLC makes a profit. But if Young Pastor William Bennett committed suicide, then the insurance wouldn't pay off."

"I don't see this, Emma," Franklyn said. "John Bennett's got too much to lose to be caught up in a scam."

"Who says it's a scam?" Thomas Shaw said. "This is a plain business deal. It's not Bennett's fault the Pastor got murdered."

"It isn't?"

"No, and besides, Sheriff Banner is on board as well."

"What do you mean, Sheriff Banner?"

"He's the other "B" in *B&B Real Estate, LLC.*"

"Well, that's it then," I said to the men. "Banner's been out to get Pa right from the start. He never looked at the idea that the Pastor might have killed himself. If he did then the church never collects on the insurance. But with a murder, the church collects and with Pastor John in charge down there, the sale goes through and Banner makes a ton of money."

"That's a wild premise, Emma," the Mayor said. "How do you dream this stuff up?"

"It just comes to me and you know what else just came to me?"

"What?"

"I know Pa didn't kill young Pastor Bennett. He didn't have a motive. But Sheriff Banner does. This land deal doesn't go through unless Young Pastor Bennett is out of the way and that deal with Clare Bennett falls through. She and the young Pastor were close, and she had all but given the church the land but was having second thoughts here at the end. But with young Bennett out of the way that was the end of the deal for sure. With John Bennett pulling the church strings to buy the B&B land, it works out for him and Banner."

"I don't know, Emma," the Mayor shook his head.

"Look, Franklyn, this might all be circumstantial, but all I care about is throwing some other options out there so you can see that my pa is innocent. Now, you get Banner to drop the charges and I'm done with the case. After that, you can take it from there. I'm not getting paid to find out who killed young Pastor Bennett. As far as I'm concerned that's your problem. I'm just interested in getting Pa out of the county lock-up. Now, you get Banner to let Pa go or I'll take this to the press and see what kind of stink it makes."

"No need to do that, Emma," the Mayor said. "I'll have a talk with Banner and set him straight."

"That's all I want."

"Under one condition."

"What?"

"You keep this quiet. I'm not sure what all Thomas and Banner have been up to with this land deal, but I don't want it coming out that we were involved in this and Pastor Bennett's death. Banner's kind of family and if he comes out smelling bad the whole family will stink right along with him."

"Okay, all I want is Pa free, but better be careful Franklyn. Remember what I said, Banner's got a lot to lose on this and he carries a gun."

***

Late that afternoon the Mayor made good on his promise and they bussed Pa back to town.

The sun setting over the mountain cast a dark shadow along Main Street. The temperature had dropped at least twenty degrees, so I bundled up, and put Blue's leash on her and walked up to Town Hall to meet Pa.

The lights in the various shops and storefronts we passed

began to come on. Several businesses had already put out holiday decorations. With many businesses counting on seasonal sales for the majority of their yearly profits, I didn't begrudge them for getting an early start. I was hoping for a big holiday rush myself, to pay off the balance of the construction costs on my renovation project.

Blue stopped and looked at the brightest window displays, like a kid at Christmas.

"They dropped the charges against me," Pa said when he came out of Town Hall. "You must have solved the case?"

"Not really," I said to Pa, remembering my promise to the Mayor. "I just got the Mayor to see reason and he talked to the Sheriff."

"I don't know what the Mayor said to the man, but the Sheriff was mad as a hornet. Banner said to tell you this wasn't over."

"The Sheriff said that?"

"Yep, I get the feeling he doesn't like you much."

"You think?"

Pa pulled his coat around him tighter, and we walked back toward the studio.

"Sorry, it took me so long to get you out. How was it in there?"

"Oh, it wasn't bad. I met up with a bunch of the old guys."

"What old guys?"

"You know, from my liquor running days."

"Oh…"

"Yes, ma'am, a couple of them have been locked up for a while."

"For liquor running?"

"No, they all graduated to drugs and stuff. Said you couldn't make money on moonshine nowadays. With the new liquor laws, the regular store-bought liquor is so cheap, especially that Russian stuff, you can't compete."

"Competition's a bear."

When we got to the studio, I asked him if he wanted to get an early dinner.

"No, I want to go back to the house and get cleaned up, you know?"

"Sure, Pa, I've got the game to shoot. Let me get my gear together and I'll drop you off before I go to the game."

After I left Pa at his house, I drove over to the stadium for a rare back-to-back home game for the Black Mountain High School Broncos.

With the cold driving the temperature down below freezing the home crowd was treated to a big first half as the Broncos rushed to a big lead. In the second half, Coach Brandon Shaw emptied the bench, and players who never dreamed they would touch the field played their hearts out for the last thirty minutes of the game. I got action shots of boys who would never play in college and whose lives might never see a brighter moment than that night on Bronco Stadium grass on a cold fall night in Black Mountain.

In a way it was all kind of sad, but I was happy for the opportunity to record it all for eternity. I was also happy at the prospects for sales. Was that greedy or what? Was I becoming a businessperson? Was I a Shaw after all?

When the game ended, I hustled out to the parking lot and passed out flyers to the crowd. It might have been my imagination, but I thought the crowd was a lot more excited than usual after the game and I saw a lot more smiles from mothers and handshakes between fathers all around.

I waved at the last few cars as they left the parking lot and pushed a flyer through any open window as they slowly went by. When finished I took a deep breath but when I turned, I saw Sheriff Banner's cruiser sitting next to my Jeep. Even across the lot, I could hear Blue barking at the man.

"What are you doing out here?" I asked him when I approached the car, as the Sheriff, and his big son struggled out of their vehicle.

"We came to see the game," Banner said, positioning themselves between me and my Jeep.

"Why? You don't have an affiliation with Black Mountain high. I'm surprised they even let you in the parking lot. Did you bribe someone?"

"We got a contract, Emma," he said above the howling from Blue, "and that allows us to be around and look after any business that goes on in town."

"Funny business?" I asked him as I tried to move around them.

"Any business," he repeated as he moved in my way again, continuing to block my path to Blue, who by this time had begun to throw herself angrily into the Jeep's driver-side window and I began to fear for her safety.

"At least let me get to my dog," I told the man as I tried to move around him again.

"You leave that dog be for a spell," Ross Banner said, stepping in my way.

"What's the matter, Ross, you had a run-in with my dog before?"

"What are you insinuating, Emma? Are you jumping to conclusions again? What gives with you, Emma, I heard you were queer and all, some kind of witch. What did they say Pa? A ghost whisperer?"

"Look…"

"No, Emma," the Sheriff said, "you look. I don't know what all you told the Mayor, but you are way off on this."

"You're not part of that land deal down at church?"

"I am, but I didn't have anything to do with Pastor William's death."

"Isn't it a little convenient that with the Pastor's death that land you bought becomes more valuable?"

"Look, we made a guess that the land would appreciate in value, sure. All the land around the lake is going sky-high. We knew the Porter sisters wanted to leave town and we decided to jump on the opportunity. And it was a coincidence the pastor died and the deal with Clare Bennett fell through."

"How did you know about that?"

"Pastor John is our partner, right? He's kept me in the loop. So, without the Bennett land, the church is looking for land and with the Pastor's life insurance policy they can afford to buy ours, even at a premium if needed."

"That doesn't explain why you kept after Pa all these days."

"Oh, we were going to let your Pa go anyhow."

"You were?"

"I got the report back from the state on the bullet in Pastor William's head. They report it was a .38. Your pa bought a .32, not a .38."

"You knew about Pa's purchase?"

"We got the report on that last week. The round in the Pastor's head was from an older gun and it looked like it had been shot through something. That slowed it down, so it didn't pass on through the Pastor's head."

"Oh…"

"Yeah, so your Pa's cleared, we were just waiting on the final report."

"So that clears him, how about you?"

"What?"

"Do you want to tell me how Ross here hurt his arm?"

"Who said I hurt my arm?"

"I felt the bandage on your arm, Ross," I explained and started to get a view of the man's aura, fluctuating among the pinks of emotional imbalance and deceit, "about the same place on the man's arm where my dog Blue got hold of a man who mugged me the week before. Is that why you don't want me to let my dog out?"

"I don't want you to let him out because I don't want to get bit."

"Her!"

"…okay, her, and I hurt my arm chopping firewood."

"Emma," the sheriff said, "the pastor was killed on a Sunday night, two Sundays back, right? Well, Ross and I sing in the church choir, and we always sing at Sunday night service. A hundred people will swear we were both in church that Sunday night and couldn't have been anywhere in the vicinity of Pastor William when he was killed."

I must have looked unconvinced because the Sheriff kept talking.

"Okay, look, I've put up with your meddling in this case. I told Franklyn I'd look the other way on your Pa evading arrest and you concealing evidence if you'd stop your doggone meddling. As long as you stay clear of this thing, I'll leave you and your Pa alone. But if I hear you're back to accusing people and fouling up this investigation, then you'll find you and your Pa back in trouble. There's still a murderer out there so I've got work to do. Am I making myself clear?"

I could only nod my head. I'd seen both their auras and though confusing and overlapping colors appeared, it looked like they were telling the truth, or at least not lying about things. So, in the end, I didn't know who killed Pastor John and I still didn't know who the other mugger was, and I guessed I might never find out.

"I got to hear you say it, Emma," the Sheriff said.

"Okay, okay, I'll leave it alone. I only wanted Pa out and free."

"Well, you got it, and no faster than it would have happened anyway for all your interfering. Now, Emma, you've been a thorn in my side ever since you moved back to town, first with Early and then with Barbara Walker. Now, here you are again. You know, Emma, detective work is a detailed process, and you can't be taking shortcuts. All it gets you is pie in the face. I hope you finally learned your lesson this time and will be leaving the detective work to those who know."

I watched the Banner duo get into their cruiser and leave

the parking lot. I let Blue out and she ran barking at the men, all the way to the end of the lot. When she came back, I knelt down to her and gave her a hug. In return, she slobbered all over me.

Thinking about what a terrible detective I turned out to be, I got in the Jeep, and we drove back to town. I thought about texting Jeff. I needed a shoulder to cry on. A woman could do anything these days. I knew a man wasn't necessary to be a success as a businesswoman or a detective, but at that moment, I could still use a kind, supportive shoulder.

Chapter Twenty-Nine

Saturday Morning

Before I knew it, Blue was standing at the foot of my bed with her leash in her mouth waiting on me to wake up. Last night Jeff and I spent some time together and I felt better when the evening ended. Smooching with him in front of my fake fireplace helped with that.

"Go away!" I yelled at Blue.

"WOOF!"

"Okay, okay, I get it."

Mercifully the apartment felt less like an igloo and more like a home. The temperature must have risen overnight because I couldn't see my breath. I wondered if the hole in the great room wall got filled in by the fireplace fairy.

I dragged myself up, put on my housecoat, and went down the steps with Blue following. Once outside she completed her ritual, and we went back in to have coffee ahead of the busy day to come.

Luckily, Sue Ellen Shaw came early with her boyfriend, Tim McBride, and they started to set up for the morning rush.

"You had a few more bookings overnight," Sue Ellen said.

"Great," I answered, trying to be cheerful, rushing back up the steps to get ready for the day which included a youth soccer game at 2:00.

"By the time I dressed and returned to the studio, our first family had arrived. Don't let anyone ever tell you that mountain folk can be lazy or tend to be tardy. So far, I hadn't seen anyone come into the shop less than ten minutes before their appointment.

The day was a small business entrepreneur's nightmare.

The system had somehow double-booked a few spots, one of my cameras stopped working, the game I shot went long due to an injury, and even after skipping lunch and eating leftovers out of my refrigerator to try to get back on schedule, we still went two hours long. At the end of the day the only thing I was happy about was being so busy I didn't have to think once about poor young Pastor Bennett's murder.

When I finally sat down and looked up, the Mayor was standing in the reception area smiling at me.

"What do you want?"

"You all look busy."

"We are. What do you want?"

"I need to talk to you about something."

"What?"

"Well, you know Randall's been publishing the Black Mountain Post for the last ten years, ever since he moved back to town."

"Right."

"Cousin Herman Shaw had published the thing for the forty years before that."

"I remember."

"Well, when Randall took it over, he reduced printing to a weekly, then in a cost-saving move went to monthly."

"I know."

"Well, come to find out, there is a market for a town paper coming out on a more frequent basis."

"What do you mean?"

"I've heard from every merchant in town on how they want to see the paper come out more regularly, for advertising purposes. Especially around the holidays. They say they would buy advertising on a monthly basis if we'd put the paper out regularly and expand distribution countywide.

"What does Randall say about that?"

"He doesn't like the idea. He said it's too much work and anyway, he says he never liked working on the paper. Said it was just a headache. He said he wouldn't put it out more than monthly."

"Oh?"

"Yep, he said if I wanted to have the paper out more than that, I'd have to get someone else to publish the thing."

"Oh…Ohhhhhh," I said, "you don't mean?"

"Yeah, Emma, what do you think about taking over the paper?"

"You're kidding?"

"No, I'm not, it makes perfect sense. Didn't you major in Journalism?"

"Photojournalism."

"What's the difference? And besides, you worked at the Piedmont paper for a while. You probably know more about running a paper than Randall did when he started."

"I don't know, Franklyn."

"Look, I know you've got your business and all, but it would kind of be a good fit. You'd be able to put some of your pictures in each run and people all over the county would see your work. Didn't you say you won an award or something for your newspaper photos?"

"I did."

"There you go. This will give you another platform. Besides, it's more of a newsletter kind of thing. No hard news. No, "If it bleeds it leads!" stories."

"I don't know…"

"Just think it over. That's all I'm asking. You and Randall could work on the holiday edition together and get the feel for it, and then you could take over starting the first of the year. It's all on the computer now, no office, you can use your office here. And no printing press to run. You just put it together and email the file over to the printer in Morgan and they ship the printed pages back for distribution."

"Still…

"Look, we'll pay you a minimum fee, plus a percentage

of all advertising. Could turn out very lucrative."

"Since when? Newspaper businesses are dying all over the state."

"That's what they said about photography, and you're making it work."

He had me on that note. The slight compliment it was. And I'd always wanted to run a newspaper. In a way, I was already halfway there with my photography business. I'd just be adding gossip and stories on sports which I was already documenting anyway. And I could use the extra income. Okay, go on and call me greedy.

"Okay, I'll think about it."

"Great," he said turning to the door. "Oh, I almost forgot."

"What else?"

"I need you to do something."

"What now?"

"The Sheriff decided it was time to move into the police offices over in Town Hall"

"Oh…"

"Yeah, I think he wants to keep a closer watch on things, probably thanks to you."

I didn't want to rehash what the Sheriff and I had gotten into the night before, so I just nodded my head.

"So, I need you to come over and clean out Early's things."

"What?"

"Yeah, when Early…you know, when he passed, we closed the office and haven't been back in there since."

"For two years?"

"No one felt like being reminded and the Sheriff never showed interest about moving in."

"Why don't you get Becky to do it?"

"She came by a long time ago and got what she wanted. This is kind of the last call before we dump everything left in there."

"Can't this wait until Monday? "I said, "I can't come right now, we're just closing up and I've got orders to settle."

"No, the Sheriff will be here Monday morning. We need to clear out what you want because he's going to dump the rest."

"I still think Becky should do it."

"Look, Becky's got what she wants and there's not much personal stuff left anyway. Now, I've got dinner plans with Shelby, so you're on your own. I'll leave Early's old office door unlocked. Just go in and get what you want. Remember, only Early's personal stuff, don't take any Town property."

"Are you sure you can trust me? I might snatch a stapler or something."

"Don't try it. We've got an inventory of everything in there that belongs to the town."

By that, he meant the Shaws.

"Whatever is left I'll figure you didn't want so we'll throw it all out come Monday morning."

I don't know how the mayor thought I'd be inclined to go through Early's things even after two years. I still missed my big brother, and the passage of time hadn't made it easier.

It was well past dark by the time we finished in the studio. Sue Ellen had finalized all the orders and double-checked payments. Tim had put up all the toys and other props we used to entertain the assortment of kids we had and then straightened up the equipment. I finished transferring all the pics from my cameras to the hard drive for retrieval later. Up until then I really hadn't thought too much about the task ahead of me.

I walked Sue Ellen and Tim out the front door and stood on the stoop as they drove off. Night had settled in on Main Street but the lights from the streetlamps and sidewalk businesses kept the darkness at bay and brought a cheer to the street.

Thinking I'd like to have some company for the task ahead I texted Jeff.

"What are you doing?"

"Closing up."

"I need your help."

"Do you want me to rough up someone?"

"No...no roughing up people. I'll explain."

"Ten minutes." Was his last text.

Even though I wouldn't have called the coming outing with Jeff a date, I still hustled in and ran up the stairs to my apartment to clean up. It had been a long day. Considering the ten-month-old that vomited on me and the sweat I worked up shooting the game, my clothes looked a mess. While changing I tried to calculate if I could squeeze in a quick shower. Since my bathroom had been finished, I had begun to really enjoy a long hot shower, a respite from troubles and worries.

I decided against a shower, no use looking desperate. I slipped on clean jeans and a clean sweatshirt. I combed out my hair and tied it back in a ponytail and used some face cream and lip balm to soften my look.

When I came out of the bathroom Jeff was sitting back on my sofa in front of my make-believe fireplace.

"Do you want me to call Hank about this fireplace business?" he said, holding his hand up to the cold breeze coming around the flimsy plywood covering the hole in the wall.

"No, I talked to him, and he is getting to it this week."

"Isn't that's what he said last week?"

"Has it been that long?"

When Jeff only smiled back, I said, reluctantly, "Okay, maybe he'll listen to you, but don't rough him up or anything."

"I won't. We'll just have a nice little talk."

Not wanting to go into what a little talk meant I said, "Ready?"

"Where to? The Black Brew?"

"No..." and then thinking I might need a drink after the ordeal ahead I said, "Maybe after."

"After what?"

On the way out the door and across the street, I explained to Jeff what the Mayor wanted me to do.

Our footsteps echoed in the empty Town Hall, eerily so, and the thought of dredging up memories of Early added to the feeling. My brother had spent the last fifteen years of his life going in and out of that office. The last seven as the town Chief of Police. People said Early was a tough cop, and he backed it up with a physical presence that could calm even the toughest situations. People also said Early was fair to a point. He had his favorites, not including the Shaws. They didn't like it. They thought they should get preferential treatment, but Early didn't give in to them. It was a noble endeavor but once he was gone the Mayor didn't waste a minute closing the office and contracting the public safety duties out to the County Sheriff. He said it was a cost-saving move, but more than likely it was a move to get someone more flexible on how they interpreted the law, as it applied to the Shaws.

The town police office looked like a movie set from the Andy Griffith show. The fact was the office had never been updated. Although every other office in Town Hall had seen a host of renovations, the Mayor never put police office renovations in the yearly budget. I think he thought if he made it uncomfortable enough Early might quit.

The office space was divided up into an eight-foot-wide pubic area, a ten-foot-wide work area with two old green metal desks and matching worn chairs, and in the rear of the space, two rooms. One room was Early's old office which looked out on the building's front lawn, and the second room housed a gun case, supplies, and files.

Solid one-hundred-year-old oak hardwood floors stretched thirty feet left to right. Two uncomfortable wooden benches sat side by side against the wall and a short wooden rail separated the visitor side of the room from the work side of the room. On the wall above the two benches, hung several rows of photos of all former town police officers. As the town was small and once in a town job, men rarely left, there weren't as many photos as you would expect. From left to right, oldest to newest, the officers' photos spread, their faces solemn with the duty they were charged. Most of the photos were grainy black and white but at some point, in the mid-50s, the photos began in color, and from then on, the faces of Black Mountain's finest stared back at you in Kodak hues.

Early and the most recent officers anchored the last column in the lineup. The last of the town's own. I didn't think the Sheriff would continue with the tradition, so I removed Early's photo and stuck it in an empty box I found. I wondered if any of the other officer's families would want a photo of a past loved one. Surely every officer up on the wall still had family in town. I wondered if the Mayor thought about saving those photos for others.

Even though the office had been left alone for the past two years, it looked clean and neat. A bulky thirty-year-old computer monitor and keyboard took up space on each desk and green trash cans sat conveniently beside them. I half expected to see typewriters.

"Emma," Jeff called to me, breaking my concentration, "where do you want to start?"

"The stuff out here is all town junk. Early's things would be in his office."

Early's office looked different than the last time I was in there. Family photos were missing leaving nothing of Early. Like he never existed.

I went through Early's desk. Most of the files I found were of old cases and not personal items. There were a few small items like pens and notebooks, but I left them for the trash. I took a silver letter opener inscribed with his name. If Becky didn't want it, I'd keep it on my studio desk. That way with every envelope I slit opened, I'd think of Early.

The lone closet in the room contained a few pieces of

clothing and I swear I could smell Early's scent in the small space.

"You should take that leather jacket," Jeff said looking over my shoulder into the closet. "Early used to wear that all the time, I remember. It's a good jacket, will last forever."

"I don't know Jeff, who'd wear it?"

"One of the boys would love it, don't you think?"

"Okay, take the jacket, but I'm done. Let's get out of here."

"Are you sure?"

"Definitely, let's go get a beer."

When I got to the office door, I saw one of Early's old backpacks hanging on a hook behind the door. Faded with half the zippers broken I remembered the thing from year before when I broke into the office looking for evidence to clear my brother. As a last memento, I grabbed the bag and stuffed it down in the box.

I was at the hallway door when I saw the wall of photos again. Throwing out old clothes and files was one thing but throwing out memories captured on film was another matter for me.

"Wait," I told Jeff, "I think we should keep all these photos."

"Why?"

"Because the families might want them."

"How are you going to find all these families?"

"I don't know, we'll do a Facebook search. People do it all the time. I could put some up in the Studio gallery. It should draw interest. Spread the word. If nothing else," I thought about the coming opportunity with the paper, "maybe the Post can do a story on the men."

"Okay," Jeff said, moving down the wall in the direction of the newest photos, "I'll start on this end, and you start here."

The first photo on the wall had a small brass plate and inscription, "Harley Bennett – First Town Police Chief – 1910 – 1932.

The Bennett family came into the Valley of the Three Forks about the same time as the Shaws and though they didn't come bearing a land grant they made out okay and staked their claim to local history in farming, the ministry, and apparently, law enforcement. Seemingly, Sheriff Harley Bennett owed his success as a peace officer to brain and not just brawn.

"Look at the town's first Chief of Police," I called out to Jeff, inviting him over to look at the photo of the man in a white shirt and bow tie. "He looks more like a schoolteacher. I would expect someone tougher looking, you know a Wyatt Earp type."

"The job of the town sheriff was different back then, Emma. I heard tell of Harley Bennett. By the thirties, the job evolved into a police department with all facets of the law from enforcement, arrest, incarceration, and probably judgment as well. It was a tough job and someone with both intelligence and toughness was probably needed."

"Do you think Clare Bennett would want this photo of her, what...great-great-grandfather? I'd hate it if the man was completely forgotten.

"I don't know, Clare or Ruth, one of them. Of course, there're plenty of monuments already around town to remember the Bennett family. I think the town garden out front was first dedicated by them back in 1910."

"I think I heard that to save the soil in the valley, the Bennetts were the first people in the area to try crop rotation."

"Where did you hear that?"

"Ruth Bennett told me."

"She did? Well, I guess they were the first environmentalists in town. I'm not much for tree huggers, Emma, but some environmental studies and techniques have proven successful. I just don't see stopping development because you want to save a frog or a flower. You know?"

I did know. I knew there were strong feelings on both sides of that conversation. Many in the mountains, like the

Shaws, welcomed the development. The more developed the more business. Being on the entrepreneur side, I understood that. But others, on the tree-hugger side, were just as vocal about development being bad for the environment.

We had a full box when we were done, and we walked across the street to the studio. Blue saw Jeff and ran to him, nearly knocking him over in greeting.

We stored the box with all the photos in a backroom supply closet. Later I'd have to figure a way to start a campaign to find the relatives. I hung Early's leather police jacket in the closet next to my parka. I hoped one of his sons would take it. Having it in there made me think Early was watching me.

I put the leash on Blue and we went out to the Jeep and drove over to the Black Brew Brewery. I hoped the night's band wasn't too loud. I was worn out and ready to relax and didn't need another headache.

Chapter Thirty

Sunday Morning

In the morning I knew Blue was watching me. I didn't open my eyes and tried to maintain my slow breathing, hoping she'd leave me for another few minutes. My head throbbed from too many beers the night before, but Blue wasn't sympathetic and prodded me with a cold nose until I gave in and climbed out of bed.

The morning temperature seemed a tad over normal, unlike the day before. Maybe signaling a late Indian Summer coming over the mountains for a warm spell. Native Americans would routinely use this brief period of warm fall weather to gather a final round of supplies before winter's hold settled in the mountains.

Some in our clan have discouraged the use of the term "Indian" in reference to the fall phenomenon. I've always been a bit ambivalent about my heritage. Being only partly blood-related to my indigenous ancestors, I'd spent a good deal of my life hiding behind my Scottish name. Did I really ever fool anyone? Did anyone really care?

I took Blue out for a walk, and we went all the way down to the lake. The sun coming up over the mountain washed the lake surface with a fine veil of mist and the scene reminded me of the eeriness of the mountain and the mystery of what you couldn't see beneath the calm water.

I thought about hanging out there all morning, but I knew Pa would expect me to attend his Sunday school class. By the time I got back to the studio my head had cleared and I proceeded to get ready.

Pa led his Sunday school class on discussions of different

passages the Pastor gave him. He wasn't doing the picking and choosing, only the Pastor did that. And with the Pastor's son just having been murdered I was curious to hear what the old man would choose. You know, something on forgiveness? Or maybe something on an eye for an eye?"

What we got was ...Romans 12:17 ... *"Do not repay anyone evil for evil. Be careful to do what is right in the eyes of everyone. If it is possible, as far as it depends on you, live at peace with everyone. Do not take revenge, my dear friends, but leave room for God's wrath, for it is written: "It is mine to avenge; I will repay, says the Lord."*

It wasn't a passage I remembered. Oh sure, there were several passages to choose from on forgiveness. Isn't that the essence of Christianity? But 12:17 hinted that God might be the one to bring a reckoning to an evil act. Like most people, I didn't doubt that in the end, evil would be repaid, but like most people, I wanted it to be sooner rather than later.

I didn't stay for the regular service and sermon. I heard what Pa and his classmates thought about the Bible topic for the week. I didn't need to hear a rehash from the Pastor to get the point of God having the final say in the matter. Didn't he always have the final say?

Remembering the morning walk Blue and I had taken, I decided to get her, and we'd go for that long walk around the lake I'd been promising. I really didn't think she remembered any off-the-cuff remark or promise I made to her over the last couple of weeks, but I still wanted to follow through on it because it might be the last nice day before winter settled in for good.

Back in the studio, I changed out of my Sunday outfit and into jeans, a sweatshirt, and my moccasin boots. I figured we'd need a snack or two during the hike, so I gathered an apple, two power bars, three doggie biscuits for Blue, and made myself a peanut butter sandwich. I filled a water bottle with fresh water and with my arms full I walked down to the studio closet. As I looked for something to carry it all in, I saw Early's old backpack. I grabbed it and stuffed everything in a compartment. I took my parka in case it got cold later in the day and stuffed that in the pack as well. Before leaving I went to my desk to get my camera. When I looked down at the mess, I saw the church folder with all the files. I decided since I'd be out that way I'd stop at the church and drop off the folder. Blue and I could start our hike from there.

While still a good way away from the church I realized I miscalculated about being able to drop the church folder off. Cars were backed up along the road indicating the faithful of *Living Waters* went longer than the typical in-town church. I heard singing and loud music coming from the church and wondered if Candi Peoples was leading the band that morning. At any rate, the church office would probably be closed until after services, whenever that would be.

I drove on past the church and decided to find a place to park, so we could take our hike before visiting the church office. To my right, among a line of cars parked just off the road, I saw that Studebaker again, parked next to an old truck. Stopping this time, I saw two people walking at the edge of the upland wood area north of the church.

Curious, I parked just beyond the Studebaker. I climbed out of the Jeep and went around to the passenger side but when I opened the door to let Blue out, she barged past me, dragging half the contents in the seat out with her. Barking and howling she lunged in the direction of the two people, me holding onto her leash for dear life.

"Blue," I shouted at the dog as she pulled. "Sit still!"

After she sat and calmed some, I started picking stuff up, and throwing it all back into the Jeep. The church files had spilled out as well. I also saw Clare's note again, *"Emma, in this file you'll find all you need."*

I went to replace the note but realized I didn't know which file it came off of. Originally, I had thought it came off the folder itself, but the note said "file", so it wasn't instructions leading me to the folder, it was meant to lead me to a specific file. But which one?

I looked at the files again, market analysis, population studies, cost analysis, and an environmental study. Harley Bennett had been an environmentalist, way before his time. What did Ruth Bennett tell me about their crop rotation practices? Of course, the Bennett sisters would have been interested in the environmental effects the church building project would have on the land around the lake. Did they contract for the study? Was that what Clare was telling me? Was I supposed to look at the environmental study? Did I miss a clue?

"Better get hold of that dog of yours," Ruth Bennett told me when she came up to where I was squatting, gathering up files and the contents of the backpack. When her son Zackary came up from behind, Blue took to barking again.

"What?" I said, confused.

"I said you need to get hold of your dog!"

"What's wrong with you, girl," I asked the dog, half expecting an answer. I put Blue in the Jeep's back seat, tossed in Early's old back pack and closed the door on her, where she continued to howl.

With Ruth Bennett looking on I apologized.

"I'm sorry about her," I said as I began to pick up the rest of the mess that fell out of the folder. When I looked down at the files again, I saw the environmental study. I paused and read the cover title again, *Environmental Impact Study*...it was an *impact* study, not just an environmental study!

"She's not like this usually," I said as I opened the file and flipped pages until I saw a page with yellow highlights about halfway through the report. The section of the study highlighted in yellow listed an endangered species; the... *White Iirisette. This species occurs on rich, basic soils probably weathered from amphibolite. It grows in clearings and the edges of upland woods where the canopy is thin and often where down-slope runoff has removed much of the deep litter layer ordinarily present on these sites. The species is only found in a few areas of North Carolina and one area in South Carolina. The rare herb is on North Carolina's endangered species list. Without protection, the species will soon disappear forever.*

What was this about? Did someone know the church expansion plan would contribute to the disappearance of a native plant?

It brought my attention back to Blue and I noticed she had stopped barking and gotten hold of the ski mask my mugger had dropped at that Friday night game, you know when he mugged me. I forgot I had stuck it in my parka pocket, but Blue sniffed it out in Early's old pack. She had it clamped in her jaws and was growling and shaking her head, like trying to tell me something.

"What are you all looking at over here?" I asked the two Bennetts. "This isn't your land."

"I know it," Ruth said, "but there's a delicate habitat here that I look after. We have the same growth down by the lake, but it stretches out all along this ridge."

"The *White Irisette?*"

"How do you know about the *Irisette?*"

"Clare left me a note?"

"What kind of note?"

"A note on the environmental impact the church building project would have on the *White Irisette,* an endangered species of plant. Is that what these plants are here?"

"Well, we don't have to worry about that. The church isn't going to go through with that project so this land and the Iris will continue to be protected."

"That's convenient for you, Ruth, isn't it? The pastor being murdered and the plans for the new church falling through?"

"What are you getting at?"

As Blue growled in the back seat of the Jeep, I said, "You know, Blue has a keen sense of smell."

"What's that got to do with anything?"

"Well, do you see that ski mask he's biting down on? We took it from a man that mugged me Friday before last. The man warned me to stay out of Pastor Bennett's murder case. Blue remembered his scent. That's why she's barking out like that. I think she's caught Zachary's scent."

"It's a coincidence."

"No, Zachary's the same size as the man who jumped me and I'm sure the DNA on that ski mask will match Zachary's DNA. That will put him there where he attacked me."

I was going to ask her if she killed the pastor but that was an obvious impossibility considering her age, so instead, I asked, "Did you get Zachary to kill the pastor?"

"I did not," she answered quickly, and her aura continued to beat a serene orange.

Knowing she wasn't lying I paused, confused. Did I have it wrong, again?

Ruth Bennett turned away from me and knelt, reaching out she cradled a long delicate vine in her hand. "You know, Emma Louise, the White Irisette used to grow all over the eastern woodlands. It's a perennial herb, quite fragrant, and rare. It's been driven to extinction by development encroaching on its habitat. There are a few populations left in North and South Carolina. Right here in Black Mountain, we are blessed to harbor a small patch, but if left unprotected, the flower will disappear from here as well. Wouldn't that be a shame? You should see the small pretty white flower in the spring. Just beautiful. I'd do anything to protect it.

"Would you kill to protect it?"

"That's nonsense. I did try to talk Clare out of donating that land. It might be a little crazy on my part, especially to some up here in the mountains, but I'd hate to see the Iris disappear from the landscape just to build some church, but I wouldn't kill anyone to save it. I'm not that crazy."

Just then Blue howled again, but when I turned to look at her, I noticed Zachary had moved over to the other side of the Jeep, out of Blue's line of sight.

"Now, Emma Louise, Zachary and I must continue our walk, so, if you don't mind, we'll be on our way."

I watched the lady and her son move off along the road. They stopped once to examine a cluster of something that looked like weeds to me, and then moved off again, approaching a slight hill.

I squatted on the ground and started gathering up the last of the mess Blue had made. I leaned back against the Jeep and regretted my random accusation against the Bennetts. It all just seemed to fit so perfectly. Ruth Bennett had a motive and the means with all those pistols back at their house, but her aura didn't confirm it.

For some reason, Blue was still in hyper mode, so as I carefully opened the door, I held her back. I looked through Early's pack for a doggie biscuit, hoping it would calm her down. While groping in the bag I found a compartment I hadn't seen before. Inside the space, I found a folded sheet of paper. When I opened it up, I saw it was a copy of a map sketch.

The last case Early had worked on was on contract with the local ATF agency. They were running a big drug sting operation in the mountains and Early had helped them locate some of the local operations. Early knew every local boy on the mountain and had provided the ATF with a list of them. It looked like he worked up the map for the ATF to help them as well.

When I looked at his map, I could identify town landmarks. The sketch showed the Swannanoa River and Lake Nebo, and the town between. Early had represented buildings with squares and roads with lines, the thickest was Main Street Black Mountain, flanked by businesses. Early had used an "X" to mark different locations throughout the surrounding foothills and included people's names and notes next to each name. It was easy for me to recognize some of the names. Most were well-known around town as families that used to run liquor.

Remembering the Church files, I pulled out the real estate study with a surveyed map of every parcel of land around the town and I spread it out on the back seat and put Early's sketched map up alongside it and compared the two. Early's map was fairly accurate. He had captured the essence of the land in relation to the town and I could identify all the roads and properties. However, when I compared his map to the surveyed map, I realized one building and an area wasn't drawn in. The missing building was the *Church of the Living Waters*. Early was too thorough to have missed it. There must have been a reason.

I looked up the road and saw that Ruth Bennett and Zachary had walked out of sight. I also noted that Blue was still growling to get out but looking in another direction. With nothing to lose I held my breath, took the ski mask away from her, unleashed her leash, stepped to the side, and let her out.

I didn't know which way she'd go but she took off, dead west, away from the Bennetts, and straight into the woods, and barking loudly, she disappeared into the thick underbrush behind the church.

She had the scent and under a dark canopy, I followed her as best I could. I crashed through low-hanging limbs, jumped over downed tree trunks, and tripped over exposed roots, as I chased her. I could hear her bark in the distance and felt my heart banging against my chest with the exertion to keep up. After a minute her barking turned into a howl. She had treed something – or someone.

When I finally caught up to her, I could see she had forced someone up into an oak tree. The man was about eight feet up on a limb.

"You need to call off your dog," the young man said.

When I got a good look at the man in the dim light, I saw he was one of Sam Lawson's boys, Larry, I think was his name.

"I don't know," I said, wheezing out from the chase, "looks like we have a problem here."

"What kind of problem?" Sam Lawson barked out from behind me, making me jump. When I turned around, Sam and his other three boys appeared out of the thick wood, like apparitions in a dream.

"Get hold of your Dog, Emma Louise," Sam said, as the four surrounded me and he pointed a 30:30 rifle at Blue.

"Mr. Lawson, we got a problem."

"Only problem you have is I might have to shoot that dog of yours if you don't get hold of her."

Until then, Blue had remained at the tree, ignoring the other men, but when Lawson raised his voice at me, she left the tree and walked to my side and growled up at the men.

"See here, Mr. Lawson," I said, kneeling down to Blue and stroking her back, but I didn't leash her, "I don't take kindly to threats, especially against my dog."

At my bravado, Mr. Lawson laughed, and his boys laughed nervously too.

"You're Early's sister, sure enough," Sam Lawson said. "He always told me you were a pistol."

"I thought you said you didn't know Early?" I asked the man as I got up and waited for his aura to come out.

"Well, we talked some, now and again."

That answer didn't help me, so I continued, "Just now and again?"

"Yep."

"Did Early know what you boys were doing out here?"

"Just what do you think we're doing?"

"If not moonshining then you're probably into drugs."

"What makes you say that?"

261

"Early worked a case for the ATF two years back. He left notes I found."

"Well, if Early was here, he'd say what's going on here is none of your business and you need to take your dog and move on."

"I can't do that, Mr. Lawson. Your boy up the tree there mugged me two weeks back and warned me off my investigation of Pastor Bennett's murder."

"What makes you say that?"

"This ski mask here," I showed him the mask. "I picked it up after your boy jumped me. Blue picked up the scent back on the road and he treed your boy. Just like a raccoon. I'm sure the DNA in it will match Larry up there perfectly. The only question I have is why warn me off the case?"

Instead of answering the four moved closer to me, causing Blue to snarl.

"What are you all hiding?" I asked, looking at them one at a time, waiting for one of them to answer.

Sometimes people's auras are hard to read, but Sam Lawson's broke out in full red of emotion, tinged in a black, the hue I've associated with anger, and he raised his rifle and pointed it at me to confirm my interpretation.

"Hold on Pa," the oldest boy said, moving between us. I had recognized the oldest boy before, George Lawson. I think he played ball with Early. "This is Early's sister, we owe Early too much for this. You need to stop and think."

"Don't tell me what to think boy!"

"Pa, hold on now, this has gone too far."

"What's all this about?" I asked the group. "Did you kill Pastor Bennett because of the land deal back here? Hoping to keep your operation secret?"

With the question, the air went out of the space, like the way it got when an IED was disarmed in Afghanistan and an explosives team took a big sigh of relief at the same time.

"Let me explain it to her, Pa," George said. "Look, Emma,

we went to pick up Mama after the social that night. When Pa saw the pastor was alone, he wanted to talk to him. Ma had told us about the Church's plans for expansion back here and Pa thought he'd talk to the man about it. Pa sent Ma and the other boys on, but we stayed behind. We caught up to the Pastor under the church steeple and Pa and the Pastor got to arguing. Pa got mad and pulled his pistol. Oh, he was just trying to scare the man, but the Pastor jumped back quick-like, and when he did, he raised his hand and his Bible up, like for protection. But in the movement, he bumped into Pa's hand and a shot went off. That old .38 of Pa's has always had a light trigger. The bullet went through the Good Book and hit the pastor in the head. He stumbled back and fell down into the baptismal fountain, dead. Well, with the whole scene in front of us we kind of panicked. It was all kind of an accident. Pa didn't want any questions because of our operation back here so we just left him there."

"What operation?"

"We've been growing and harvesting marijuana for years, back in a clearing we made."

"Did Early know about it?"

"Early knew but with us being friends and all he looked the other way. Your brother was good like that with people. He knew how hard it was for us backwoods folk to get by so he helped out when he could."

"Is that why he didn't turn you guys over to the ATF?"

"That's why. When you told us you were looking into the Pastor's death, Pa sent Larry out that night after the game, to warn you off the case."

"And in the Alley?"

"That was Ricky."

"But if it was an accident like you say, why didn't you all just tell the law what happened?"

"Accident or not," Mr. Lawson said, "we'd be out of business, and we couldn't get by without the income from

263

selling. We've still got little ones at home and now grandbabies too. No, I just couldn't stand by and watch the family suffer through winter."

Last Chapter

Sheriff Banner found Pastor Bennett's Bible at the Lawson house, with a hole in it. The State lab later confirmed Sam Lawson's gun was the one used in Pastor Bennett's death. The low-velocity bullet from Lawson's gun slowed as it passed through the Bible and into the Pastor's head. That's what made it appear the Pastor was killed by a small round bullet and had cast suspicion on Pa.

Bartholomew Shaw sent Sam Lawson over to the county jail until the trial and let his boys out on their recognizance but warned them they were accomplices and could face charges at some future date, although exactly what charges anyone would face was still up in the air, considering the circumstances.

Soon after, I finally got to meet Clare Bennett. Pa brought her into the studio one day to introduce her. She had clear light blue eyes, long gray hair pulled back in a ponytail, and wore a pair of worn jeans and comfortable-looking boots. I liked her smile, almost flirtatious, and her aura burned a bright tint of love. I was happy Pa had found a friend after all the years.

Pa said they'd been working out at the old Bennett farm, tilling up the land ahead of the season, putting out some winter wheat to get the soil set for next spring's corn. It looked like the two were all in on the cornmeal project to feed the hungry. It amazed me the couple had so much energy. Is that what love does for you? I had a hard enough time just getting up in the morning.

After the introductions, we went up the walk to pick Jeff up and the four of us went to the *Bean* for lunch, just like a double date. After we'd eaten and settled back, I asked Clare about the note she left in the file on the church property.

"I knew you were kind of a detective, Emma, from what

your Pa told me. I didn't know who killed Pastor Bennett but figured the land was somehow the key."

"Where have you been all this time?"

"We've been staying out at my old family farm in the valley."

"We?" I asked looking at Pa.

Pa said, "I couldn't stay at the house, Emma, the Sheriff was looking all over town for me."

I asked her about that pistol Pa bought for her.

"Oh, I didn't get it for any protection or anything," she said. Blue got up and put her head in her lap where Clare took to scratching behind one of the dog's ears, making her a friend for life. "I wanted to meet your Pa and heard he had been in the military. I thought if I showed an interest in getting a gun, he'd help me out and we'd get to spend some time together. I couldn't think of any other way to meet him."

"I thought the way to a man's heart was through his stomach?"

"Not if you can't cook!"

Good to know.

The End

Ruben D. Gonzales was born and raised in East L.A. but has called North Carolina home since 1976. The Black Mountain Mystery series is developed out of his love for the heritage and mystery of the North Carolina mountains. After college, Ruben spent five years with the Peace Corps in various capacities and stations including two years as an elementary school teacher in a small African village without electricity or indoor plumbing. Ruben spent evenings reading and writing by candlelight and during this time he wrote a short story that was bought by the BBC for world broadcast. His first published novel, *The Cottage on the Bay*, a historical novel, takes place on a fictional plantation outside of Wilmington, NC, and his second book, *Murder on Black Mountain*, the first in his series, takes place in the foothills of the Blue Ridge Mountains. Since retiring from full-time work, Ruben spends his time writing and teaches part-time with the local community college.

www.ingramcontent.com/pod-product-compliance
Lightning Source LLC
Chambersburg PA
CBHW070727280626
47159CB00023B/2857